TAKE YOUR MEDICINE

TAKE YOUR MEDICINE

PAMELA CRANE

Rockin' C Reads
Raleigh, North Carolina

Thank you for supporting authors and literacy by purchasing this book. Want to add more gripping reads to your library? As the author of more than a dozen award-winning and bestselling books, you can find all of Pamela Crane's works on her website at www.pamelacrane.com.

To any woman who has ever been told to fit in better, to smile more, to shut up and listen, to make yourself smaller, to follow the status quo, to *take your medicine like a man…* don't be afraid to spit it out.

Chapter 1
March 18, 1970

Samantha Stanton's father often joked about her killing him with kindness, until the fall of 1965, when his death became the punchline. Sam called it *murder*, her mother called it an *accident*. Potato, potahto. In the end, it didn't really matter, did it? He was gone, and that's all anyone knew for sure.

Except four and a half years later it *still* mattered to Sam. Her father wasn't coming back from the grave, not until Jesus came a'callin', and Sam couldn't let this bygone *be gone*. By the arrival of the Disco Era, she decided to pull the trigger on avenging him. Figuratively speaking, that is, because in the spring of 1970 Sam didn't own a gun, and she couldn't purchase one even if she wanted. It was one of many things women couldn't have. But retribution, Sam decided, she *would* have.

The easy part had been figuring out her father's killer.

The hard part was figuring out how to get back at him.

Then an idea came to Sam on the tail of her home's foreclosure notice. It was an idea that would probably get her fired and most certainly get her on someone's hit list.

"Are you *trying* to get yourself killed?" Sam's mother had yelled into the phone receiver when Sam called to tell her the plan.

"If I could prove that the drug industry is corrupt, I could then explain to people why natural remedies are a better alternative." Sam's breaths came heavy as she packed her car for the long drive ahead.

"And how do you plan to do this?"

"By educating the biggest consumers in America."

"Honey," her mother began with the sharp tone Sam recognized before every lecture, "I know your dad always supported your dreams, but he's no longer here to protect you. This vendetta will only destroy you."

Sam closed her blue train case with a click. "At least I won't go down without a fight."

The grim reality was that after Sam's father—the only person who truly understood Sam's unconventional dreams—passed away, along with him went her ambition. The domino effect of losing her father, and subsequently losing faith in herself, rattled down through the past four years.

But recently she had found her resolve, and a plan formed—pulling her to the only place where Sam's message could reach America's biggest consumers, the magazine-reading masses: *Ladies Home Journal.*

"You really think going back to New York is a good idea?" Sam's mother lamented.

"Stop worrying so much. Everything will be fine, Mom."

Thus, her father's fateful passing led Sam through a series of twists and turns, much like the Pennsylvania turnpike she was now driving along.

It was a brisk March morning when she kissed Fido's muzzle with an affectionate goodbye, left her suburban Pittsburgh home well before dawn to hit the highway, and had no idea what waited for her at the end of the 350-mile journey to New York City. But even if Sam could have predicted the upcoming bruise to her face, stint in jail, escaped pony, and incriminating byline in tomorrow's newspaper, she would have done it all the same.

That's the type of woman Sam was: reckless and resolute, emphasis on *wreck*. As Sam had been reminded at her father's funeral, the family curse of losing everything seemed to be her birthright. And believe it or not, it all started with a parking ticket...

Chapter 2

The drive from the Steel City, where the three rivers ran brown and the air hung with smog, to the Big Apple, where skyscrapers pierced the clouds and bodies jostled like jockeys along the sidewalks, took all morning.

Road-weary Samantha Stanton sniffed, wrinkling her nose at the fragrance of gasoline and tire tread, with notes of travel sweat and anxiety. Opening the eggshell-blue train case on the passenger seat beside her, she spritzed herself with the Ô de Lancôme she'd stolen from her mother, then parked her dead father's 1965 Chevrolet Impala SS smack dab in the middle of 54th street.

"You can't park there!" a meter maid shouted as she waved her pink ticket booklet in warning.

Sam glanced up and down the street, where every square inch of parking was occupied in front of the entrance to the *Ladies Home Journal* headquarters. The middle of the street would have to do. She had bigger problems than a $25 parking ticket to worry about. Like punishing her father's killer.

"Then ticket me if you must," Sam dared, slamming the car door behind her. What did a parking ticket matter when her father was dead?

The cherry-red white-top convertible looked exactly like the midlife crisis purchase her father had intended it to be when he bought it brand new five years ago. His effort to chase youth and vigor proved fruitless, however. Months after he traded in his family-friendly, paid-off Ford Galaxie and signed the $4,900 muscle car loan at a whopping 12 percent interest that the steelworker couldn't afford, he fell to his knees and clutched his chest in his living room watching *Bonanza* while his wife cooked chicken a la king in the kitchen not even twenty feet away.

One minute later he sprawled face down on the persimmon orange carpet.

Five minutes after that Sam's mother rushed to his side, unable to find a pulse.

Within thirty minutes Sam consoled her weeping mother as the ambulance attendant wheeled his body to the back of the Cadillac Superior ambulance that reminded Sam of the nearly identical style hearse she knew would soon follow.

The funeral expenses emptied their family's meager savings account, and by Christmas of 1965, a home foreclosure notice arrived in the mail. Death had become the gift that kept on giving. With hopes of saving her childhood home, off to the bank Sam went. As luck would have it, borrowing money was out of the question:

"You'll need to bring your husband to cosign on a loan," the banker had explained.

"What if I don't have a husband?" Sam had a habit of questioning poor logic.

"What about an uncle?" the banker suggested. "Or a cousin?"

"I have none of those either."

The banker offered only poorer logic in return: "I suggest

you pretty yourself up and try harder to find a mate, miss." But Sam knew *that* was a hopeless cause.

Past the point of desperation, Sam decided to do something that went against every fiber of her being. No, she didn't solicit a potential husband or find a long-lost uncle, but instead accepted a fate much worse:

A job in the food service industry.

Her typist position during the day left her evenings open just enough to fit in a waitressing stint that went terribly wrong. During one night shift in particular, she came to discover that she was either too forgetful or too clumsy—or possibly both— to turn it into a career. Patrons didn't tend to like wearing their beverages, or appreciate *alfredo* when they ordered a *potato*.

The last straw broke when Sam promised free soft serve to a table full of boys after a Little League victory game—not realizing the ice cream machine had broken hours earlier. When Sam asked the cook what she could offer the kids instead, she misheard his British-speak "eff all" as "waffle" and proceeded to order a round of waffles on the house... the bill for which came out of Sam's final paycheck before she was promptly fired (and told to get her ears checked).

The $0.89 per hour cashier job that Sam's mother had reluctantly taken at Gimbels department store helped supplement her Avon door-to-door sales, but it still wasn't enough to make ends meet.

Sam never told her mother that she had applied to college and was one of two women accepted into their plant pathology program. Along with a full ride, too. The day Sam tore open the acceptance letter felt like the first day of the rest of her life... until she saw the foreclosure notice for the house, which her mother failed to hide. So Sam respectfully declined the scholarship and settled into her life of mediocrity.

It wasn't a total loss when she accepted a typist position for *Women's House Magazine,* a small-time Pittsburgh-based rag, because in a twisty unexpected way, it drew her back to New York City, to this very moment.

That singular event—the death of her father four and a half years ago—eventually came full circle, bringing Sam back to the city that never sleeps, in this busy street, in front of this towering building where nearly a hundred women waited for her on the Manhattan sidewalk. Just as zealous. Just as single-minded. And just as fed up with traffic.

"Don't say I didn't warn you," the meter maid announced as she slid the pink ticket under Sam's windshield wiper.

Sam was already marching across two lanes toward the glass and chrome building where she would, for the first time ever, do something that would land her in jail. It was just shy of 9:00 a.m., but the city was already wide awake and abuzz.

A pulse of adrenaline—along with a horn beeping behind her—quickened her gait toward the pack of women. *Radical Feminists,* the media had pegged them, as if it were an insult. But it was 1970, and *radical* now held a whole new definition. And *feminism* was growing as fast as a hippie's hair, if last year's Woodstock music festival was any indication. They might as well have called them the *Groovy Equalists*, as far as Sam was concerned.

Despite the group's muted colors of conservative thigh-skimming suits, their expressions conveyed the same defiant passion that Sam felt with each click of her platform clogs on the concrete.

A yellow checkered taxicab skirted around her, nearly knocking her onto the wide sidewalk while spraying her with last night's rainfall.

She gave the driver a hairy eyeball. "Watch where you're going!"

"Do you have a death wish or something?" a woman in a mandarin leisure suit asked, drawing all eyes and ears on Sam, their designated leader. "You can't be too careful on these crazy streets."

But Sam already knew this from the years she had lived in Brooklyn as a fresh-faced naïve careerwoman—minus the career. At least a *real* career had been within reach, she consoled herself. On the same day she had been offered a promotion to the coveted columnist position at the prestigious *Ladies Home Journal*, a rare weekday long-distance call rang through her tiny apartment. The three-minute and $12 call from her sobbing mother was just expensive enough to use up an entire day's wage, and long enough to wreck Sam's world.

"Your father needs you," was what her mother had opened with when Sam had answered the phone. "The medicines and treatments aren't working. Your father's heart is barely hanging on by a thread."

So Sam, the ever-dutiful daughter, turned the columnist promotion down, left New York, and headed home to Pittsburgh to care for her ill-fated father and soon-to-be-widowed mother. Mere months later, when her father's heart gave up anyway, she was burdened with the shame of failure and bills they couldn't afford.

Even after regaining her footing as a typist for *Women's House Magazine,* with an unprecedented 140 words per minute, undoubtably the skill that secured her the job, Sam's meager salary was no match for survival in this world. But money—or lack thereof—didn't stop her from filling up her gas tank at $0.36 a gallon and driving across Pennsylvania to New York with a resolve to right old wrongs.

And finally take down her father's killer.

"Are we ready, ladies?" a gorgeous gal in argyle called out.

"Remember, do not give in, no matter the cost," another said, her sleek and severe middle-part catching the tail wind of a passing truck.

The *cost*—that was the lingering detail that gave Sam a slight hesitancy. They would certainly be breaking a law—or two or three—today. The cost could end up ripping mothers from their children, wives from their husbands, businesswomen from their only source of income.

"This is no small sacrifice," Sam reminded them.

Not that Sam wasn't familiar with sacrifice. She had given up the only guy she ever loved—regretfully. Then gave up her dream columnist job to help her sick father—willingly. She turned down a college scholarship to support her mother— selflessly. She spent her evenings alone studying plants that could heal others—happily. But to petition all these women to risk their own comforts for a greater cause... this was asking a lot. And every cell in Sam's body resisted the urge to ask for anything.

"We're ready for it!" Argyle Gal urged. "Any wise words to inspire us before we make history, Sam?"

Sam thought a moment, tapping her chewed fingernail on her chin. The cool sensation of the gold heart necklace skimming her collarbone gave her the words she needed to say:

"I'm proud of you all for showing up this morning and risking so much. Each of you is braver than you realize! And it won't be in vain. As we know, choosing silence is choosing our own downfall. As long as we padlock our tongues, all women will continue to wear chains. So here's to making some noise, ladies!"

A collective cheer boosted morale as the women surged ahead. A chorus of "You're our hero, Sam!" and "Lead us to victory, Sam!" filled the street.

While they had become Sam's comrades of a sort, there remained a chasm that she couldn't quite cross over into genuine friendship. Not one of them invited her to a Friday game night. Or to a Saturday night of disco. Or even to a Tupperware party. Not that Sam would have gone anyway. It could have been due to her lack of interest in typical feminine things, like the latest hairdos, makeup, or fashion trends. But she sensed it was something deeper. Something about her that didn't quite vibe with other women her age and status.

Her mother had plenty of opinions on why—her strange passion for plants, her apathy toward appearance, her indifference to dating—but Sam worried it was something off-putting that a coat of foundation and a man on her arm couldn't fix. But there was one person whose vibe matched Sam's perfectly. It had been friendship at first sight.

She eagerly searched the pool of faces for his in particular. She had been certain he would come—she had given him plenty of notice—but his infectious energy was missing and his goosebump-inducing smile nowhere to be found.

When her gaze settled on a lone figure, her fury surfaced. Hanging along the outskirts of the throng was a sole cameraman and local news reporter from a no-name network Sam didn't recognize. Was that it? Where was *Eyewitness News*? Or *Report to New York*? Her rebellion—and all that was at stake—wasn't even important enough to draw the attention of any major news outlet?!

No matter. Once they accomplished what they set out to do, ABC and NBC—and all the letters in between—would be chomping for interviews like a shoal of piranhas.

"Check out that stone fox," the cameraman muttered to the reporter with a hungry gaze. He twirled the tip of his thin mustache around his finger with a lewdness that grossed Sam out.

Sam already knew he wasn't referring to her, for no one could mistake her homely features and outdated haircut as foxy. But the sexism so effortlessly slipping off his tongue still irritated her like a nasty rash.

"The things I would do to her…" he added with a groan.

"Oh, sit on it!" Sam turned on him. "You think you're a real Casanova, don't you? Pigheaded men like you are the reason we're here."

The cameraman laughed her off, which maddened her all the more. "Stop trippin', lady, and take a chill pill. I wasn't talking to you. I was talking to that chick in argyle. You're just jealous no one's checkin' you out."

Sam scoffed.

"And you're lucky anyone showed up to your silly little ra-ra rally," he continued, waving his arm at the empty sidewalk behind him as a cruel smirk lifted his lips. "The real news is over in Vietnam. Or covering the Manson murders. As you can see, no one cares about your man-hating cause."

"Man-hating? I'll show you man-hating!" The words flung out as quickly as her hand, followed by the slap of her palm on his cheek.

The cameraman's eyes widened with shock. His face reddened with embarrassment to match the handprint. Sam's shoulders straightened with satisfaction. Then she turned on her wedge heels and led the charge.

A more conventional woman would have known her place and sheepishly apologized. But Sam wasn't a conventional woman. And there wasn't a sheepish bone in her body. In fact, there was not a single conventional woman among the group that now migrated through the glass front doors of the *Ladies Home Journal* office building, with Sam forging the way to one of two outcomes:

Their *prize*, or their *demise*.

As it seemed to happen to generations of Stantons before her, the two most often ended up colliding, becoming one and the same. The higher Sam rose, the harder she would fall.

Chapter 3

"Samantha Stanton!" a voice boomed amid the bodies clustered like grapes in the *Ladies Home Journal's* front office.

They were packed wall to wall in the bullpen, from the receptionist's neat-as-a-pin desk to the lead editor's slammed-shut door. Women of every age, dress size, and background—from homemakers to hairdressers, busybodies to businesswomen—angled for seats and standing room, talking excitedly about their petitions: Fair wages. Better jobs. And dare they demand daycare?

"Has anyone seen Samantha Stanton?" the voice repeated, louder and angrier.

Upon hearing the gravelly sound that all these years later still sent a chill up Sam's suddenly-weakened spine, she ducked into the crowd. Chairs screeched against the floor as a man rammed through like a Spanish bull.

"I know you're here!" His declaration bounced like a Ping-Pong ball against the chatter.

"Is this who you're looking for?" the cameraman tattled, pointing Sam out.

If given the chance, Sam would have bashed the cameraman over the head with that hefty recorder attached to him like a backpack. Such a strong dislike of someone wasn't typical for Sam, as she didn't tend to make enemies—except for one. For a moment she forgot all about the pharmaceutical company responsible for her father's death. Now she had a new nemesis, and his name was… well, she would call the small-time news station advertised across his Portapak video camera and find out.

"I see you, Samantha. Don't you hide from me!" the voice thundered out a warning.

There was no avoiding the magazine's head honcho, Calvin Dreyfuss *the third*, he always introduced himself as, clinging to the two former generations of publishing tycoons that had passed their mantels of greatness down to him, lest anyone doubt his qualifications. Which no one dared to do. He hadn't acquired the nickname *Callous Calvin* for nothing. Luckily he had never caught on that *Cal* was short for his unlikeable personality, not his namesake.

As Sam spotted his bald head bobbing its way toward her, sensibility told her to run from her former boss. But she had already lost all sensibility when she hand-planted the cameraman, then stormed through the office doors, so her feet remained glued to the mustard-yellow tile as Mr. Dreyfuss lurched out of the crowd, huffing and puffing like he'd just finished a marathon.

"Hello, sir." Sam stood, motionless, like an awestruck teenybopper at a Beatles concert. But Mr. Dreyfuss was no John Lennon, and Sam was no prepubescent girl. She was a grown woman with a mind of her own, and she would remind him of that, if need be.

"So," he stated. "There you are. Always in the middle of drama."

"It's good to see you, sir," Sam offered, though it was never good to see Callous Calvin, especially on a bad day. Today would prove to be the epitome of bad days.

"I can't say the same for you, Miss Stanton. You look like something the cat dragged in."

Shiny and rotund, Mr. Dreyfuss grumbled as his gaze wandered over Sam, her heart racing, lips chapped, and the scent of Ô de Lancôme fading amid the stench of too many bodies in too small a space. Unlike most women she knew, Sam was rarely plagued with nerves—or big feelings of any kind. She would simply logic her way through most problems, and leave emotions out of it. But today was different. Because it wasn't only about her. The lives of all her sisters-in-arms were at stake alongside her. She feared not for herself, but for them.

"Uh, thank you, sir?"

"Enough pleasantries," Mr. Dreyfuss barked, spittle spraying, although there was nothing pleasant about this conversation. "What are you doing back here in New York? I thought you moved to Pittsburgh."

"I did, sir. I came back to support my former co-workers…" Then Sam remembered her father-avenging agenda. "And ask for a favor."

"So you're here to bring chaos to my doorstep, are you?"

"Chaos? No. We're here to negotiate about—" Sam began, only to be promptly cut off.

"You call this *negotiating*?"

Behind her the cameraman chuckled with satisfaction. Sam didn't like the way his glare dawdled on her as nearly one hundred women crammed into the offices where secretaries and publishing executives watched with helpless bewilderment as Mr. Dreyfuss took charge.

"I should have known you were behind this... whatever this is!" he yelled, even though she stood barely a foot away.

"Negotiations," Sam reminded him, only making him angrier.

A haze of cigarette smoke veiled his ruddy face that looked like an infected zit about to pop, which a dab of tea tree oil could remedy. "One of these days you're going to give me a heart attack from all the stress you cause."

"That cigarette is more likely to trigger a heart condition than my being here. Might I suggest some hawthorn berries to lower your blood pressure?"

"Might I suggest you lose the know-it-all attitude?" he grunted back. "You always seem to attract trouble, don't you, Samantha?"

"It's *Sam*, not *Samantha*," she corrected him, like she had done a million times back when she had worked for him.

The Twiggy-haired receptionist looked up from her blue typewriter, the clack of keys pausing. Mr. Dreyfuss shrugged and rolled his eyes, like he had done a million times back when Sam had corrected him.

"Whatever you say," he said, the cigarette dangling precariously from his mouth. "You're making me regret not firing you instead of letting you transfer to our Pittsburgh rag. Do you cause such problems for your boss at *Women's House Magazine*?"

When Mr. Dreyfuss had agreed to transfer Sam to their smaller imprint after her father's prognosis, she soon discovered the editor at the Pittsburgh-based publisher could have cared less about his magazine's success. It was no secret he was simply counting down the days to retirement, so when Sam had approached him about taking over the neglected advice column, he sent her to the bigwigs in New York City to deal with her. So here she was, ready to plead her case and issue some ultimatums. Only, the ultimatums remained stuck in her parched throat.

"If you'd just listen, you'll see I'm not *causing* problems. I'm *fixing* them."

"Ha!" he huffed. "You started a riot that's going to put a bunch of women behind bars."

His sheer ignorance bolstered her confidence to say what she came here on this brisk March day to say. "It's not a riot. All I'm asking is for you to listen to our requests."

"*Requests?*" Mr. Dreyfuss coughed a cloud of smoke into Sam's face. "No, you're a herd of crazy feminists storming in here as if you own the place, making ludicrous *demands*! This is tyranny! Trespassing! And I'm pretty sure illegal!"

"We're not storming anything, sir. It's a sit-in." Another of her corrections that she was certain he would shrug off and ignore. "What we want is simple: our voices to be heard—and read. In here." She lifted the stack of *Ladies Home Journal* and *Women's House Magazine* she had brought with her as evidence.

"You're lucky I haven't called the cops... yet. But when I do, you're going to bring a lot more trouble on a lot more people, *Samantha*. Are you prepared to start a war?"

Suddenly uncertain, scared, and self-conscious, she smoothed her androgynous shag, tucking a few aimless hairs behind her ears. Her mother called it an "ape drape," and credited Sam's perpetual singledom to the haircut that would go out of style by 1972, since apparently every other woman could see just how tragic it looked except for Sam. But as she saw it, if the haircut was good enough for Jane Fonda, it was good enough for her.

"I'm not trying to start a war, Mr. Dreyfuss. Women simply want representation in the magazine, that's all."

"I gave you your chance to run a column five years ago, Samantha. You turned it down."

"To take care of my sick father. Who died shortly after, by the way."

"Tough luck." Mr. Dreyfuss lacked the empathy gene, a common male trait when raised on phrases like *boys don't cry* and *man up.* "The job's already taken."

"By a man who doesn't know what he's talking about!"

"He's a *doctor*, mind you."

"Look at this." Sam thrust out last month's issue, page open to the latest advice column where a reader confessed about her husband beating her over burned meatloaf, asking if she could justify divorce. "Your columnist told her to take cooking lessons and learn how to do her job as a housewife better. What kind of advice is that—to stay married to a wifebeater? She'll probably end up dead before she ever learns how to master meatloaf!"

Sam leafed through another issue, aiming her finger at even more absurd advice. "And this one validates an employer for firing a girl when she refused his sexual advances!"

"And I'm sure she flirted heavily in the first place to get that job. You can't blame a guy for acting on it." He swatted the magazines away. "There are two sides to every story, Miss Stanton. You should know that if you ever plan to be a journalist. Which you clearly are not equipped for."

Certainly Mr. Dreyfuss could see the injustice so blatantly

splayed across the pages. It disgusted her, hearing the same story with different characters again and again. Sam—and all the other women before her and those who would endure it after her—were sick and tired of feeling sick and tired.

"Do you think it's rational to solicit an unqualified man's advice to answer distinctively women's dilemmas?" she inquired.

Mr. Dreyfuss's eyes glazed over as if Sam were explaining the antimicrobial properties of lemongrass instead of basic human rights.

"I don't see the problem with this advice," he said bluntly. "One is a tease who deserved to get fired, and the other is a bad cook. Which makes her a bad wife. She's lucky to have a husband who would keep her."

"*Keep her*—like she's a pet? That's exactly my point! Do you think your readers want to hear this? You claim this magazine is *for* women, but it's not written *by* women."

"That's because men know better what women need than you do. We pay for your extravagant face creams and overpriced wardrobes, so we deserve a decent meatloaf in return. After all, isn't the way you dress, the way you act, the way you look... it's all in order to find and win over a man who will take care of you."

He yanked a magazine from Sam's hand, his wrist glistening with a thick gold chain that probably cost as much as her Impala still parked in the street six floors below. He jabbed a finger at the name credited to the article—a Dr. Something-or-other, as if the *Dr.* gave the writer license to prescribe bad advice.

"Only a *man* can help guide you in achieving that goal."

The goal of securing a mate was why every article was paired with an advertisement for the latest cooking class, or hair product, or anti-aging makeup, or fashion brand. Because according to Mr. Dreyfuss and Dr. Something-or-other, and possibly all men in 1970, women lived for men. Cooking for them, cleaning for them, and raising their brood.

"You don't think women are capable of determining our own happiness?" It was a question Sam had only recently come to terms with. She had always relied on the validation of her father to pursue her dreams of becoming a writer—or botanist, if such a career existed—but when that stopped with his death, she simply gave up at the first obstacle. But not anymore. She had become a different woman since then, a woman who would not only make her father proud, but herself as well. This, here and now, was the first step toward that. And an arduous step it was proving to be.

"Women have no idea what they want or need!" Mr. Dreyfuss retorted. "Look at how fickle you are—one day you want men to pay the bills and put food on the table, and the next day you're complaining when all we ask for is a decent meatloaf. Men give women stability... and yes, happiness. You should be thanking us instead of biting the hand that feeds you."

"Thanking you?" Sam recoiled.

"With that said, I'm done here. Either get these nutjobs out of here, or face the consequences." Mr. Dreyfuss turned to the receptionist who had yet to resume typing. "Twyla, call the cops on these terrorists. Now!"

"I believe the meter maid already took care of that, sir," Twyla replied with a wince, a meek apology to Sam written on her face.

28

"Then I hope the New York Police Department has enough room in the holding cells for all of us," Sam dared.

"So you're willing to risk all of these women's freedom just to make a point?"

"You call this freedom? It's 1970 and we can't even get a loan without a man's signature. We *can't* get birth control if we're single, but we *can* get fired for getting pregnant… and since we can't open up a checking account without putting a man's name on it, it makes being a single working woman nearly impossible! Tell me, in what world do women have freedom?"

"Why would you want to do any of those things on your own when a man can do them all for you? In this world, all you have to worry about is raising kids and looking pretty."

"No, sir, that's *your* world, not a woman's world. Has it ever occurred to you that we *want* to work, and not all of us care about looking pretty?"

He scrutinized her up and down. "Yeah, I can tell that's not something you concern yourself with. Maybe if you dolled yourself up a bit you'd find a husband and wouldn't be so disgruntled. A new haircut and some lipstick can go a long way. Well, maybe not *that* long of a way for a homely gal like you, but you know what I mean."

Behind her she heard the snicker of the cameraman. Would he ever bug off? She couldn't wait to file her complaint against him to his superiors… which would inevitably be dusted under the rug. Pivoting around, she found him filming their conversation, still wearing that smirk she hadn't managed to slap off his face. That smirk only widened as the distinct piercing sound of sirens six floors below drew everyone's attention to the window.

"Someone called the pigs!" Argyle Gal cried.

Another woman cried out, "No one told me we could be arrested for this! I have four children at home." *And a fifth on the way*, Sam realized as she noticed the woman's huge pregnant belly beneath her pink shift dress.

"My husband will kill me if I'm not home before school lets out," a flowy-skirted hippie cried out.

It was in this moment that Sam realized she had taken an entirely wrong approach. She could never convince someone like Mr. Dreyfuss that women should be the ones representing women's wants and needs in his magazine. But there was one thing that spoke to businessmen like him more than human rights or logic. If she was right, they could revolutionize the entire publishing industry. Perhaps even change the world.

But if she was wrong, the swish of the glass office doors opening, the beat of heavy footsteps, and the mass of blue uniformed officers predicted their fate.

"NYPD! We got a call about an illegally parked car blocking traffic. Who's in charge here?" an officer yelled. A glint of silver handcuffs hanging from his hips evoked visions of cuffed wrists and jailcell bars clanging shut.

"And who is causing all this ruckus?" another officer added to the pandemonium.

Everything rode on this moment. Sam—and that ever-daunting muscle car payment—could not afford to lose the only thing that mattered: freedom.

Chapter 4

One thing spoke louder than words. One thing could grab Callous Calvin Dreyfuss's attention above the demands that peppered the offices on the sixth floor at the corner of 54th street. And having dealt with people like Mr. Dreyfuss her entire life, Sam knew exactly what that one thing was.

"Money," she stated.

Behind another puff of smoke Mr. Dreyfuss's face scrunched with confusion and intrigue. "Money?"

"Yes, money," she echoed. "What if I can guarantee to draw in more readers, increase magazine sales, and thus earn you more money?"

Mr. Dreyfuss leaned in. Sam held her breath. She would endure his cigarette coffee breath if it meant holding his interest.

Always follow the money, her father had once told her when she questioned why his doctor had prescribed him a heart medicine with documented adverse side effects that could kill him. And it eventually did. But the silver lining for the doctor was the substantial kickback he got from Cook Pharmaceuticals for prescribing the popular heart disease drug that Sam was determined to expose to the public as ineffective—nay, *dangerous*—if everything went as planned. As far as Sam was concerned, the doctor *and* his kickback could go down in flames together.

"Go on." Mr. Dreyfuss gestured for her to continue. "Money talks. What's the skinny?"

"It's one small favor I'm asking for..." Sam inhaled a lungful of audacity. "I want my own advice column for *Women's House Magazine*, and free rein to write what I want. With no interference from the higher-ups."

"And how do you propose *you* getting a promotion will benefit *me*?" he shot back.

Touché, Mr. Dreyfuss. But Sam already had an answer locked and loaded.

"That's only the first part. The second part is that you do the same with *Ladies Home Journal*. Promote women to columnist positions and let them write what they want..." And here was the tough sell she knew he wouldn't buy: "Without advertisements pushing products."

Straightening up, he stepped back, closing negotiations. "No can do. Those advertisements are our bread and butter."

"Cal, hear me out," Sam pleaded.

His bushy eyebrow shot up in an upside-down V. He wasn't used to being addressed as *Cal* outside the boardroom or off the golf course... at least not by an *inferior*, a *woman,* of all people.

Gaze narrowing, Sam skimmed headlines on the enlarged, framed magazine covers of years past lining the wall:

How to Cure Your Singledom if You're Ugly

Five Bedroom Tricks to Make Him Forget His Secretary

The Three Most Important B's He Needs: Bedtime, Breakfast, and—

Sam flushed and returned her attention to Mr. Dreyfuss.

"Look, your target readership is *supposed to be* women." Though the article headlines she had just read suggested otherwise. "If you give us a voice, we'll tell all our friends that your magazine offers something no other has: real-life women's advice. You'll resurrect this outdated magazine to something fresh and original. Something women want. Something we *need*."

"Hm." He didn't look convinced.

"*And* you'll become the leader in modern journalism, which will give you an advantage that I am confident will bring in massive profits while you kill the competition. Imagine your name on the door of the coveted corner office, Cal, when you destroy previous sales records."

Leader. Massive profits. Kill. Destroy. Corner office. Sam had used all the right buzzwords that would appeal to a power-hungry businessman with a penchant for violence when a housewife burned the meatloaf. She even dared to use his first name, which showed confidence. Unless he took it as insubordination... which of course could backfire.

"I've done the homework," she continued. "I already know your subscription numbers are dwindling, so what do you have to lose—other than a lot of readers once we start boycotting the magazine if you turn us down?"

"So that's how it's going to be—you'll bite the hand that feeds you if I don't cave?" Mr. Dreyfuss had a point, since such actions would most certainly get Sam fired from the smaller sister magazine.

"Do you think I have any allegiance to a company that underpays me and a boss who dislikes me regardless of what I do?" Sam posed a truth that was worth remembering. In fact, she had reminded herself of that the entire drive here, lest she be tempted to chicken out. Which she had considered at mile marker 162, then again at mile marker 236.

"Gee, I can't possibly understand why your boss hates you," Mr. Dreyfuss muttered.

Gesturing to the mass of women around her, Sam wasn't above making threats. "Look, the bottom line is that we can do a lot of damage if we want to. Or we can do a lot of good. Your call."

She watched his expression shift. Slowly. From cynical… to curious… to captive.

A greedy gaze clouded his eyes. His hands rubbed together in a ravenous motion. "You think this will work?"

"I really do, sir."

"You're making big promises I hope you can deliver, Sam."

Sam, not *Samantha.* Well at least she'd made *some* progress in the fight for her voice.

"I will prove it to you. And the women will work harder than any man on your staff. Give us thirty-six issues running it our way, and you'll see the women are worth the pay raise."

"Thirty-six issues? Pay raise?" he snorted, then hacked up a lung. Sam would have suggested marshmallow root to soothe that cough, if she had been bold enough to interrupt him. "That's three years! Dream on. I'll give you six issues—and no raise for these gals' promotions until after I see results."

That wasn't even enough time to convince a woman to switch shampoos, let alone start a revolution. No, she needed time. Much more time. "How about thirty months?" she countered hopefully, then added between gritted teeth, "Consider the savings as they write the magazine for half the pay."

A frown drooped across Mr. Dreyfuss's face. One look at

that sour expression informed Sam she had already lost as tensions rose around her. The congregating police were still searching for the leader responsible for the mounting chaos. And for the owner of the illegally parked red 1965 Chevrolet Impala SS.

"If one of you doesn't turn herself in for starting this riot, I'm arresting the lot of you!" bellowed the loudest lawman of the bunch.

Judging by the wild eyes, flustered cheeks, and nervous twitches, one of the sisters-in-arms was about to throw Sam to the wolves, and she couldn't blame whoever the Judas would be. This whole thing was her idea, after all. Fear flew like aimless darts:

"The pigs are here to arrest us!" the hippie declared.

"I can't afford another bail after getting thrown in the slammer last year at Woodstock. I gotta skitty," the pregnant mom-of-four surprised Sam with.

"Wait—we're allowed to leave? Peace, love, and granola!" Argyle Gal realized aloud, weaving her way to the door. She halted at Sam's side, then patted her on the shoulder. "It was an honor fighting alongside you, Sam. You're the real deal. We did our best, but some battles just can't be won. Not by us, at least."

As Sam watched her leave, the cameraman hustled to catch up, aiming a harsh elbow directly in Sam's eye as he carelessly passed. He paused only a moment to glace back unapologetically.

"Oh, that's gonna leave a bruise." With no further sympathy offered, he instead raised his hand, pointing a finger down at her. "Officer, here's your culprit!" Then he scuttled away, camera and recorder bouncing off his legs, in pursuit of Argyle

Gal while his mediocre hit-on trailed behind him: "Hey, gorgeous, wait up! Need a personal escort?"

Sam's troops were steadily retreating. The police were encroaching. The door to negotiations was closing as quickly as the iron bars of that imminent jail cell.

Glancing at the panicked mom-of-four, Sam didn't know what to do. Mom-of-Four earned the right to keep a job even when she was pregnant. Argyle Gal deserved the respect of her employers, no matter how beautiful she was. Hippie should be assured the choice to remain single and self-sufficient, with access to loans and reasonable pay. Sam couldn't give up, not when she was this close.

"What do you say, Mr. Dreyfuss? Thirty issues to turn the magazines around. I'll even put my job up as collateral." At the time Sam offered this, she had no idea it would in fact cost her more than her job. It would cost her everything.

By now the bellowing bobby had arrived, whipping out his handcuffs. "Ma'am, you're coming with me."

"But sir—" Sam pleaded.

The cuffs clicked nonetheless. Sam could feel her eye socket purpling with pain and her neck pinking with embarrassment.

"There's no need to arrest her," Mr. Dreyfuss attempted a rescue. "Everything's as sound as a pound, Officer."

"Sorry, Mr. Dreyfuss, but we've been given orders," he rebutted, dragging Sam to the door. "You can pick her up at the station and post her bail. Or not."

One look at Sam's pathetic surrender seemed to do the trick, because the last thing she heard as she trundled through the office doors was a frustrated but white-flag-waving Calvin

Dreyfuss calling above the din:

"You win, Sam!"

They were the three most beautiful words she'd ever heard.

"You have until the May 1972 publication. That's twenty-four issues to turn it around or you bow out and I never see your face again. Final offer!"

Sam enthusiastically accepted.

"If you fail," he added a warning, "you'll be blacklisted from every magazine in the country. I hope it's worth it."

"It's worth everything, sir." Her heart soared unlike anything she'd ever felt, those dormant emotions blooming. "I promise you won't regret it!"

He would regret it the very next day.

While Sam was hauled off to the first of many incarcerations to come, she couldn't have been happier. That happiness would eventually water down into despair and deliberation over where it had all fallen apart. Only in looking back did the realization punch her right in the gut, leaving her breathless.

Everything wrong always cycled back to one person, the only man who could mete out such a blow: Raul Smothers.

Chapter 5

It was too quiet. As anyone who has children—or normally noisy pets—knows, that unusual hush is not in fact tranquility, but trouble.

"Something's wrong." This was Sam's first spoken thought in hours, as she swung open her front door after a long day in the slammer and a longer night driving home. Despite all the things that felt wrong about living in her dead grandmother's mausoleum of memories, it was something else altogether that bugged Sam in this moment.

Heading straight to the fridge, she grabbed a bag of frozen peas and held them to her eye socket, while the other eye adjusted to the morning light that poured in through the kitchen windows.

The mid-century ranch house was nestled comfortably in a suburb populated by widows of a nearly extinct generation who wore flapper-dresses in the Roarin' '20s and survived on giggle juice during the Great Depression. Alcohol seemed the only way to endure a dozen children sharing two bedrooms while living off of liver loaf and creamed lima beans.

"Hello?" Sam called out, waiting.

It wasn't the mothball scent of her long-deceased grandmother's wardrobe infusing the wall-to-wall shag carpet that bothered her. Nor was it the hideous checkered avocado green wallpaper that Grandma Stanton had claimed matched Sam's eyes. No, it was the eerie quiet that shouldn't have been there… along with the light on the state-of-the-art PhoneMate answering machine that Sam's mother overpaid $300 for, which Sam swore she didn't want and would never use, but was now announcing a message with that demanding red glow.

"Fido?" Sam called, listening for the familiar trot across the kitchen linoleum.

She knew she had left the sliding back door open, as families in the safe suburbs often did on a nice spring day. Who needed locks when you had nebby neighbors? But when Fido didn't immediately show, Sam dropped her train case with a soundless thump and headed to the answering machine.

A white *Message Received* flag appeared across the reel-to-reel tape that claimed the potential to hold twenty messages, although Sam hoped to never find out. No one with that many friends had freedom to do as she pleased, and doing as she pleased was the one thing Sam valued most. Clicking the knob to *Playback Calls*, Sam secured the earphone in place and listened as a familiar treacly voice filled her ear canal:

"Is this recording? Hello? Oh, hello, Samantha! This is your mother calling. Am I your first message? How exciting! I knew you would eventually find use for the answering machine. Rather than jot down a note, I figured I would leave you a personal message saying I stopped by to collect your mail and water your plants, which are getting out of control, I must add. The house looks like a jungle, Samantha. Really, it's ridiculous!"

Minnie Stanton never could understand her daughter's draw to botany, or how an eighth-grade science fair project studying the effects of chebula on wrinkles could turn into an obsession with alternative medicine. Not that Minnie hadn't been happy to let thirteen-year-old Sam experiment on her aging skin, the Polaroids showing clear signs of smoothing those fine lines after a mere four weeks.

A science fair project was one thing; the joy of youth lost to weekends filled with experiments and research instead of friends and discos was another. Not that Sam could ever relate to the "youthful joy" her mother referred to. Girl gossip bored her, and loud psychedelic rock paired with pulsating bodies didn't appeal. But the silence and solitude found in her garden… now *that* was joy!

As much as Minnie wanted her daughter to fit in, she couldn't deny the fact that Sam was gifted. The grapefruit Sam prescribed had lowered her father's blood pressure. And the aloe vera Sam lathered on Minnie's arthritis soothed the inflammation. Sam had even gotten her article on local honey curing allergies published in a little-known medical journal that no one but her best friend, only friend, Raul Smothers had read. He owned fifteen copies of the journal, which he never told Sam about but she had discovered hidden on his bookshelf one evening as he cooked spaghetti on a hotplate, the "fanciest" dish he knew how to make.

Maybe if Sam had ended up saving her father's life, perhaps Minnie would have become a believer in the homeopathy Sam offered, but as it stood, it was a pastime that Minnie felt was past time to give up on.

The message continued as Sam's mother picked up steam: "I should also mention I locked Fido outside. I know you think it's sanitary to let that awful beast wander in and out of the house as he pleases, but honestly, Samantha, you need to find him a proper home."

It was the same song every time Minnie stopped by or called—or now left a message—which was far more often than Sam preferred from her mother who simply refused to cut the umbilical cord: a plea for Sam to be someone she wasn't.

Fido, much like his human housemate, also preferred to do as he pleased. He was not some unwanted stray that didn't deserve a home just because he wasn't a typical pet. In fact, that was exactly what had appealed to Sam about him in the first place.

"Anyway," Minnie continued, as if chatting over coffee, "an old friend of yours contacted me trying to locate you. A gentleman by the name of Raul Smothers? The name rings a bell, but I cannot for the life of me remember why. What is he— Puerto Rican? Now that I think on it, with a surname like that, maybe British? Perhaps from Cheshire? Even so, he sounded quite handsome on the phone, a real charmer. He gave me his phone number to pass along to you, and I told him where you worked. I would have instead provided your home address, but I didn't want to scare him off if he happened to stop by. God forbid he sees what you've done to your grandmother's house, God rest her soul. She'd be rolling in her grave."

Apparently Raul had picked up on some stalker tips during the four years since they'd last spoken—the day after Sam's father's funeral. Although, who needed to invest the energy in stalking when Minnie Stanton was handing out personal information like it was trick-or-treat candy?

No matter. Sam had no intention of returning Raul's call. Not after what he had done.

41

"I'll keep this short and sweet, darling." Except Minnie Stanton kept nothing short and even less sweet. "Let me know when you arrive home from New York and I'll bring by a casserole. You're getting too thin, Samantha, and we don't want Raul to think you're one of those girls who starves herself, now do we? Oh, and I know someone who works at a dog food company and might be willing to take Fido off your hands—"

Click.

Perhaps the PhoneMate was a good investment after all, intuitive enough to cut her mother off from rambling and threatening Fido's life, which convinced Sam that she would keep the machine after all.

Sam slipped into the kitchen, a quandary presenting itself. She examined the rows of potted herbs along the Formica counter wrapped in shiny chrome, which replaced Grandma Stanton's every color of Tupperware, bread bin, and butter molds that had once filled the space. A decision had to be made. Four years had passed since she'd last spoken to Raul, and for good reason. To Sam, betrayal was an unforgiveable sin, and that man was exceptionally talented in the fine art of treachery.

Raul didn't start off that way, as no one ever advertises such a trait from the get-go. In fact, from the first moment Sam stumbled into the downtown New York deli *and* Raul Smothers, literally knocking the triple-decker club sandwich out of his hand, she sensed he was someone special.

It wasn't his status as an up-and-coming *New York Times* reporter that impressed her, even after he'd arrogantly mentioned it twice, as if she cared about such things as status, having none herself. What *did* impress her was the way he had ignored the salami splayed across the floor and instead smiled.

At *her*. Which was a rarity when surrounded by the Sophia Lorens and Audrey Hepburns waltzing around every corner of the most beautiful and *arrogant* city in the world—as long as Raul lived there.

What Sam lacked in beauty she made up for in smarts and a doggedness to educate others in alternative forms of medicine. Homeopathy offered hope and healing. Health remedies that didn't come with a side effect of death. But as is often the case with an outspoken woman, the proper ladies avoided her, the single men slandered her, and her own mother disapproved of her.

Until Raul Smothers came along and turned her heart inside-out.

Chapter 6

Within six months of meeting Raul Smothers in a New York City deli, Sam shared her ardor for ashwagandha. The charm of chamomile. Why she went gaga over ginseng. Raul was the first to listen, to ask questions, to even take her unsolicited advice and apply her methods—with success! Cured was his pesky cough. Gone was his painful gout. Raul Smothers became her guinea pig, her cheer captain, and eventually her dream come true.

Except...

Except Sam didn't allow herself to dare dream of anything more than friendship. There was a long and complicated backstory to why, but she never found the courage to share it with Raul. So they remained more than friends but less than lovers until Minnie's phone call came and inevitably broke them up and dragged Sam away from the city that never sleeps to take care of her ailing father. The autumn of 1965 was her and Raul's first official fight, but it wouldn't be the last.

"Something's wrong," Raul had stated plainly the moment he opened his apartment door to find a sodden, shivering Sam.

New York City had four days in a row of nonstop sleet, which Sam had trekked through with a postman-like determination to bring news that could only be bad in this weather. Sleet was nothing to this lake-effect-snow Pittsburgh native, as she had spent many a winter's night as a child shoveling the snow off her roof.

"My mother called." Sam offered nothing more than that as she stood in the hallway.

Raul held his breath. "And...?"

"And... I have to go home to Pittsburgh. My dad's heart is failing and they need my help taking care of him." Her voice faltered. "Apparently Dad's been getting worse ever since he started his new medication. I'm sure his poor diet isn't helping. Anyway, I'm going home to try to cure him."

"I'm so sorry, Sam." Raul pulled her into his apartment that was twice the size of hers, and into a hug that put Sam's neck at an awkward angle. The cramp was worth feeling held. "Can I do anything to help?"

Raul was a problem-solver by nature, often offering his own version of a "solution"—sometimes solicited, but more often not. Sam was one of few who liked that about him, but her father's condition was beyond his knowledge base. She shook her head against his chest while Raul held her like her life depended on it. Sometimes it felt like it did.

"What about your new column for *Ladies Home Journal*? You just got that promotion after working so hard for it."

"I had to quit."

"Quit? No, I'll talk to Mr. Dreyfuss about holding the position open for you." There was that fixer in Raul coming through again.

"Please don't, Raul. I don't know how long I'll be gone."

"I know his boss's boss. You're finally getting your foot in the door. Now is not the time to walk away. If I talk to him, I'm sure I can convince him to—"

"Stop!" Sam didn't mean to yell, but it was already hard enough to say goodbye without Raul giving her a reason to stay. "This is on me to deal with, I'm afraid."

Raul opened his mouth to say something, pausing as he thought better of it, then spurted it out anyway. "You do know your plants and herbs may not fix what's wrong with your dad, don't you?"

"What do you mean?" Sam stepped out of his grasp. He should have trusted his instinct to keep his mouth shut. "You don't think my methods are effective."

"I'm not saying that, Sam. I just… want you to have realistic expectations. The doctor helping him has a medical degree. You don't."

Sam's cheeks warmed, despite the cold chill still lingering on her wet clothes. "My *realistic expectations* were that you believed in me and my research."

"I do believe in you, but you don't even know what's wrong with your dad."

"It's his heart, his high blood pressure. And I've already been looking into ways to fix it. In fact, I just found out that grapefruit is one of the most effective ways to lower blood pressure. I figure I can start with his diet and go from there."

"Grapefruit can only go so far, Sam. He's in good hands with his doctor. You don't have to give up everything to help—"

"You don't understand because you have never had a father!" The moment the words came out Sam wished she could shove them right back in. But it was the cold, hard truth.

Raul would never understand Sam's sacrifice, because he had never had someone worth sacrificing for.

"Raul," she continued softer, gentler, "My dad is the only reason I have something worth giving up—because he always supported me. The least I can do is be there with him, force-feeding him grapefruit if need be."

Raul grinned and cupped her cheek. "You always seem to do the right thing. Just promise me something."

"What?"

"In the event that you don't find a cure-all, I don't want you to blame yourself if..." Raul choked down the rest of the thought.

"If what, *Raul*?"

"If it doesn't save your dad."

They both knew what Raul was saying without saying it. "I knew it. You think my work is a bunch of hippie fringe quackery that doesn't help anyone. One of these days I'll prove myself to you and everyone else."

What Sam didn't realize was there was nothing to prove with Raul, because even when her research let her down and her father died shortly after, Raul would still believe in her. Still want to be her guinea pig. Still yearn to be her cheer captain.

"I never called you a quack, Sam. I just don't want you to be putting so much pressure on yourself to save the world."

"Someone has to, and it sure as heck won't be the men willing to destroy it for a buck. So it might as well be me. Look, I've got to start packing," Sam said, glancing at the door.

"I guess I'll see you when you get back," Raul concluded.

"You don't get it. There no coming back, Raul. I'm moving home... for good. I don't think I'll ever see you again. This," Sam turned her gaze to his window that was also twice the size of hers, afraid to meet his eyes and lose the last remains of pragmatism that held her tears back, "is goodbye."

Raul scoffed at the insinuation. "Goodbye? Sam, there will never be goodbye between us. I... love you."

There went the pragmatism, right out the window. "You can't possibly love me—"

"And of course you'll see me. I'll come visit the first chance I get," Raul bulldozed ahead, as if he hadn't just spoken the three most precious words strung together that Sam had never been given.

"And I'll write you once I get settled," Sam vowed.

Raul never visited, and Sam never wrote. When her father died, the first—and only—person she called was Raul.

"My dad passed. Please come to his funeral next week," was the last thing she had said.

"I promise I'll be there," was the last thing Raul had replied.

Raul didn't show up (on time), and Sam couldn't forgive him (ever). The memory was as dramatic as an episode of the soap opera *All My Children*, minus the illegitimate child and shocking affair. The Raul she knew used to make good on his promises. But one week *and a day* later, Raul showed up at Minnie's house out of the blue, and out of time.

After Minnie directed him to find Sam at the cemetery, he found her standing under a tree of golden leaves. The poor girl stood staring at the fresh mound of dirt that had been piled atop her father's casket only twelve hours earlier.

While leaves fell around them, Raul apologized and begged her to return to the city, to her old job, to their life together. Not quite friends, not quite lovers, but something more meaningful in between. An *I love you* had been professed, after all. But Sam couldn't join him. There was no longer a *together* for them. The one time she had truly needed Raul as she buried the only other man she ever loved, he had shown up a day too late.

"I said I was sorry for missing the funeral. Gimme another chance, Sam!" Raul had demanded as they both stood at the foot of her dad's freshly turned plot. Though Raul knew Sam didn't cave to demands.

"Raul, I don't belong with you. Or with anyone. I don't know what I'm doing with my life, or even what I want, but it's not in New York anymore," she had tried to explain through tears.

"You're wrong, Sam. That city is just as much a part of you as I am," Raul had also tried to explain through tears.

But Sam was done crying for the lost city and her lost love. All the tears left were for her lost father.

"I need to figure out who I am, and I can't do that with you around. I'm sorry." It was the most honest thing Sam had said in a long time.

As she turned away to head back up the concrete path that meandered between lines of headstones like gapped teeth, Raul pleaded, unaware that he was about to light a fire in her that would never quite burn out.

"Wait. Please. This isn't about me, it's about you. You once told me you wanted to make a difference in the world with your plants and your writing."

"And I had meant it when I said it. But that's gone now, Raul." The weight of the admission felt heavy in her steps, just as the weight of her father's burial felt heavy in her tears. "My stupid plants couldn't save my dad, and my writing won't save the world. It's all pointless."

"You can't give up, kid. Your dream means something! And

I can help you."

Sam stopped. Looked back at him. The wind bit her wet cheeks and the cold stung her eyes. "How can you help me when I can't even help myself? Sometimes you just have to let go. This is me. Letting go."

"So that's it then? You're going to settle, working as a typist for a tiny women's magazine when you're destined for so much more?"

She scoffed at that word: *destined*. "I don't know, but I'll figure it out. Goodbye, Raul."

It was their second goodbye, and this time Sam meant it. She walked away thinking little of Raul, an arrogant, clueless man with the privilege to dream risk-free. What could Raul possibly know about her *destiny*?

Apparently he knew a lot.

The sit-in was plotted three and a half years later. Sam arrived at the *Ladies Home Journal* head office another six months after that. As of mere hours ago, Mr. Dreyfuss, the magazine's editor, had just given women carte blanch to revolutionize a publication that reached millions of readers. And now here we were.

Raul had called and spoken to her mother. Presumably to offer a weak, belated apology for not showing up to report on the sit-in in New York City, but Sam would never know because she vowed then and there not to find out. There would be no return phone call, no reunion for Sam and Raul.

He had been given his chance to prove he cared four years ago at her father's funeral, and he arrived too late. Then she handed him another chance yesterday to support her cause and he blew it again. With 373 miles—she knew the exact number as she had counted them down from the minute she left the NYPD police station to the minute she pulled up her driveway—of distance between them, it wasn't like she would ever simply run into him. Goodbye, Raul. End of story.

Opening the locked back door—a testament to her overly cautious mother whose brain brimmed with worst-case scenarios—Sam placed her fingers between her lips and she blew out a shrill whistle. Across the next-door neighbor's backyard Fido came trotting, his short legs frenzied and his tail and mane catching the breeze as the neighbor scowled from her porch.

"My God, your face!" Miss Posey shrieked, curlers pinned in neat rows across her pink scalp. At her slippered feet a mass of black curls yapped at Sam.

Sam absentmindedly covered her eye with her palm. "It's just a bruise."

"That's why they invented concealer, dear." Miss Posey turned her attention from Sam's apparently freakish appearance to Fido. "Your *nuisance animal* escaped and pooped in my yard."

"You're welcome. Manure makes wonderful fertilizer." Sam smiled warmly.

"I wasn't thanking you." Miss Posey scowled. "You know those things don't belong in the suburbs, don't you?"

"This *thing* is a Shetland pony, ma'am, and he belongs wherever he'll be loved and taken care of," Sam replied coolly.

"I can't imagine the mess he's made of your floors," Miss Posey grumbled. Dangling from the back porch awning were tin cans on one end and milk jugs on the other, both of which mystified Sam. "And you're bringing our property values down with that beast roaming around. It's uncivilized, what you're doing. Uncivilized!"

"I'll have you know that Fido is quite intelligent, and more housebroken than your dog."

Sam knew this to be fact upon hearing the countless reprimands coming from next-door about the poodle's *oopsie-poopsies* in the living room. And kitchen. And at least once on the brand-new bedspread. That, and the constantly used pooper-scooper sitting at the ready on Miss Posey's back porch that never seemed to be applied in the backyard.

"Archibald Maverick Emerson Posey the Sixth"—and yes, that was the dog's actual name, as if Miss Posey had hand selected the most pretentious names she could think of—"is in training, I'll have you know! But your *mule* is a disturbance to our peaceful community. A nuisance, that's what he is. And dog food, that's what he should be!" But Sam could barely hear Miss Posey's reply over the poodle's barking.

Then Miss Posey ruffled her housedress with a huff, turned on her slippered heel, and slammed the metal screen door shut behind her, catching a tuft of the dog's bum fur in the door that made the pooch yelp.

Sam slipped into the solitude—and silence—of her kitchen, Fido following at her hip, his tiny hooves click-click-clicking after her. She kissed his outstretched muzzle and ran her fingers through his forelock, then dug through a pot of dirt beneath a grow light she had purchased from an off-the-grid marijuana farmer. Pulling a tassel of green leaves out, she washed off the carrot and offered a bite to Fido.

"Don't listen to that grouch," she assured him. "You're a far-out pet. And much quieter too."

Most days Sam appreciated the paid-off house in a stuffy community that she had inherited upon her grandmother's passing. Other days she loathed it. Particularly the days when the beady, judgmental eyes of traditionalist widows and status-quo-following housewives eyed Sam and her eccentric ways with disdain.

Sometimes she even felt the displeasure of her grandmother seeping from the very walls that Sam had been forbidden from redecorating—as per stated in the will. Apparently Grandma Stanton wanted her style to live as long as her legacy... which was as nonexistent as the abstract expressionist wall art that Sam had taken down on moving day and now collected dust in the garage.

Grandma Stanton's outdated tastes were woven into every detail. Built twenty years ago by Grandpa Stanton as an anniversary gift to his wife and a retirement gift to himself, within a year of moving in, the steelworker life—like father, like son—had caught up with him when he was diagnosed with lung cancer and his clinician blamed the working conditions. Though, Sam suspected the pack a day of Marlboros to be another contributor, despite the flood of ads endorsed by Mickey Mantle—"they're mild and swell tasting!"—and Jackie Robinson claiming "the filters made them finer!" If tobacco helped Hank Aaron achieve his .355 batting average, what harm could it possibly cause Grandpa Stanton, he reasoned.

Checking the time on the wall-hanging sunburst clock—the one decoration Sam kept of her grandmother's that made sense—she figured she had enough time for a bus ride into the city. She couldn't wait to give her boss at *Women's House Magazine* the good news—which he would most certainly not find to be good—that she now officially had her own big-wig-approved advice column.

By nine thirty Sam stood at the foot of the Gulf Building, its pyramidal top reaching for the sky and lit up in a steady blue, which forecast cool, fair weather. At nine forty-five Sam walked into the open bullpen office that matched every other office on the floor. And at nine forty-six Sam gasped with surprise—and well-deserved indignation—at the sight of the person filling up her tiny corner of the room, sitting in her stiff chair, with his dirty shoes propped up on her clean desk.

"Did you miss me?" he asked.

Sam barely heard him over the fury boiling her blood.

It didn't take more than a moment for her to reply, "Not in a million years."

Chapter 7

There was a sensible yet strange reason Sam refused to dream. Dreams, as they often did when the dreamer was exceptionally determined, led to achieving them. But for the Stanton family, achieving them led to certain death.

Grandpa Stanton had first taught his doe-eyed granddaughter this hard fact of life in 1950 after building his post-retirement dream home in an up-and-coming suburb, then dying from lung cancer shortly after the final brick was laid.

Sam's father reiterated the point in 1965 when he bought his dream car—a brand new cherry red, white-top, chrome-accented, 300-horsepower Chevrolet Impala *SS*, the initials alone a sign from God to purchase the convertible, as they instantly reminded him of his first and only-born: *Samantha Stanton*. He dropped dead—literally, on the living room floor—before he even put 1,000 miles on it.

Grandma Stanton's unexpected passing drove the point home, the final nail in the coffin (an apt analogy, considering the family history). Inspired by a neighbor's newly carpeted living room, Sam's grandmother, who was affluent in taste but not in money, set the curse in stone in 1966, months after installing her coveted wall-to-wall avocado green shag carpet that coordinated with Sam's eyes. Despite months of prayers for the modern luxury, God saw fit to decline her request until, refusing His higher wisdom, Grandma Stanton squandered her husband's death benefits on the plush feet-pleasing novelty. She died of a broken heart mere weeks after losing her son, and before the carpet had yet to be permanently imprinted with the feet of the sofa.

When it came to dreaming, Sam avoided it like the Spanish flu. Hope for nothing, be disappointed in nothing. And the most important part—do not die in the process. That was Sam's motto to live (and avoid death) by. But Raul Smothers came along and set her dreams in motion.

The words he had spoken over four years ago often slid between her thoughts: *"You're destined for so much more..."* She had resented him back then for filling her with hope, and she resented him now for knowing her better than she knew herself.

Raul, with his big, wide grin flashing from across her small, crowded office corner.

Raul, with his crushed velvet elephant bell-bottom-clad butt (which she hadn't failed to appreciate—she was a hot-blooded young woman, after all!) planted in her scratchy, orange chair.

Raul, with his black cowboy boots defacing her organized, metal desk.

Raul... holding a very confidential sheet of paper that belonged to her and her alone?!

"What happened to your face?" he asked, pointing to his own brown eye that sparkled with flecks of gold... not that Sam would admit to noticing.

Sam blinked herself out of his orbit. "It's just a small bruise."

"Some makeup could help with that!" a secretary who had

been eavesdropping chirped as she glided past.

As Sam reached over to snatch the paper from him, Raul pulled back just in time to evade her. She didn't offer a warm hello. Didn't show an ounce of joyful reunion. In fact, the only expression she showed was anger. She couldn't believe Raul Smothers had the gall to come to her place of work, put his rear in her chair and his feet on her desk, read her private words, and sit there smiling after letting her down... again. And she would tell him exactly why she was prepared to never speak to him... except for the part of telling him so.

"You never showed up," she stated emotionlessly.

"Well hello to you too!" Raul held the grin as he stood up, moving around the orange-topped desk, reaching out to hug her. "I can't believe I'm finally looking at you. In the flesh!"

Sam shuffled back a step. Raised a palm at him.

"There will be no hugs for friends—or should I say *ex-friends*?—who don't show up, Raul." She had selected the word *friends* carefully, lest he hope for anything more.

"Is this about your dad's funeral *over four years ago*? How many times can I apologize for getting the day wrong?" he exclaimed.

His exasperation colored his cheeks. He looked endearing when he was flustered.

"No, this isn't about my dad, though I still don't understand how you could mix up a Friday and a Saturday. I mean, how hard is it to buy a calendar? You can find one at any drugstore, you know—" She stopped herself then, not wanting to transform into her mother. "That's beside the point. I'm upset that you didn't come yesterday," she said so matter-of-factly that Raul assumed it had been something he should have known.

Her birthday? No, while he was terrible with dates and numbers, he was certain that wasn't it. An anniversary, maybe? While he vividly recalled the way Sam looked when he first met her all those years ago, standing awkwardly in the deli line, her unconventional beauty hidden by a hideous brown frock that did nothing for her complexion, he couldn't recall the exact day they met. Which was to be expected since, as previously noted, he was truly awful at remembering dates.

Having not seen Sam for years, their "meet anniversary" didn't seem like a logical answer. Nor did it resolve the question of the location for this supposedly vital event he had missed. But the way Sam assumed with such certainty that he should have known whatever *yesterday* was, it made Raul fear asking.

"I give up. Can you just tell me what exactly I did wrong... this time?" He matched her irritation tone for tone.

"I was in New York at the *Women's Home Journal* headquarters for the sit-in yesterday. You were supposed to interview us and help spread the word about the cause. But you didn't bother to show up or report on it." Sam rolled her eyes as if this sit-in was major news... and no thanks to Raul, it wasn't. "I suppose you had a more pressing story to chase."

"How was I supposed to know about your sit-in? I don't live in New York or work for the *Times* anymore. But you'd know that if you ever called."

"I did call you and left a message with your mother," Sam insisted. "Last week. With explicit instructions for where to meet and what time. I explained how important this was to me."

Raul sighed. "My mother's been dead for over a year, Sam. Which you would also know if you ever called."

"Oh." Well, *this* was uncomfortable. "I'm sorry to hear

about your mother, Raul. Are you okay?"

"Yeah, I'm fine. You know how complicated my relationship was with her."

Sam would have further asked what happened to his dear mother, who was anything but a dear. Sam had only met her once and hoped to never meet again after the way Lilith Smothers had treated her devoted-to-a-fault son. And since Mrs. Smothers was dead, now she'd never have to.

The woman was so full of toxic bitterness at the world, and cruelly took it out on Raul, that Sam could only assume her body had gone so septic that even licorice root tea couldn't help save her. But there were too many competing questions swirling in Sam's frazzled brain for her to continue speculating on what eventually took the old hag out.

"Well, then, who did I leave a message with at your apartment?"

"Beats me." Raul shrugged. "Probably whoever is renting my old apartment now. But it wasn't me or the ghost of my mother, Sam."

"Why on earth didn't the woman mention she didn't know you when I left the message?"

"I don't live there anymore, Sam. How would I know the logic of a crazy lady who likes to take messages for people she doesn't know? Anyway, now that I've exonerated myself of the crime of not showing up yesterday, can I get that hug?" Raul fished, arms stretched out wide.

But Sam's irritation hadn't yet thawed. Her gaze flicked to the flapping page that he continued to grip, which he had leisurely picked up off the top of her paper tray. She plucked the sheet from his hand.

"That is private."

"And it's good," he replied.

As one who never minced words or freely handed out compliments, if Raul Smothers said it was *good*, that meant something.

Having escalated the ranks to top reporter at the *New York Times*, and not because of a rich daddy or university connection, Raul knew a ripe scoop when he smelled one. And he possessed a unique gift for delivering it. He could massage every pertinent detail from a story and navigate the most sensitive ethical landmines with ease. In a word—or two—Raul Smothers was a media marvel.

Within one year he was promoted from telegraph messenger to mailroom clerk, and by his second year he had stolen the sought-after position of journalist, skipping the line of ivy-league college-educated applicants who looked better on paper and had paid their dues. But talent like Raul's couldn't be taught or bought. The first time he tossed a hastily-typed draft of a news report on the staff editor's desk, with the simple statement, "You should print this instead," his boss laughed Raul right out of the office. Then he read it and called Raul right back in. He knew he had found a gem in the rough.

Unfortunately, Raul was also quite aware that he was a gem in the rough. This made him arrogant, and arrogance made him intolerable.

Like most arrogant people gifted with charm, his overinflated ego smothered everyone else's opinion of him, both spoken and unspoken. Which made Raul's last name— Smothers—a perfect fit. Combine the qualities of egotistical and extroverted, throw in charisma, and you had a journalist with the confidence to pursue the biggest features, the unreservedness to chase the most evasive connections, and the magnetism to win everyone over... until they hated you again for that darn arrogance.

This circled back to what also made him intolerable: he always had to win.

Win the National Journalism Award. Win the Pulitzer Prize for Local Reporting. But for some reason Raul couldn't quite understand, he could never win *the girl*. The only girl that mattered, at least. Or any girl, if truth be told.

As a self-aware non-winner might secretly admit if plied with enough inhibition-reducing agent like valerian root, there was a love-hate relationship with any successful, intelligent charmer like Raul Smothers. You couldn't resist grabbing for the attention he doled out sparingly, but you'd walk away hating yourself for wanting it.

After one conversation you'd learn never to ask, "What story are you working on now?" unless you were prepared to hear about everything from the hot topic of the "Great Society" to the cold war in the Soviet Union; from the awful details of Charles Manson to the amusing toy soldier uniforms President Nixon appointed to the White House guards (which two decades later would be worn by a high school marching band).

At some point he would inevitably throw in a mention of the journalism award he earned for his ironic article on medical malpractice after reporting on a man who was pronounced dead, only for said dead man to wake up in his half-submerged coffin in front of grief-stricken relatives, pull the cotton swabs from his nose, and instantly die from a heart attack upon realizing he had been buried alive.

Despite establishing his professional credibility, Raul had never quite established his personal credibility. He wasn't ugly enough to scare women away, but not handsome enough to guarantee a date. This meant he had to work for that "yes," but after all that hard work wooing, and all that money spent impressing, he hoped to at least end the night with a kiss. Which rarely, if ever, culminated. To his dismay, women never seemed to find the gory details about Helter Skelter a turn-on.

There is a common misconception that arrogant men tend to be good-looking. Raul was one of many to prove this untrue. He was neither attractive nor unattractive. He simply... was. What he lacked in a hideous, villainous facial scar he made up for in brown-eyed, brown-haired forgettability. People didn't give him a second look, which made it easy for him to slip into the darkest corners of the city to observe the crime that he would later report on.

Unfortunately for him, what wasn't forgettable was his personality. His friends could only handle small doses of him at a time, and no woman on earth wanted to date a man who looked for a newsworthy story under every nook and cranny. During one memorable lunch date—for he was too "economic" to splurge on dinner for a woman he barely knew—it started off bad when he took her to a hole-in-the-wall diner, and it ended even worse when the conversation took an unusually dark turn.

"There's a new disco club that opened. I hear it's out of sight. Wanna go tonight?" the girl whose name Raul couldn't remember had asked. Not only was he terrible with numbers, he was bad at remembering names too. Unless they were newsworthy.

"Actually, I would love to. I heard Carlo Gambino was

laundering money through clubs now. I could talk to some of the employees and gather intel while you get your groove on," he had replied.

"If you don't like to dance, we can do something else. How about we go see *The Love Bug* film that just came out?" she offered, thinking light comedy could do this date some good.

"You want to support an hour-and-a-half-long Volkswagen commercial after knowing Germany's history of genocide, which led to World War II?" he countered, oblivious to her scorching glare.

By this point the nameless girl had tired of trying to meet him halfway, because Raul was not a meet-you-halfway kind of guy, and his forced smile could only take him so far. Needless to say, there was no discotheque or *Love Bug* or second date over a higher price-tag dinner.

One time Raul made the mistake of recounting the sour experience to his mother.

"What is wrong with you? I don't even know where to begin! A disappointment, that's what you are," Lilith Smothers would yell through the phone line at him one Sunday night a month, at 10:00 p.m., during the cheapest time to call. "It's probably your posture," she surmised. "You hunch over." Which he didn't. "Or maybe it's your hair. You're getting a little thin on top." Which he wasn't.

He learned during those once-a-month phone calls home never to bring up women, or work, or anything, for that matter. No number of dates he went on or prestigious awards he won would ever be good enough. His mother had been the only person blunt enough to confirm his worst fear over and over and over, in every phone call and letter and Western Union telegram: He was a failure and a disappointment, and probably the reason his father left them.

After the one and only time Sam endured Raul's mother in person, she knew exactly what his feigned arrogance stemmed from—feigned because Sam knew it was all an act, but she would never call him out on it. Everyone had their own breed of coping mechanisms, so who was Sam to judge? Thus Sam became the girl who endured Raul Smothers and all his idiosyncrasies, partly out of kindness but mostly out of pity. Despite all this, Raul was a good man who knew good writing. And he had just concluded that Sam's advice column draft was *good*.

"You really think so?" Sam asked, the cold anger gone and replaced with warm hope.

"Sure." Raul's practical approach to compliments left much to be desired.

"You're not just saying that?"

Not that Raul was saying much more than that it was passable. But Sam needed to know she hadn't fought for a chance at this advice column for nothing.

"I wouldn't lie to you. You've got talent, kid. I always knew you did, and this proves it."

Then Sam remembered she was in the *Women's House Magazine* bullpen with her ex-not-quite-friend-not-quite-lover, and she still had yet to find out why he was here.

"So we've established that you're not here to apologize about missing the sit-in. Why are you here then—in Pittsburgh, in particular my workplace?"

"Oh yeah. That. You wouldn't believe me if I told you."

Chapter 8

Sam wasn't sure which was scarier: knowing why Raul Smothers had shown up in her workplace in her town, or not knowing.

"I came to tell you I quit the *Times*."

Sam's jaw dropped open. "You quit your dream job?" It seemed like an awful long drive just to share that piece of news. "Congratulations?"

"And to tell you I now live a few minutes from here. In the city. Near you."

Sam wasn't quite sure what to make of this. Was this career change a chess move to win her over? Or was it something far worse, the only thing that Sam simply could not survive:

"You're not working for *this* magazine, are you?"

"Me—working *here*?" Raul laughed a little too hard for Sam's liking. "Not a chance." Then Raul noticed her glare a moment too late. "And I'm not trying to demean your job, Sam. It's just... you know how I felt about you leaving an actual writing career to become a glorified secretary."

Sam held up the page that Raul had called *good*. "It just so happens that I'm no longer a glorified secretary. I got promoted—thanks to the sit-in you didn't support."

"Because you left a message with a lady who wasn't my dead mother," he interjected.

"And I finally got my own advice column now."

"Really? That's far out!" Raul clapped, a genuine happy sound that made Sam smile. Finally Raul cracked her frown! "You earned it, kid. I expect big things from you."

"What about you, though?" Sam couldn't understand why Raul, the publishing prodigy, had lost his job and left the city he loved more than anything. Even more than his own mother, although that wasn't saying much.

Had this gem lost its luster?

"What about me?" Raul asked.

"What drags you to Pittsburgh, if not the distinguished *Women's House Magazine*? Because I can only imagine you came here kicking and screaming."

"You wouldn't believe me if I told you," Raul answered.

"Try me," she goaded.

"Okay. I'm working at a children's television show."

Sam's jaw dropped. She couldn't decide what was more unbelievable—his below average face donning every television set across the nation, or his child-allergic temperament shaping little tykes' minds. God save America.

"Have I heard of the program?"

Raul glanced at the floor. "Probably not. It's small potatoes and is pretty low-budget."

"I'm all about the small potatoes, Raul. I work here, after all."

"It's called *Mister Rogers' Neighborhood*. If you ever decide to watch after-school children's programming, check it out."

"Maybe I will." She absolutely would watch it the first chance she got. "Care to explain why you left a prestigious journalism career for a no-name children's television show? *And I'm not trying to demean your job,* Raul."

Raul grinned. "Well, it's complicated."

"I like complicated." Sam did like Raul, after all.

"Okay, well, I needed a break from all the dark stuff. The death and conspiracies and crime. It was exhausting and turning me into someone I didn't like." And someone most other people didn't like either. "But when I heard the show's creator—Fred Rogers—was looking for a writer, I checked it out and valued what he stands for. Plus, the job was here. Near you. It's crazy how things worked out."

"Crazy indeed."

So he *was* stalking her, Sam realized, if stalking involved quitting one's job and relocating to a new city just to be near a girl. Not that she totally minded this possibility.

"This calls for a celebration," Raul announced. "Let's go for drinks. On me."

"It's not even noon yet."

"Then how about coffee?"

He gently rested a hand on Sam's shoulder, then slipped his hand into hers, guiding her around the rows of desks, through the bullpen, and toward the lobby doors.

"I'm not sure this is a good idea," Sam concluded.

"Oh, c'mon. I'm betting you haven't had breakfast yet."

But Sam knew breakfast would lead to dinner, and dinner would lead to talking, and talking would lead to heartbreak.

"I can't. Besides, you look ridiculous in those pants. I'm not going out in public with you wearing those."

"Why? These are all the rage." Raul saw the twitch of her lip, the crease across her brow. Her objection wasn't about his magnificently large bell bottoms. "Look, I promise no funny business. We'll toast to your new column."

"Maybe another time, Raul," Sam decided. She had a new job to focus on, and she didn't need any distractions. Raul was nothing if not a distraction.

Raul took her arm and rolled up her sleeve with a gentleness that betrayed his size. He grabbed a pen off of *Betty Number Five's* desk. That was how everyone at the magazine referred to the newest fresh-faced Betty addition after human resources nixed *Babelicious Betty*, as there were four other Bettys in the office due to the popularity of Betty Hutton's 1950 role as Annie Oakley in *Annie Get Your Gun,* the year all of these Bettys seemed to have been born. Raul pressed the pen's tip to Sam's wrist. When he was done, a series of black numbers ran up her arm.

"It's my phone number. In case you need anything," Raul explained, tossing the pen back on the desk as Sam walked ahead.

"I won't ever need anything from you, Raul." Sam wanted this success on her own terms, by her own talents. Not by grabbing hold of the nearest coattails that waved past her.

"Just in case you do. That way you have it. So, what's it called—your new column?"

The reality hadn't yet set in until now. She had a column to name!

"I haven't come up with one yet."

Raul stopped mid-stride. "Hmm." He drummed his fingers on his lanky thigh. "How about…" He raised a single finger in the air with an Einsteinian flare. "*Samantha Says…!*"

The name rolled effortlessly off his tongue and invitingly

PAMELA CRANE

into her ear.

"It's a bit simplistic…" Sam replied.

"It's on-the-nose," Raul countered.

"And you know I *hate* the name *Samantha*. I prefer Sam."

"But then your readers might assume you're a man, which would defeat the whole purpose."

He had a point. A logical one.

"*Samantha Says*," she murmured. "I think I like it."

"Of course you do. Because it's perfect, like you."

Already Raul was imprinting himself on her skin, worming his way into her life, influencing her decisions, and now naming her column. Sam glanced down at his number etched across her body. No, this would absolutely not do.

With a swipe of her palm, Sam rubbed across Raul's numbers, smearing them into a blur.

Raul's jaw dropped open. "So just like that you want to wipe my number off of your arm and me out of your life?"

"I need to do this on my own," Sam stated.

"And that means ending our friendship?"

"You'll always be my greatest distraction, Raul. I need to focus on doing this myself, which is why I have to let go. It's for the best."

He could never understand how easy it was for Sam to ask of him simply because he was there. In the same way, she could never understand how easy it was for Raul to give to her simply because she was there. Both Sam and Raul knew—desperately wishing it didn't have to be this way—that the only way their friendship worked was for there to be no friendship at all. It was the curse of being stuck between friendship and love.

And so the day that *Samantha Says* was born was the day

Sam laid her feelings for Raul to rest.

Women's House Magazine
May 1970 Issue

SAMANTHA SAYS…

Q: Dear Samantha,

I wanted to open with a congratulations on your new column. I was thrilled to discover that the magazine's dedicated readers will at last get a fresh perspective from a person who understands the discomfort of menstrual cramps and the release of removing a bra at the end of the day. Advice for women by women? Who would have thought we could offer anything more than recipes and cleaning tips, let alone real advice for real problems!

Speaking of real problems, I come to you with a marriage dilemma. My husband works in the steel mill and is always tired when he gets home. While I understand the hard labor and long days he suffers, it is taking a toll on our relationship. He is too exhausted to eat, too tired to talk, and too sleepy to… you know what. What hot-blooded man is ever too tired for that? As a result of our dry spell, he is not only weary but irritable with me!

I have suggested he quit and get another less physically demanding job, but losing his union benefits would bring on a whole other set of problems. Leaky roofs and empty fridges don't remedy themselves.

As my children are getting older, my life revolves around his unpredictable moods, and I am at my wits' end waiting and wondering how he'll feel when he arrives home from work each day. Worry keeps me up at night with thoughts of "Can our marriage survive this?" and "What will happen if he leaves me?"

As the esteemed artist Vincent Van Gogh said: "I dream my painting, and then I paint my dream." My dream is to stop those fears and help our marriage thrive. What can I do?

Sincerely,
Dry-spell Debbie

A: Dear Dry-spell Debbie,

I wanted to open with a thank you for the vote of confidence. It means a lot to me personally that I get this opportunity to connect with my readers, and hopefully educate you on more than how to repurpose leftover Spam or style the perfect asymmetrical bob (which I have no experience with anyway).

I applaud your courage to reach out for help. This sounds more like a health issue than a marriage dilemma. Considering your husband's working conditions in a steel mill, he is more than likely exposed to myriad chemicals that could be causing his symptoms of lethargy and other unrealized health problems. Thus, all of this could be more than just a hard day at work taking its toll.

My first recommendation would be for him to do a daily cleanse to detoxify his body. This could include drinking green tea and adding turmeric to his diet. And don't forget to replace that Schlitz beer with water!

In addition, he'll want to consume more vitamin B12 to boost his energy. I won't bore you with the details of how B12 can promote methylation pathways, but trust me, it helps. And since B12 is found in red meat, I'm sure your husband won't mind an extra steak dinner or two each week!

An extra tip for curing the under-the-covers drought: chocolate for you and epimedium plant for him. It's not called horny goat weed for nothing!

Last, but most importantly, you should not be waiting and wondering for anyone. As the esteemed Van Gogh also said: "If you hear a voice within you say, 'You cannot paint,' then by all means paint, and that voice will be silenced." Find your passion and silence the voice that keeps you up at night. Your husband is not the only one who deserves to thrive.

Sincerely,
Samantha

Chapter 9

"Houston, we've had a problem!" Franklin Getty yelled, quoting the famous line from last month's *Apollo 13* oxygen tank explosion that had the world watching in horror on the edge of their seats.

"What kind of problem?" Sam stared at her boss numbly, wondering what she had done *this time* to upset him.

"What is this hogwash? How did we publish this?" Mr. Getty waved a newspaper at Sam while the now-disbanded Beatles sang "Let It Be" from a state-of-the-art stereo coffee table.

He tossed the article Sam had spent weeks drafting, then writing, then editing, at the garbage can beside his desk and missed it by about five feet. A stack of copies of the already-published May 1970 issue that Mr. Getty apparently hadn't proofed sat in front of him, and Sam wondered if he planned to toss every last one of them.

"Do you mind?" Sam waited inside his office doorway, aiming her finger at the Drexel stereo that cost more than her monthly wage, then pointed to her ears.

The room was littered with empty bottles of champagne, crushed cans of Schlitz beer, and a tray with two deviled eggs left over from the office mixer Sam hadn't been invited to. A pair of white go-go boots lay haphazardly on the floor next to the orange sofa that Mr. Getty sat on. He snuffed out his cigarette in an overflowing ashtray, rolled his eyes, then clicked the music off.

"You need to appreciate technology more, Samantha. That was Vibrasonic reflected sound energy with dynamic sound focus and a three-channel output. Swell, huh?"

"Yes, swell." Sam could care less about any of those words, let alone what they meant. All she learned from it was that when Mr. Getty told her a raise wasn't in the budget, now she knew why.

He looked at her expectantly, but she was only standing in the editor-in-chief's office because he had beckoned her. And when Mr. Getty beckoned, you came. Or else you were demoted to mailroom, which was considered by many to be the tenth circle of hell.

"Did you call me to discuss my column for the May issue?" Sam ventured a guess, growing irritated.

"Oh, right." Mr. Getty gestured to the other end of the sofa. "You'll want to sit for this."

"I prefer to stand."

"Suit yourself."

Sam entered the office and stood rather than sit on a mysterious woman's fur coat that was far too warm for the balmy spring weather, and which took up the other two cushions that Mr. Getty didn't occupy. The coat looked suspiciously a lot like Betty Number Five's, who was young enough to be Mr. Getty's daughter but overeager enough to be his mistress. Sam scribbled a mental note to have a chat about self-respect with Mr. Getty's new secretary later.

"So, about your article," he picked up another copy and

glanced at it, "what is this crap?" Then he slammed Sam's newly minted advice column on the coffee table as he revved up for an ear beating that Sam had already steeled herself against.

"It's called *Samantha Says*, sir. I take it you don't like it?"

It was obvious that he didn't, but Sam dutifully adopted the role of naïve simpleton because the only way to calm the raging lunatic down was to make him pity her. He couldn't berate someone who didn't know better. Like a starving stray puppy, or a dumb female advice columnist. *Pity poor, stupid Samantha...*

"Does it look like I like it? I hate it. It will ruin us!"

Ruin seemed a bit extreme, given that the *Women's House Magazine* circulation numbers were in the low thousands and couldn't get much lower before hitting nonexistent.

"They why did you approve it for publication?" Sam asked.

"Because," he muttered begrudgingly, "I didn't proof it first."

It had been months since Mr. Getty had last checked out a copy of the magazine he was editor-in-chief over, because Mr. Getty had already mentally checked into retirement.

"Regardless, sir, I think you're overreacting. You clearly don't understand the depth of my content."

Oops. That crossed a line, Sam realized too late as Mr. Getty's face purpled.

"Did you just accuse me of *overreacting*? Are you hysterical? I should fire you on the spot!"

"Fire me? My column is not *that* bad."

"This is exactly why I didn't want to give a woman this position. None of you know the first thing about writing."

"And you don't know the first thing about women—" Only

too late did Sam realize her mistake as she hastily added, "sir."

Mr. Getty hmphed at this. "If you know what's good for you, you will take your medicine like a man and shut up, Samantha."

God forbid a woman show the slightest emotion, or offer an alternative logic to the one held by her male counterpart, because when she did, the label *hysterical* was slapped on her as if it was a formal diagnosis, and a script for one sedative or another was imminently prescribed.

"Wait until my cousin Jean Paul sees this," he groaned. "I'll be the laughingstock of the family."

Franklin Getty claimed his second cousin was none other than the world's richest—and stingiest—man, J. Paul Getty. In a building full of journalists, not one had been able to successfully substantiate this claim, no matter how often Mr. Getty dropped the miserly oil magnate's name into every conversation with a familial ease devoid of anything personal that would prove it.

"Mr. Getty, hear me out. This is real advice to a real problem. Dry-spell Debbie wants to help her exhausted husband, and I gave her a very logical, very helpful solution."

Getty laughed, his lip curled up in a cruel smirk. "Green tea and turmeric? Are you kidding me with this?"

"Don't forget the B12," Sam added. "It's necessary for producing S-adenosylmethionine to improve mood and immune function—"

"I don't care about any of that nonsense you're spouting, Samantha." Getty refused to use Sam's preferred name just as Callous Calvin Dreyfuss had done before him. And every boss before him. What was so difficult about pronouncing *Sam*?

"And none of our readers will care either. All I care about is magazine sales, and this is not the way to do it."

"You think women don't want to know about the benefits of B12?" Sam asked. "I could go into more explanation about how it works with folate to improve red blood cells, if that would help."

"No, that will *not* help. I thought I told Mel to work with you on your column."

Mel had told her to skedaddle, but there was no point tattling on him, because in the offices of *Women's House Magazine*, the men stuck together. So instead she said, "I did ask Mel for help, but he felt it best I learn on my feet."

The actual conversation went more like Sam begrudgingly approaching Mel, the dethroned advice columnist of *Tell Mel*, and him yelling at her to scram before he put a foot up her rear. Then she got nothing but a cold shoulder and silent treatment after what she thought was a threat or two mumbled under his breath for her stealing his job.

She was perfectly happy with Mel's refusal, since she had never wanted his advice—whether reading it in his column or on how to write hers—in the first place. Despite his years of marital experience and a PhD in accounting, Mel knew nothing about women's troubles, other than how to multiply their dividends in his own marriage as he belittled his wife and turned her into the butt of every office joke. In Sam's mind, Mel was a narcissist, and the advice columnist world was rife with them. They excelled at assuming everyone else was the problem and they held the only solution.

"Obviously you don't have the natural talent Mel does," Mr. Getty concluded.

"Because I offered different advice from what he would have given?"

"You're missing my point! First of all, you're promoting undocumented therapies that have not been proven to work. There are real scientists curing real illnesses with real medicine. Second of all, women don't care about vitamins. They want to know about the latest Memorial Day party cake recipe. Just write what I tell you instead of this trash."

"With all due respect, it's not trash. How many variations of pineapple upside-down cake do you think women need? I'm trying to write about something new. Something relevant. And health and wellness are relevant. Dry-spell Debbie at least thinks so."

"Fine." Getty sighed exasperatingly. "You want to talk about health? I've got a compromise."

Grabbing a pen, he scratched ink across Sam's pages, scrawling frantically in an illegible script, then handed the papers to her.

"Replace the B12 with those black beauty pills that give you energy and help women lose weight. Then we can plug an ad in for the pills, along with a clothing line to bring in some extra advertising revenue. I can see the ad tagline now: *One pill tonight, and your pants won't be tight!*" Getty raised his hands, as if boxing the slogan in mid-air.

Black beauties—a dangerous mind-altering drug made by the same manufacturer that created Nosartin, the heart medicine that had killed Sam's father. There was no way on earth—or in hell, as Sam speculated Mr. Getty could very well be Satan's second cousin—that she would endorse something so harmful. This was no compromise. This was a dictatorship.

"Sir, for centuries homeopathic remedies have been used in Eastern cultures and have proven to be effective. And safe. I'm not saying modern medicine doesn't work, but just because something is modern doesn't make it better."

"That's exactly what *modern* is—better! Otherwise we wouldn't use it!" Getty bellowed.

Sam did not want to waste oxygen trying to explain how during her grandmother's youth, highly addictive cocaine tablets could be purchased at your local Sears Roebuck, or consumed in your Coca-Cola soft drink. During her mother's youth, children were offered Bayer aspirin laced with heroine for the common cough. And a mere three years ago, in 1967, Dr. Walter Freeman was still performing legalized lobotomies, including brain-hacking President Kennedy's sister, which resultantly left her an invalid. All *modern* medicine, and all eventually proven ineffective. In fact, quite the opposite of healthy: *deadly*.

But none of these examples would break through Franklin Getty's thick, stubborn skull, because men like him only believed in one truth. The one stuck inside his huge ego.

Sam thought of her dad, and the Nosartin that had killed him despite its FDA stamp of approval and Cook Pharmaceuticals' assurance that the side effects—including but not limited to blurred vision, rapid heart rate, anxiety, panic attacks, and stroke—were perfectly normal, completely safe. For the sake of her father, and all others who suffered at the hands of medical malpractice, Sam refused to give in. Especially to an uneducated tyrant like Mr. Getty who aided and abetted the murder of countless people at the hands of Cook Pharmaceuticals' negligence.

"Do you realize what pharmaceutical companies put in drugs?" Sam glanced at Mr. Getty's desk, where an orange prescription bottle sat next to a ceramic coffee mug with an image of Jackie Gleason's *Joe the Bartender* emblazoned on the side. She picked up the bottle and read the label: *oxyphenisatin*. "Did you know this laxative can cause liver damage?"

Mr. Getty's eyes widened in horror as he yanked the bottle from Sam's grip. "Laxative? Uh, that's not mine."

"It says your name right there—" Sam pointed at the label as Mr. Getty slapped her hand away. "They are already trying to withdraw it from the market because it's toxic."

"My doctor never mentioned that."

"I thought it wasn't your prescription."

"Okay, okay, you got me. I'm constipated because of the stress of this job, and you're not helping matters, Samantha."

"That's exactly what I want to change!" Sam exclaimed. Finally Mr. Getty was getting it! "Instead of promoting outdated norms, I'm suggesting a *fresh* alternative, if you will. Something no other magazine is offering."

"What you're doing is trying to branch into investigative journalism, not entertainment journalism. Stay in your lane, Miss Stanton, and leave the reporting to the reporters."

"I was given carte blanche to write what I want to write. I put my job security on the line for this. If I end up *ruining* the magazine, as you so clearly think I will, then you can have my head and my job. But if I increase subscription numbers, like I know I can do, you can thank me later. I'll even save your liver *and* cure your constipation, if you give me a chance."

Mr. Getty scoffed. "Not likely." Then his gaze lingered on the prescription bottle. "If you can give me proof—tangible evidence—of your outrageous claims, I'll let you run your advice column the way you want it."

"I intend to."

"By the end of the week."

"The end of *this* week? How am I supposed to prove—"

"Figure it out. You want to be a journalist, then this is what it takes. Deadlines, pressure, chasing leads, fact-checking… now get out of my office before I change my mind."

Before Sam could reach the door, Getty stopped her with an earnest, "Wait!"

She turned to him, already knowing the words before they parted his lips.

"Drink more water, and I'll bring you some psyllium to loosen your bowels," she said. Mr. Getty's face contorted in confusion. "It's an herbal seed packed with soluble fiber. You'll see results within a day or two."

Seemingly satisfied, Mr. Getty grunted approval. "I'll expect it on my desk by lunch. Oh, and Samantha?"

"Yes, sir?"

"I'm getting complaints from the secretaries that you're too… uptight. Relax a little. Show some teeth once in a while. You look prettier when you smile."

She closed Mr. Getty's office door, mumbling, "I'll show *you* some teeth," under her breath as the Beatles resurrected in the silence behind her.

Already a plan formed in her mind, the details whirling and swirling in her dark matter. This task would either take her all the way to the top, or throw her underfoot.

A constipation cure by lunch, and proof of Cook Pharmaceuticals' dangerous drugs by the end of the week? Sam liked a challenge, but this would require journalistic finesse that she severely lacked. Luckily she knew someone who had it in spades and who would travel the ends of the earth—or at least from New York City to Pittsburgh—to help her.

Chapter 10

Desperate times called for desperate measures. And Sam was nothing if not desperate.

It had been more than a month—thirty-four days to be exact—since Sam had last spoken to Raul, but not for lack of thinking of him. In fact, his smile plagued her waking thoughts every morning. His laughter haunted her afternoons, the only company she kept as she ate her triple-decker club alone at the deli across the street from her office, where she imagined bumping into him—and subsequently knocking her own salami sandwich across the floor as she had once done to him the first day they met. And Raul's was the last face she conjured as she drifted off to sleep each night. But her instinct for self-survival made her hands heel any time she reached for the phone to call him.

Until today.

Today was an exception, because her career depended on a man's help. On Raul, specifically. The one who had already created a habit of letting her down twice now. But Sam, against her better judgement, had no other option than to risk it all—her pride and her heart, the only two things that mattered—as she picked up the telephone receiver. Placing her finger in the rotary dial, she carefully spun each number Raul had handwritten on her wrist before their last parting, the ink of which she had subsequently smeared to oblivion, but not before she had memorized each digit.

Unlike Raul, Sam had an excellent memory when it came to numbers.

"Hello?" Raul answered breathlessly on the first ring, as if he had been expecting her call.

"Hi," Sam stated simply, betraying her racing heartbeat. "It's me."

"Me who?" Raul asked.

Suddenly Sam flushed with embarrassment and itched to hang up. Perhaps he had already forgotten the sound of her voice, even though she intimately knew the way his words quickened when he broke a story, or how his voice thickened to a low murmur when he shared something deeply personal.

"I'm kidding, Sam! Of course I know it's you. So you decided to keep my phone number after all, huh?"

Sam glanced up from her typewriter, where people dashed across the bullpen, weaving through rows of desks and idling secretaries. She dropped her voice to a lower decibel.

"Can't a girl change her mind?"

"But you said, and I quote, that '*you won't* ever *need anything from me.*'"

How *Raul* of him to quote her verbatim.

"Some things change."

"They sure do, Sam. So what caused the change of heart?"

"Change of *mind*," Sam corrected, lest Raul get the wrong idea. Nothing with her heart had changed. Of that she needed to be clear.

"Okay, I'll bite. What's the skinny?"

While Raul sounded so casually confident, Sam's heart rate

hadn't yet returned to normal. She pushed through the apprehension regardless.

"I was hoping I could ask for your help with something."

"What kind of *something*?"

"I need to get in touch with an untouchable person."

"Ooh, I'm intrigued. Who is the unlucky fellow?" There was that rush of sound that Sam recognized as Raul's interest grew.

"Thomas Cook."

Raul scoffed. "The CEO of Cook Pharmaceuticals?"

"The one and only," she said.

"Why on earth would you want to contact *him*?"

"Because he is the man responsible for my father's death. And finding him is the only way I'm going to bring him and his evil empire down."

"Evil empire? Sam, you're not Carol Danvers trying to take down Doctor Doom." When Raul noticed that Sam was unusually silent, he went on to explain, "Carol Danvers—you know, Ms. Marvel, the superhero?" Sam remained contemplatively confused. "From *Marvel Comics*?" Still nothing. "Were you born under a rock?"

In all likelihood Sam could have been. Minnie Stanton had birthed her on the side of the highway on the way to the hospital after being stuck in bumper-to-bumper traffic inside the Liberty Tunnel, one of the many tunnels built into the Allegheny mountains that surrounded the city.

Tunnels, bridges, and steep roads—these were the proudest claims to fame by Pittsburgh, Pennsylvania, along with the toxic wastewater from the coking process used in steel production that bled into the three rivers that supplied questionable drinking water to the city's residents.

"Anyway, Sam, Thomas Cook is a powerful man, and powerful men are dangerous men. Just stay away from him. Please."

"His toxic medicine killed my father. I'm not letting it go. This was why I fought so hard to get this advice column in the first place."

"So that you could make a public spectacle of him and exact your revenge?" Raul scoffed. "Are you crazy?"

"Maybe. But if you won't help me, I'll do it without you." Sam always had, after all.

This statement was followed by reticence. Sam knew she was asking the impossible. After hours of research, she had gone from dead end to deader end as she discovered Thomas Cook was unlisted in the phone directory, inaccessible for appointments, and refused any and all meetings, according to his spiteful secretary who had bluntly rejected Sam's requests for an interview the first and second time she had called. By Sam's third call, the ruthless assistant had simply hung up at the sound of Sam's voice.

Sam had even gone so far as to sit outside the Cook Pharmaceuticals' US Steel Tower headquarters, the newest and tallest skyscraper addition to the skyline, not even open to the public yet. So she waited until the brimming city had emptied its bowels, watching the lobby doors late into the evening for Thomas Cook's departure. Only by the pity of a young intern who worked on Cook's floor, identified by the ID badge hanging from a lanyard, did Sam discover why the man was so successfully evasive.

"Rumor has it that Dr. Cook paid off the builders to give

him his own private entrance and exit," the intern explained when Sam had approached her outside the black-marbled atrium, asking if she knew when Dr. Cook usually left the office. "When you control the drugs that save lives, you can afford just about anything."

Which made Thomas Cook the richest—and most elusive—man in the city.

"So will you help me or not, Raul?" Sam spoke into the static phone line.

Raul sighed. "I wish I could, but even I can't get access to him. Trust me, I've tried."

"You have?"

Sam wondered why Thomas Cook had landed on Raul's radar in the first place. During his *New York Times* journalism days, Raul had only pursued scandals and injustices, not entitled rich businessmen... unless the entitled rich businessmen happened to be behind the scandals and injustices, which was more often than not.

Did Raul know something about Thomas Cook that Sam didn't?

"Years ago I tried to investigate him. I think Cook knew his heart drugs were killing people—"

"Like my dad," Sam interjected.

"Uh, right, like your dad," Raul continued, "but I failed to get the story. And now Cook is still getting away with it."

"That's why I need to stop him!"

"No, Sam, it turns out it was for the best that I never exposed it."

"For the best? How can you say that?"

"Trust me, you don't want to know. Please leave it alone."

"I can't. My job depends on it."

In a sparse bachelor pad on one side of the city, Raul stood at his kitchen counter, twirling the phone cord around his finger wondering how he could possibly tell Sam the truth of what he knew.

In a skyscraper bullpen on the other side of the city, Sam sat in her scratchy orange office chair, twirling the phone cord around her finger wondering what Raul could possibly be hiding.

"Why did you give up the story, Raul?" Sam needed to know. Raul never gave up on a lead, not even a dangerous one.

Raul silently debated, then said, "The moment my boss got wind that I was looking into Cook, they pulled the plug on my research and demanded I stop... or lose my job. I couldn't give up the job when it helped expose so many wrongs."

"So then you understand my dilemma," Sam persisted. "I can't lose this job. Please."

"All I've got is a flimsy file on the guy, which you can have. Maybe you'll have better luck with it than I did."

Sam would need a lot more than luck.

"Do you happen to have a home address in that flimsy file?"

"Home address, work hours, relationship status... I even managed to dig up his home phone number. Though I think his number has been changed since then. As for getting access to Thomas Cook, he's as shifty as President Nixon on tax day. You'll need to get creative in order to get close to him, Sam."

Creative, Sam could do. Getting close to people, though? That wasn't Sam's strong suit.

"Any suggestions for how to do that?" she asked.

"You could always date the guy, assuming he's still single."

Raul laughed at that, but the idea wasn't half bad. "That was a joke, by the way. You're not actually going to try to date him, are you?"

"I just might, Raul. For the story, of course. Unless you don't think he'll go for a girl like me?" Sam wasn't sure she wanted to hear Raul's reply. She knew she wasn't most men's type, but she didn't need it spelled out for her.

"I've looked into the women he's usually seen out in public with. Brainy types. But he's also got a womanizing streak. You've got the intellect to hold his interest, but you'll need to work on your wardrobe and makeup…"

It would require a makeover of epic proportions, but Sam knew someone who could assist with that.

"So you'll help me then?"

Raul hesitated. "I don't know, Sam…"

"Are you going to make me beg?" Sam had a feeling it would come to this, and she was prepared for it.

"No begging required," Raul finally concluded. "But I'll only help you on one condition."

"What's that?"

"That you agree to go out with me."

"Together? In public?"

"What other way is there?" Raul chuckled.

"I'll agree to your terms, as long as you agree to mine."

"Name your price."

"I get to pick the location."

"Deal," Raul hastily accepted, unaware that Sam was plotting what would be his worst nightmare incarnate. "That sounds fair."

Whether this was intentionally set up to give Sam the upper

hand in this agreed-upon date, or simply to amuse her, Raul would never find out, but it ended up serving both purposes.

Chapter 11

"This is totally unfair!"

Raul stood at the entrance to the newest roller-coaster addition at Kennywood Amusement Park, watching in horror from the safety of the ground as the cart climbed and plunged and twisted and turned along the tracks, already flipping Raul's naturally sensitive stomach. Screams of excitement joined the sounds of metal clanging as Raul imagined his own eardrum-splitting cries soon joining theirs.

"You really thought I would enjoy going to 'The Roller Coaster Capital of the World' for our date?" Raul lamented.

"Don't be a baby, Raul. We can't stay in Kiddieland all day. A grown man riding children's rides? That is just plain old creepy. And it could probably get you thrown in the slammer."

Sam had already dragged Raul across the park, from the Skooter bumper cars to the Turtle tumble bug. The jarring motions and centrifugal forces had already done him in, but Sam wasn't done with him yet. To conclude their date, she had given him the choice of two rides: the Jack Rabbit, famous for its double-dip drop, or the Thunderbolt, known for its double helix. Both double the trouble for poor Raul and his bilious belly.

When he couldn't pick the lesser of two evils, Sam chose for him. Thunderbolt it was. The Potato Patch French fries tossed around in Raul's gut, a warning of what was to come if he got on that ride.

"You know I get motion sickness easily," he whined.

"I brought ginger root to help with that."

"And I hate heights."

"Then close your eyes."

"But I'm terrified of roller coasters."

"Which is why I'm going to help you overcome your fear of death-defying fun. Statistically speaking, you had a 99 percent higher chance of dying in a car accident on the way here than you do riding the Thunderbolt."

"Especially with the way you drive, the pedal to the metal," he murmured as sweat pooled on his worry-creased forehead.

Sam grabbed his slippery hand, tugging him along the moving line of eager riders. "Come on. You'll have fun. Just give it a chance."

Raul shook his head, pulling away from Sam and stepping on the clog of a teenage girl behind him, who yelped in response. Raul sputtered an apology, wondering why anyone in their right mind would wear platforms to walk around in all day at an amusement park. However, if modern teens were anything like teenager Raul—who drag raced down highways at two o'clock in the morning, or on an impulse traveled cross-country with the Freedom Riders protesting segregation, which subsequently earned him a lifetime grounding sentence from his mother—most teens were not in their right mind.

"I don't want to ride. I'll get sick."

"Eat this. Problem solved." Sam handed him a shriveled root she plucked from her pocket, as if this would lessen the prospect of him vomiting all over her.

"I'm not eating that." He grimaced at the gnarled brown

lump that he was certain would only make his symptoms worse. "And I'm warning you—I *will* throw up on you, Sam, if I go on that ride."

"I never liked this shirt anyway."

Though Raul could tell she had picked out the white peasant blouse especially for this date, as it was the only fashionable top he'd ever seen her wear.

"No."

"Please?"

"I can't. I'm afraid."

"Of what?"

Raul thought for a moment. "Of getting hurt, I suppose."

Sam squeezed his clammy palm. "Everyone is afraid of getting hurt, Raul. But some things are worth the risk, don't you think?"

Raul couldn't waste this opportunity to throw a little jab at the girl who kept getting away. "I'm done taking risks, Sam. You're the one who taught me that."

Her eyebrow lifted. "What is *that* supposed to mean?"

Crossing his arms over his chest, he stiffened and leaned against the metal railing that wove a maze toward the roller coaster loading dock.

"It just means that I risked everything to come to this city to be with you, and I haven't heard from you in a month. Clearly I don't mean to you what you mean to me."

"I never asked you to move here."

"You didn't need to ask, Sam. I came because I... I care about you and wanted to help you."

"And I never asked for your help."

"Until now," Raul reminded her.

"One request in all our years of friendship!"

"Doing the one thing I wish you wouldn't—going after Thomas Cook. Alone, for that matter."

"There's no other way for me to prove myself capable of handling my new job otherwise. If I relied on you, it wouldn't be *my* credit. It'd be yours. Because you're Raul Smothers, award-winning journalist, and I'm just Samantha Stanton, low-level advice columnist."

"Don't forget Samantha Stanton, who doesn't call her friends unless she needs something."

Sam huffed. "Don't pin that guilt on me. You didn't exactly make friendship with you easy. I was quite clear that I wanted to pursue my own path, a career… and if we were to…" she wordsmithed carefully, "become more than friends, you know it would derail everything I've worked for. I would end up exactly like my mother—a housewife barefoot in the kitchen with a baby on her hip and supper in the oven and her dreams in the toilet. That's not me, and it will never be me."

"What's wrong with having a family, Sam? You act like that is the worst possible thing you can imagine."

"To me, maybe it is. Women are not all built the same. We are not all supposed to be married, popping out kids, and cooking beef stroganoff while doting on our hapless, helpless husbands."

Just the thought of stroganoff sent Raul's reflux in a whirl.

"If you like the idea of family so much, why don't *you* do the housekeeping and child-rearing and cooking?" Sam challenged.

"Maybe I will," Raul accepted.

"The day I see a man barefoot in the kitchen with a baby on

his hip is the day I'll marry you, Raul." Sam laughed as she imagined it, because in 1970 it was laughably unimaginable.

"Samantha Stanton, one day you will eat those words."

"The only one among us eating anything is *you*—" she took the ginger root from his hand and popped it into his mouth, "before getting on the ride."

By now they were standing on the narrow roller coaster platform, bodies bumping, kids careening, ride operators barking orders. Sam stepped into the metal cart, waiting for Raul to join her.

"Are you coming?" she asked.

He stood, feet frozen to the wooden platform in fear.

"You trusted me enough to follow me across two states, Raul. Trust me enough to follow me now."

Raul felt her point prick his heart, and that was all it took. Anything Sam wanted Raul would have given her.

Ten minutes later they exited the ride with Sam wearing Raul's lunch and Raul wearing an *I-told-you-so* green-faced grimace. And he would suffer through it all over again if it meant hearing Sam laugh so freely, his damp hand clenching hers.

Chapter 12

There are many ways for a writer to get into trouble, but only one that could get them killed. And Sam had found that exact one:

Picking the wrong thread to pull.

"Are you sure you need to do this?" Raul confirmed one last time, standing across from Sam on an empty sidewalk beneath a frowning moon and starless sky. "You can't undo what you find out."

"Stop worrying so much," Sam replied.

"I'll never stop worrying about you."

The flimsy yellow folder Raul handed Sam when she dropped him off at his apartment was less impressive than she had expected of a renowned investigative journalist. Only bare bone facts were tucked into the file that Nancy Drew in her sleuthing infancy could have dug up. But at least Sam now had the one thing she needed—Thomas Cook's home address— which was enough to get the ball rolling. And rolling quickly, she reminded herself as she parked in her driveway.

She was down to mere days before Mr. Getty's deadline to prove that Cook Pharmaceuticals was selling dangerous drugs… and that Thomas Cook himself knew it. It was a daunting challenge, but one that Sam had been anticipating for the past five years since her father's death.

Evening fell like a dark curtain as she headed up her front walkway, eager to change out of the blouse stained and stinking with Raul's amusement park lunch. She paused halfway across the yard. The suburban streetlight illuminated something peculiar next door.

A stout metal *For Sale* sign hung crookedly in the neighbor's front yard, listing a phone number with the wording: *To any purchaser regardless of race, color, or creed.* A pity it wasn't Miss Posey and Archibald Maverick Emerson Posey the Sixth who were relocating, whose hatred for Fido knew no end.

Sam had met her other next-door neighbor only once, a vampiric recluse of a man who avoided sunlight like it was deadly, and detested vegetables unless they were deep-fried. The day he had beckoned Sam from his open window, she hadn't made it past his living room before she spotted fast-food bags of every chain and variety, from Roy Rogers roast beef to Winky's hamburgers and French fries. After offering him a mild nutritional scolding, along with fennel seeds to cure his indigestion complaints, she had never been invited back and occasionally wondered why.

"Dead," a voice spooked Sam from behind in the dark.

Sam turned to find Miss Posey had meandered into her yard, with Archibald making an oopsie-poopsie in Sam's herb garden.

"What happened?" Sam asked.

"His estranged daughter found what was left of him decaying in his living room. Apparently he'd been dead for weeks before she showed up."

That explained the lack of invite, along with what he had done with Sam's fennel seeds and nutritional advice. Considering the vitamin D in sunshine was integral to calcium absorption in the bones to prevent osteoporosis, it was no surprise his body eventually crumbled to dust in his grease-stained plaid club chair.

"Can you believe his house sold within a day?" Miss Posey continued, rambling over any thoughts Sam might have had about his death that barely merited a footnote in the obituary. "Who would buy a house a man just died in?"

"Most people, I assume," Sam concluded, assuming most homes had someone die in them at some point. With the exception of hospitals and the occasional fatal car crash, where else were people dying, if not in their own beds?

Miss Posey shook her head. "Someone with something to hide, I bet."

"Or someone looking for a good deal?" Sam suggested.

"I'd give my left kidney to find out how much they paid for it. Probably got it for a steal… I just hope they're not dirt-poor hippies, bringing drugs and rock 'n' roll and all that New Age nonsense onto our quiet street."

It was no wonder Miss Posey was head of the neighborhood gossip chain. She was naturally talented at it.

"I'm sure whoever it is will be a welcome addition to the community." Sam generally liked hippies. They seemed to be the only ones who appreciated nature, unlike Miss Posey and her dog, who just dug up Sam's rosemary and was pawing at her ginseng with reckless abandon.

"We'll see…" Miss Posey sounded doubtful. "I saw a U-Haul rental van earlier this morning loading all the old furniture out of there. No sign of the buyers yet. All we can do is pray we get a better neighbor this time around. One who actually tends to his yard…"

She gestured to the barely ankle-skimming grass that looked pretty well tended to Sam, and which Miss Posey certainly shouldn't blame a weeks-old dead man for neglecting.

Then Miss Posey cast a glare at Sam. "Or perhaps a neighbor who doesn't turn our nice, clean neighborhood into a foul-smelling mule farm."

"Pony, not a mule," Sam corrected, then wished Miss Posey a pleasant evening and retreated inside to change into her one-piece dotted culottes.

Sam had big plans with a small file tonight, as she looked forward to leafing through Raul's notes and coming up with a scheme to stop Cook Pharmaceuticals once and for all.

By the time Johnny Carson's *Tonight Show* came on television, Sam's AAA map was unfolded across her dining room table and she had charted her directions to Morewood Heights, home to the richest men in Pittsburgh. But driving to Thomas Cook's mansion was only the first plan of attack. The real battle would be grabbing his attention—and holding it long enough to find proof of malpractice, which was a much loftier war. There was only one person who could help Sam with that.

A master manipulator. The most deceptive dame Sam knew. And professionally pretty.

The front door swung open.

"Avon calling!" Minnie Stanton chimed from the entryway, nudging the door shut with her rear. "Mummy to the rescue!"

Sam's mother whirled into the dining room like a dervish, lugging a blue floral tapestry tote, which she slung with a huff onto the table. Fido trotted his way over, nuzzling Minnie's elbow with his nose despite her attempts to shoo him away.

"Can you please put this thing outside? He is going to poop

all over the floor."

"That's why he wears a manure bag."

"And he won't stop bumping me with his nose."

"Those are his love nudges. You should be honored, since Fido doesn't approve of just anybody. Horses can smell pheromones, which determine if you're friend or foe—"

"Thank you for the science lesson, dear, but let's move on to more important things." Minnie patted her magician's bag of tricks and miracles guaranteed to turn Sam from homely to hot-to-trot in one sitting. "Now, this won't be easy," Minnie warned, unzipping the sack full of color palettes and creams. "Do you need a Valium before we start?"

"No, Mom, I can handle it."

"And it might be downright painful," Minnie added, holding up a pointy metal object that glinted under the dining room light.

"I've got a high pain threshold."

"You probably won't recognize yourself afterward, Samantha," Minnie concluded with a *click-click* of the tweezers.

Sam squirmed. "That's the whole reason I called you, Mom."

Minnie giggled gleefully as she clapped with excitement. "My little girl is finally becoming a woman!"

"You've been waiting for this moment since I was born, haven't you?"

"Well, you never did like dresses or makeup or dollies as a child. So yes, as a mother who specializes in beauty, this is a landmark day for me." Minnie grimaced, leaning forward with a curious expression, then plucked a stray hair from Sam's brow with a flourish. "One down, thirty to go!"

By the time Minnie's makeover was complete, and she held up her silver hand mirror in front of her daughter's face, Sam couldn't decide if she looked more like an *It Girl* or Cousin Itt. Her eyebrows were rimmed with angry red blotches, her lips stained an unnatural pink, and her bronzed face no longer matched her pale neck. But she looked feminine. Pretty, almost.

"Were you paying attention to how I applied your makeup so you can replicate it?" Minnie asked, stacking bottles and jars and tubes into a canary yellow train case, then handing it to Sam.

"Yes, Mom. I took notes." Sam held up the notepad on which she had written each step down, from the eye liner to the lip pencil and everything in between.

"Maybe try smiling, dear. And don't act so quirky."

"But quirky works for me."

"Oh, honey, quirky doesn't work for anyone. You know there's a pill for that."

"Mom, I'm not taking a pill to change my personality."

"Okay, okay." Minnie waved off Sam's scowl, giving up the battle she knew she would never win. "So who is all of this for, anyway?"

"I never said it was for anyone."

"Oh, come on, Samantha. It doesn't take a mother's intuition to know this is obviously for a man. You've never shown an interest in cosmetics or beauty before. And certainly not at eleven o'clock at night. Is this about that Raul Smothers fellow?" she wondered with a wink. "I had a feeling about you two."

"Can't a girl decide she wants to learn how to act like a proper woman without an interrogation?" Sam deflected, knowing a woman's propriety was her mother's—and society's—correct answer to almost any question.

"Fair enough," Minnie conceded. "I can't say it doesn't make me happy that you might at last find a husband."

And marriage was the solution to almost any dilemma.

"I can assure you there is no husband waiting in the wings. Just me, Fido, my plants, and my column."

"I really wish you'd quit daydreaming and be practical, Samantha," her mother chided anytime Sam revisited her passion for botany. Or writing. Or both. "Writing and gardening won't pay the bills. Stick with secretarial work. That's where the money is. Along with the eligible bachelors," her mother added with a wink.

Minnie went home feeling optimistic that her daughter would finally, most certainly, assuredly land a man. And Sam went to bed feeling terrified that she would undoubtedly, most certainly, assuredly lose her job. But more than that, as Sam gazed at her reflection in the bathroom mirror, she hated the version of herself staring back. Lips sticky with gloss, eyes hooded under a velvet purple, floral hairpins probing her scalp...

She had been forced to become someone else in order to become herself. In her tight-fisted grip to keep the job she fought so hard for, and made enemies over, she had exchanged her very dignity. With a splash of water and a dollop of face soap the makeup disappeared, but the worry over the secrets Raul knew about Thomas Cook stuck to her long into the night.

Chapter 13

If the next evening proved to be anything like her day, Sam would simply give up without a fight. There were only so many punches a person could take before a knockout.

Like every other day since Sam had gotten her own column, she stepped into the *Women's House Magazine* bullpen ignoring her co-workers' whispered slander, dodging Mr. Getty's "deadline" reminders, and tiptoeing around Mel's evil eye. By the time she got home, transformed into her mother's mini-me, and bumped into Miss Posey on her way to infiltrate Thomas Cook, Sam fell to pieces. Literally speaking.

Eager to catch Sam on an unprecedented night out and looking uncharacteristically made up, Miss Posey blocked Sam's path to her car with the full force of her five-foot-tall three-foot-wide frame. The moment Miss Posey noticed the glisten in Sam's eyes, she adjusted a stray pink curler, straightened her housedress, then proceeded to hold Sam as she crumbled into a tearful waterfall of sadness.

"My dear, what's got you in such a sad state?" Miss Posey consoled Sam with rigid pats on the back.

Sam swiped the tears away, smudging the mascara and stinging her eyes, only prompting more tears and smudging and stinging.

"It's been a difficult day. The people at my office don't like me much."

"I suspect it's because you don't know your place. You're an odd bird, and you don't fit in. If you packaged yourself correctly, I'm sure they'd like you."

But Sam didn't want to fit in. She never had. When the other little girls wore poodle skirts and ballet shoes, Sam sported overalls and camp shirts. While the other teenagers collected Troll dolls and went out go-go dancing, Sam collected plant cuttings and hid in her room reading. The only way to appease them was to become them. What was the correct *female packaging* anyway?

While Sam would have preferred pants, pinstripes, and pockets, she'd been scolded more than once that a typist's *correct* attire were pantyhose, miniskirts, and pussybow blouses. For that is exactly what everyone saw Sam as: a typist. An assistant. A subordinate. But never the respected columnist she worked so hard to be.

"I'll be fine, Miss Posey." Sam inhaled a breath and rummaged through her macrame purse for her car keys. "I really need to get going."

"Are you going on a date… at this hour?"

"No, ma'am. It's not a date."

"Oh, well then, I'll just say you look very nice for your non-date, Samantha." It was the first pleasant thing Miss Posey had ever spoken to Sam. "Now if you could adjust your homemaking to match, you might actually have hope, my dear."

Of course the niceties would be cut short. It was Miss Posey, after all. But considering Miss Posey's porch was littered with tins hanging from the eaves, Sam found it ironic that the woman would challenge Sam's housekeeping when her porch looked like a cannery.

"What part of the city are you venturing into? Only trouble happens after dark. And I imagine you know it's improper for a single woman to go out alone. People will assume things."

Miss Posey was the only one making assumptions.

"And rumors will spread."

She was also the only one likely to spread them.

"I am meeting a friend." Sam offered nothing more than that, for already she could see the urge pulsing behind Miss Posey's quivering lips to call the rumor mill pronto.

Sam nudged past the muumuu-wearing blockade, nerves buzzing, makeup freshly streaked, and her prettiest peach prairie dress donned, ready to woo Thomas Cook. She glanced at the house next door, finding the *For Sale* sign gone... and in its vacancy two more had popped up further down the street.

"What's that about?" Sam asked, gesturing at the suddenly available real estate.

"Dire times, my dear," Miss Posey said, returning to her natural doom-and-gloom state as she trekked back to her perch on the porch. "I hear you are now living next to a criminal."

"A criminal? In the suburbs?"

"Where else would they live? It is a lot easier to commit crime when you are surrounded by unsuspecting victims who are only a front yard away. If I were you, I'd sell your house before the neighborhood's market value plummets. At least that is what *I* would do if I had somewhere else to go," Miss Posey advised with a wise shrug.

"What makes you think I have somewhere else to go?" No way in hell or on earth would Sam's mother permit her to move back home, bringing all of her plants... and especially not Fido, no matter how sweetly he nuzzled her.

"You'll eventually move in with whomever you marry. And soon, I hope? Your biological clock is ticking away, my dear."

"I don't plan on marrying. Or having children," Sam stated matter-of-factly, as if those were two perfectly acceptable choices for a woman in her twenties.

"Ha!" Miss Posey laughed.

Sam should have known better. How could single women thrive in a society where employers could discriminate against hiring them, the laws of which remained unchanged because women were forbidden from becoming lawyers or serving as judges, a plight that persisted because universities refused to admit them? While childlessness made a woman a pariah, singledom was her death sentence.

"Single *and* childless?" Miss Posey cast Sam a scrutinous gaze. "Are you mad? You can't possibly consider that an acceptable life. It's an abomination!"

"Why not? *You're* single and childless. And you seem… content with that status." As content as any lonely curmudgeon could be, Sam figured.

"I most certainly am *not* single *or* childless! I am a widow because the Korean War stole my husband from me, which is a very different thing. And my son is an ungrateful, selfish youngblood who moved across the country to California without me to work with silicon, of all things." She cackled mirthlessly. "Good luck with that worthless venture."

Sam suspected Miss Posey was referring to Silicon Valley, the newest hot-spot for science and technology development. *Worthless venture* it was not, but Sam was in a hurry, and Miss Posey clearly wasn't.

"Be careful, dear," Miss Posey warned as she examined one of her dangling cans. "Looks like a storm's a-brewin'."

"How can you tell?" Sam asked, certain the weatherman had called for a clear night.

"My homemade barometer is showing low pressure." Miss Posey pointed to one of the cans with a toothpick gauge. "It'll be a doozy tonight!"

How accurate Miss Posey would turn out to be…

By the time Sam shrugged off Miss Posey's weather assessment and slipped into her car, driving past one, two, three more *For Sale* signs, she had forgotten all about her new scandalous neighbor or her sinking home value. She had much bigger problems to worry about tonight.

Chapter 14

Another dead end. It seemed only Sam's bad luck was on a winning streak these days.

After Sam knocked on the massive iron lion's head knocker at Thomas Cook's residence, the housekeeper gripped the edge of the front door protectively, then shortly announced that "no, Dr. Cook isn't home," and "he does not take kindly to uninvited guests."

"But we had plans…" Sam lied. Even if Sam had plans, her bad luck would have inevitably rose above them.

You see, plans were meant for people who could successfully execute them. People with a natural predisposition for good luck. Sam, on the other hand, had a knack for the exact opposite, her life proving to be a domino effect of events cascading randomly every which way, impossible to stop and frustrating to clean up.

"Well, I'm sorry I can't help you," the housekeeper replied. "Dr. Cook isn't exactly known for keeping his appointments."

This put a kink in Sam's carefully laid plan of duping Thomas Cook into permitting her entrance into his 11,000-square-foot brick mansion with the claim that her car had broken down conveniently outside his home. Part 1 of the plan segued into a glass of wine and intimate conversation through the wee hours of the night, at which point Sam plotted Part 2: a little

PAMELA CRANE

snooping once Thomas Cook passed out, which he inevitably would, thanks to Sam's ingenuity. After that, well, Sam hoped the evidence she needed would fall into her lap. The ploy sounded so much easier in her head.

"Do you know when Mr. Cook will be back?"

"You mean *Dr. Cook*, don't you? You should know he insists on the *doctor*."

"Of course. How forgetful of me," Sam apologized, mentally noting it.

The housekeeper was used to strangers arriving on the estate uninvited wanting one thing or another. Long-lost relatives begging for money. Ex-girlfriends digging for gold. Reporters hungry for an interview. All the same characters, just a different story. But something about Sam felt different. Apparently the pathetic look on Sam's face garnered a morsel of pity from the frazzled housekeeper as she paused before she would usually slam the heavy oak double-entry doors in the intruder's face.

"He usually doesn't get home until late. Is there anything else I can help you with?"

"Actually, yes, ma'am. I noticed that your fingernails are purple," Sam commented.

The housekeeper released her grip on the door and self-consciously assessed her fingertips.

"So they are," the housekeeper noted with alarm. "Do you have any idea what could cause this?"

"It can be a sign of cyanosis, which is caused by lack of oxygen in the blood," Sam explained. Glimpsing the housekeeper's mildly stained teeth, Sam deduced a possible cause. "Do you happen to smoke, ma'am?"

"You got me. A bad habit, I'm afraid. I've been trying to

111

quit, but the stress of this job… and my night classes…"

"Say no more." Sam raised a hand to halt her. "I completely understand. But smoking is most likely diminishing your lung capacity, thus causing the cyanosis, and if it gets any worse, well, life will become a lot more stressful."

"Oh dear."

"I think I can help, though."

"Really? How so?"

Sam tapped a newly manicured Georgia Peach-painted fingernail against her chin. "Quitting cold turkey can be tough, but I have some lobelia that can make it easier. It's a flower that can stifle the nicotine craving and relax your airways by halting the production of inflammatory proteins in your lungs." Sam rattled off facts while the housekeeper looked perplexed but grateful. "Then I can mix the lobelia with ginseng, which will help your body adapt to the stress. All safe, all natural, and all freely grown in my garden." Or what Archibald had left of it.

"I can't thank you enough, Miss…?"

"Stanton. Sam Stanton. And if natural remedies interest you, I run an advice column called *Samantha Says* that can address any ailment you might have, whether it be emotional or physical. Write to me any question, any time."

"I truly appreciate that. No one, let alone a stranger, has ever been so considerate of me. Not even Dr. Cook," the housekeeper exclaimed gratefully. "By the way, what is it you're here to see him about, miss? Maybe I can help."

Sam realized her broken-down car alibi required a quick change in tactic, preferably one where she could serendipitously run into Thomas Cook in person.

"I, uh, was interested in Cook Pharmaceuticals' research

division and was supposed to meet Mr. Cook—I mean *Dr. Cook*—after hours." Sam hated fibbing to the woman, but as Raul had emphasized more than once, it was a necessary God-approved sin exclusive to investigative journalists. A tiny white lie Raul assured her God would overlook. "We were supposed to meet for dinner tonight to discuss a new drug trial. But I can't recall where."

"Oh, that would be the Gaslight Club. But certainly you know that it's a gentlemen only club?"

"So I've heard."

Sam first learned of the exclusive establishment when the news had covered the two dozen nude paintings that had created quite a seamy controversy. Rumors had even circulated that the Gaslight Club would be hosting its own private showing of *Oh Calcutta!,* a nude risqué revue that had only recently made its Off-Broadway debut. A gentleman's club, they called it? Sam was fairly certain there would be no *gentlemen* present.

"Even if you did manage to make your way inside," the housekeeper cautioned, "you are asking for trouble as a stray woman mingling among those types of men. They tend to be attracted to a certain... class of woman, if you know what I mean."

"Thank you for your concern, but I assure you I'm not the type to attract sleazy men." Or any men for that matter.

"Good luck, then. You'll need it."

Trouble, however, was one thing Sam was good at attracting.

Chapter 15

"No women allowed," the Gaslight Club's balding doorman barked at Sam while a sexy woman in heels clicked past, her sparkly red dress matching the velvet red rope that kept Sam out. The woman blew the attendant a red-lipped kiss as she disappeared into the speakeasy.

"Hey, what about *her*? You just let her in," Sam shot back.

"She belongs here. Yinz don't."

As Sam nudged forward in line, she knew the doorman was right. She would have rather been at the DMV than the posh three-story private club exclusive to its elite male-only members with more combined wealth than most third world countries. Sharing space with the city's finest chauvinistic bachelors wasn't Sam's idea of a good time, but it was the only way to get close to Thomas Cook, who she suspected was one of them.

"Haven't you heard of the Unruh Civil Rights Act?" Sam asked.

"Huh?" The bouncer's forehead scrunched halfway up his bare scalp.

"It's a law that prohibits businesses from engaging in unlawful discrimination based on sex, race, color, religi—"

"Okay, okay, I get it, lady," the bouncer growled. "What's your point?"

In all likelihood, few people had heard of the Unruh Civil

Rights Act, which only applied to California and did not, in fact, apply to private clubs such as the Gaslight. Nor was the act enforced in favor of women. But Sam hedged her bets that anyone who worked at the Gaslight Club was none the wiser and would prefer not to debate litigation when the line of antsy members waiting behind her was growing around the block.

"My point is that you're discriminating against me as a woman, which is illegal and can be prosecuted in a court of law."

"It's the club's rule, not mine. Why don't yinz go dahntahn?" he asked, his Pittsburgh dialect coming out more with each syllable.

"I don't want to go *downtown*. I want to go here. Why don't you take me to the club's owner and I'll talk to him about it. Or," Sam paused, "simply let me in and I'll be out of your hair… what's left of it."

He ran his hand self-consciously over a few stray strands on the sides.

"Fine," he mumbled under his breath as he unclipped the velvet rope to let her through, "what's up yinz nose with a rubber hose?"

When she entered the dark lobby, Sam stopped at a poster hanging on the painted brick wall featuring upcoming events, one of which was *the* Maxine Sullivan—flugelhorn sensation, jazz singer, and the only woman entertainer given stage to perform at the Gaslight Club to date. A step, albeit a small one, toward progress, Sam supposed.

Meandering through a dimly lit corridor that led to the cozy speakeasy lounge, round tables dotted the room with votive candles centered on each one. Men in suits, legs casually crossed, sat laughing and boasting as scantily-dressed waitresses endured slaps on the rear in hopes of a bigger tip.

Avoiding the crowd, Sam found herself wandering up to a bare stage where a man—sweaty, ruddy-faced, and clearly plied with alcohol—stood in front of a humble audience of about twenty. His gaze locked on Sam's face, then he sputtered something that resembled poetry, but terribly so:

"When I see your face,
It reminds me of you.
In every place,
With every cue.
If I were Shakespeare with a heart-shaped quill,
I'd write a sonnet from my heart,
And bring you a heart-shaped daffodil.
If I had Cupid's arrow and a heart-shaped dart,
I'd pierce the sun with your golden lingerie
And tell the sun to never go away."

A smattering of claps and hoots echoed around the room as an elbow from behind pushed Sam up the single step onto the edge of the stage. The spotlight swung to her, instantly blinding her as the sweaty man reached for her. Avoiding his touch, she fumbled backwards in heels she wasn't used to wearing, frantically searching for stage right.

The backdrop curtain tangled in the hem of her dress, tripping her up and sending her windmilling off the platform. As she made her graceless landing, knocking a waitress and her tray of drinks over, the whole room erupted in laughter. She sunk into the first empty chair she found in a tight corner, mortified and ready to admit defeat and go home. Until her eyes locked on those of the dreadfully mediocre rhymester.

Something felt strangely familiar about him as he approached her.

Chapter 16

The moment the woman with the horrible haircut entered the Gaslight Club lounge, Thomas Cook became acutely aware of her presence. It was not her out-of-place attire that commanded his attention, or her flushed cheeks that drew his gaze, but the crash of glass as she bumped into a waitress while falling off the stage and into a vacant seat in the corner.

From where he waxed poetic, Thomas Cook watched her with interest. This enchantingly clumsy gal was definitely one he wanted to know more about.

He bowed as the mixed clapping and laughter subsided, then left the stage and made a beeline for her table.

"Dr. Thomas Cook," he introduced himself, holding out his hand that the woman had moments ago avoided. But not this time. His name held power in this city, and he knew it.

She shook it, dumbfounded. "I thought I recognized you on stage."

"You probably know me from *Time Magazine*. I was nominated for Man of the Year last year," he stated proudly.

She nodded. "I vaguely remember a much less sweaty version of your face on the 1969 issue that touted your accomplishments in modern medicine. Congratulations on the accolades."

"Yes, well, I wasn't under hot stage lights when they did

that photo shoot, so…" He swiped at a trickle of sweat dripping down his temple.

"Did you know Adolf Hitler won that very same prestigious claim in 1938?" she replied mildly.

At the least, both Hitler and Cook shared a similar claim to fame—the reason for the death of millions. But the comparison seemed to elude Thomas as he probed, "And you are?"

"Oh, me? Samantha Stanton. But my friends call me Sam." Not that she had friends to speak of, but if she did, she would have insisted they call her *Sam*.

Uninvited, Thomas sat next to her. "Then I'll call you Samantha, because I have no intention of becoming your friend."

In Thomas's liquor-addled brain he thought his words smooth, charming even, but to Sam they sounded downright disrespectful and a bit unsettling.

"Those were some pretty impressive acrobatics up there," he said, gesturing to the stage Sam had fallen from.

"Thanks. I'm a natural, I guess. Do you come here often?" she asked.

"When the mood suits me. Which is every Tuesday, Thursday, and Friday night. What about you?"

"It's my first time here."

"Speaking of first time, I've never had a lover named Samantha before. You could be the first."

"Oh, uh, how kind of you to offer, Mr. Cook."

"*Dr.* Cook," he corrected with a wink. "I didn't study my way through eight years of pharmacology to be a simple *mister*, you know."

"In that case, I also prefer people call me *Sam*," she

reiterated, awkwardly turning her knees toward him until they bumped kneecaps.

"A pity. *Samantha* sounds more… feminine. You really ought to reconsider."

"Samantha it is, then." Sam decided she could put up with it long enough to get the proof she needed to take this narcissist down.

"So…" In spite of all of his connections and wealth and womanizing, Thomas still had a lot to learn about dating, and casual conversation was not one of his strong suits.

"So…" Sam echoed.

"Samantha Stanton. Hm." Thomas chewed on the words. "Why does your name sound familiar?"

"Maybe you've read my advice column?"

"I doubt it," he answered too quickly.

Thomas only read medical journals, and anything written by a woman would have instantly been used as kindling. In all truth, Thomas didn't care where he knew Samantha Stanton's name from. All he cared about was whether she would remember his name later tonight in his bedroom… and hopefully forget it by the following morning in the event that Samantha got too attached.

A relationship with an advice columnist was certainly not one he wanted to invest in—he preferred his women less opinionated. It was this type of detachment that made him so very good at investing and so very bad at relationships.

"So you're a lyricist?" Sam used the term loosely.

"Not professionally… yet. Only for pleasure—mine *and* yours. You liked my poem, I take it?"

"Oh yes, it was quite good."

"You inspired it. Especially the part about the golden lingerie," he said, eyeing her chest.

"Wow. I don't know what to say. Thank you?"

"I like to dabble in the fine art of spoken poetry once or twice a week. One of these days I hope to write it down and get published."

Sam smiled agreeably, wondering if he'd pay off a publisher to create his terrible book of poems just like he paid off the FDA to approve his terrible case studies on medicines.

"How do you tap into such... meaningful prose?" Sam asked, entertained by the way Thomas's blotchy face grew thoughtful.

"Poetry is easy. Anyone can do it," he said, unwittingly belittling the talent of the literary greats to mere ordinary. "You should go up there and give it a try."

Sam shook her head emphatically. "No thanks. As you can tell, I don't belong on a stage."

"Oh, I beg to differ. Every beautiful woman belongs on a stage."

"I prefer to watch."

"But it's exhilarating being the center of attention," he persisted, standing up and reaching for her.

Sam scooted her chair back, blocked by the wall behind her. "Nope. Not going to happen. I'm perfectly happy sitting right here listening to everyone else." Sam wasn't perfectly happy, but Thomas Cook didn't mind her unhappiness if it contributed to his indulgence.

"I insist!" He grabbed her hand and yanked her to her feet. "We've got a new poet in our midst!" he bellowed, shocking every table in the room to silence. "Fellas, give Samantha a warm Gaslight Club welcome."

The blinding spotlight swung back over to Sam. Cupping her eyes, she realized she had two choices: Appease Thomas the Man-Child and make up a poem on the fly, for how much worse could her lyrics be? Or run with her tail tucked between her legs and lose any chance of getting access to Thomas's files.

A couple claps and a stray wolf whistle followed her up on stage.

While Sam's home library held plenty of poetry books, a poet she was not. Nor did she want to play one tonight. She doubted a single man in this room had ever heard of Edna St. Vincent Millay, let alone read her riveting poem "I, Being Born a Woman and Distressed." So Sam, awkward with words and even worse with emotions, conjured the long-ago written verse of the literary icon and recited them from memory:

"I, being born a woman and distressed
By all the needs and notions of my kind,
Am urged by your propinquity to find
Your person fair, and feel a certain zest
To bear your body's weight upon my breast:
So subtly is the fume of life designed,
To clarify the pulse and cloud the mind,
And leave me once again undone, possessed.
Think not for this, however, the poor treason
Of my stout blood against my staggering brain,
I shall remember you with love, or season
My scorn with pity—let me make it plain:
I find this frenzy insufficient reason
For conversation when we meet again."

No one clapped. No one hooted. No one even seemed to notice that she had poured out a soul—Ms. Millay's as well as her own—for all to drink of. Sam was disheartened but not surprised as the room's din returned to normal, so she returned to her seat next to Thomas.

"*Zest*, huh? And *my weight on your breast*. I take it that poem was about me," he assumed, leaning toward her hungrily. "So you're agreeable to my plans for us later tonight?"

Sam was right. Not a single man in the room had ever heard of the poem or understood its interpretation.

"It's actually about the power a woman has to walk away from a man. The point is that women aren't made to be possessed."

"As if any woman would *want* to walk away… from me." His lips curled up in a smirk. "Anyway, that wasn't bad for a first time," he complimented the best he could. "You could use a little work on your rhyming, but overall pretty good."

"Thanks. I don't think anyone else cared for it much."

"Well, it was a bit… pretentious, maybe?"

Apparently being a woman and talking about it was pretentious. "I did warn you that spoken poetry wasn't my thing."

"Don't be too hard on yourself." Opening his legs, he pulled her chair closer between his knees, then lowered his hand to her thigh. Sam squirmed away, but his grip followed. "The spoken word doesn't come easy for everyone. You'll get there." He looked at her pitiably as if Sam were a child nursing a boo-boo.

By now another bard had bumbled his way on stage. The crowd heckled as he loosened his tie and rolled up his sleeves, sweat pooling in circles under his armpits. Sam covered her ears as the noise grew.

Thomas glanced around the raucous lounge. "So... do you want to get out of here?"

With the noise pounding in her temples, Sam exhaled an easy "yes," never having been asked this kind of question by this kind of man before. How could she know what he had planned?

They barely made it out before the foretelling lyrics resonated from the man on stage:

"You will be mine, whether you like it or not.
Sweet and spicy, cold and hot.
Fight against your will, you will not..."

When Thomas placed a possessive hold under Sam's elbow and towed her out of the club into the silent night, a most unholy night, she realized too late what she had gotten herself into.

Chapter 17

"I work at *Women's House Magazine,*" Sam told Thomas over wine on the leather sofa in his home office, which was bigger than Sam's entire home. And it had taken a breakdown of Sam's morals to get here. But finally Part 1 of Sam's plan was coming to fruition.

They had started their conversation in the formal living room where an original Picasso hung on one wall and a taxidermy zebra's head hung on another. After a glass of $5-a-bottle Blue Nun, cheap enough that even Sam could have afforded it, Thomas wasted no time asserting they relocate to his bedroom suite. But Sam, prudent enough to pace her drinking, still had her wits about her and instead suggested a tour of the estate. Thomas hadn't been as committed to pacing his own gulps, so he affably agreed, lumbering room by room through the mansion until Sam had lost her sense of direction.

When they landed in front of his padlocked office, Sam knew she needed to get inside. When a peal of thunder shook the walls, she knew she needed to do it quickly if she were to get home before the storm hit. Miss Posey's makeshift weather instruments had been accurate after all.

If Thomas kept any confidential business documents at home, they would be somewhere secure, behind lock and key. But getting Thomas to focus on anything but her chest, or her rear, was difficult, so she offered another refill for him and a top-off for her, then begged for a glimpse of Thomas's workspace.

Sam's suggestion of "give me a closeup of your office desk," seemed to do the trick, as Thomas's brain instantly fantasized about things he could do to her—or more likely *her do to him*—on that desk. So he pulled from his pants pocket a keychain with a single key dangling from an ivory sculpted C, unlocked the door, and inside they went.

Sam didn't feel good about what she was about to do, immoral even, but there was not much choice as Thomas grew touchier and sloppier every minute. After he had emptied his wineglass for the umpteenth time—Sam had lost count after the third refill—he was too horny to keep his paws off, and too drunk to hear her insistent *no*.

So Sam did the unthinkable. She executed Part 2 of the plan.

With a sleight of hand and a dash of kava root, Sam handed Thomas his spiked drink. Nothing dangerous; just a little nudge toward Sleepytown. Partly to calm his hungry urges for her flesh, and partly to knock him the heck out. Within minutes he had drowsily flopped onto the sofa, eyelids heavy and breathing slow, and Sam took the break from his groping to observe the room.

Full of every type of medical journal and pharmacology book, his office library held few—if any—works of fiction or literary entertainment. It was no wonder the man was clueless when it came to poetry and romance. He had nothing to compare his to, when his limited literary diet consisted of the chemical compound of penicillin or symptoms of gonorrhea.

"You work at *Women's House Magazine*? No kidding," he

slurred. "And what are you again—a typist?"

She grinned stiffly. She had already told him *twice* that she was a writer, but like most men she knew—Raul being the exception—they rarely found anything she said worth listening to.

"No, I'm an advice columnist, remember?"

He frowned. "I didn't think that magazine employed female columnists…"

"I happen to be the first."

"Interesting. What kind of advice do you give your readers?" He wasn't too drowsy to give Sam's waist a squeeze. "Cooking and housekeeping and… *womanly duties*?"

"Something like that," Sam said, gaze wandering. There *had* to be evidence she could use against him somewhere in this room of locked secrets. "But with a more feminist slant."

"So you promote homewrecking then?" Thomas thought he was reading between the lines, but in truth he was reading a completely different book.

"Homewrecking?"

"Yes, breaking up marriages. You advise women to leave their husbands, don't you?"

"A woman leaving an abusive marriage is not homewrecking because there is no home to wreck. It's freedom."

"Freedom from her cushy life eating bonbons and painting her nails while her husband pays the bills?"

Sam stomped her foot and rolled her eyes. Why was it that men saw themselves as a woman's savior? As if being born with ovaries and a uterus somehow replaced her brain.

"No. Freedom is being able to practice law, or attend an Ivy

League college. It's when a married woman can make medical decisions for herself." Sam noted Thomas's puzzled expression.

"What about all that Civil Rights Act garbage? I thought the law changed that."

"Laws only matter to the people who follow them. And since that law is only a few years old, no one knows about it so no one enforces it." Sam huffed. "Did you know that a woman isn't permitted to receive direct consultation from her doctor about her health? All conversations go through her husband. As if we're too dumb to discuss our own bodies!"

"Hey, I'm not calling you dumb." Thomas raised his hands in surrender. "But I have never met a woman who understands the first thing about medicine, let alone wants to discuss it."

"Then let me introduce you to the first." Sam held out her hand, shaking his. "I would love to discuss it, and I happen to know a lot about medicine."

"Do you?" Thomas challenged faintly. It was apparent the kava root was kicking in as his eyelids drooped.

"I research homeopathic medicine and lifestyle changes as alternatives to certain prescription drugs," Sam added after a beat, wondering if he was still awake.

Thomas shifted, and his eyes blinked wide open. "Oh, that's what I do—I own a pharmaceutical drug company. We share something in common: We both cure people."

"Well, they're not exactly the same thing. Yours are made in a lab, while mine are made in nature."

Thomas chuckled. "Ah, you're one of *those* types, aren't you? A tree-hugger."

"And what's wrong with hugging trees? The oxygen they supply is essential to all life, you know. They could use a little gratitude."

"Just because pills don't grow on trees doesn't make them inherently evil."

"I'm not suggesting that all medicine is bad, but it shouldn't be the first reaction to a health issue. It should be a last resort."

"Not every illness can be cured with whatever potion you've thrown together in your cauldron."

"You make it sound like my work is a joke."

Thomas slid closer, tucked her hand in his, and kissed her knuckles. An unwanted rouge spread up Sam's neck as she sensed trouble.

"Samantha—*Sam*," he corrected, a courtesy Sam appreciated, and he pressed her hand to his heart, "the people that consistently make easy choices that destroy their bodies will never make the tough choices to save them. Modern medicine offers one thing that your natural cures never will: a quick fix."

"And I would argue that nothing truly offers a quick fix. It's like a get-rich-quick scheme—there is always a catch."

Sam felt his heartbeat quicken beneath his shirt as he leaned toward her, still holding her hand to his chest.

"You want to cure cancer your way? Get rid of all the food on every store shelf and tell the people to start growing their own. But wait! You can't use pesticides, so there goes most of your harvest to bugs. And those powerlines? You've got to get rid of those dangerous electromotive forces. Then we've got the steel mills probably giving most of the city lung cancer, so say goodbye to all those jobs and hello to homelessness and dire poverty." He released her hand and exchanged it for his wine glass. "Until the people you want to help start helping themselves, your way will never work and my way will always end up as their lifeboat."

Sam reconsidered Thomas Cook, a man she had regarded as carelessly evil but now realized was necessarily evil, not because he wanted to hurt people but because people continued to hurt themselves. Maybe they weren't at such odds as she had thought.

"What about when your drugs do more harm than good?"

"That's why we put warnings on the labels."

"Warnings that doctors fail to inform their patients."

"Can't patients read for themselves? It's called *personal accountability*, Samantha."

"According to you, women are too dumb to be personally accountable, Thomas."

Thomas was growing irritated while Sam was losing her resolve to go through with her clandestine plan. He didn't want to argue with her, just as Sam didn't want to defend herself.

"Look, I went into this field wanting to give people a chance at a longer life, with a better quality of life. Why do you assume the worst about me?"

As she heard the conviction of his words, she felt guilty for what she was about to do. "But what do you do when those medicines prove dangerous? Do you pull them off the market... or cover it up so you don't cut into your profit margins?"

She had stumped Thomas as he faltered for a response that didn't make him sound as money-grubbing as he was.

"Isn't it enough that I do rigorous testing, and clinical studies, and get FDA approval? After all of that, if doctors choose not to prescribe it properly or patients abuse it, that's not on me. That's on them."

His rant stopped there, because the truth was that Thomas also felt guilty, but not over what Sam thought he was guilty of. He hadn't told Sam the full truth.

As much as he wanted to warn her of what was to come, telling her his secret would slam shut any open door to a fun night together. Maybe even a fun summer together, if she played her cards right.

Despite her know-it-all arrogance and suffragette brashness, Samantha Stanton was beginning to grow on Thomas Cook. It wasn't every day a woman challenged him... and Samantha—rather, *Sam*—could prove to be quite the challenge.

"Perhaps if there was more transparency in the medical field I would agree with you," Sam stated. "But as it is, pharmaceuticals have become a money-making scheme that preys on the health-compromised. I've lost trust in medicine. But nature, well, it will always remain trustworthy because it has nothing to gain."

She took a deep breath, ready to launch into all the ways nature served mankind better than anything he could create in a lab, but she had already lost Thomas at the mention of *transparency*. His snores vibrated the room, a guttural sound from within the deepest slumber.

Slipping her hand into his pocket, his wheezing faltered as she pulled the C-shaped keychain out. She held her breath and waited, wondering how many elephants were poached to procure this novelty ivory letter. A moment later, the nasal whistle resumed and Sam carefully rose from the sofa.

A long marble cabinet lined the wall behind his mammoth neat-as-a-pin desk that would have made her mother proud, but a quick open-and-shut glimpse into a dozen drawers proved worthless. As she reached the last cabinet, she checked the time on her watch. She didn't know how long the kava root would last, as she had never drugged a person before, but she didn't want to be rummaging through his files when he woke.

Pulling on the last handle, it wouldn't budge. She leaned over, searching for a keyhole, but all she saw was the letter C imprinted in the marble. As if Thomas Cook needed a reminder of his infamous last name.

Then Sam saw it. She held up the keychain. The C in the marble was the exact shape and size of the ivory keychain. Pressing the ivory into the marble, it became a button that pushed open a drawer that bumped into Sam's hip. Inside were several items, but one looked particularly incriminating. Sam picked it up, read the single word on the front, and knew this would change everything.

Thunder rumbled overhead. The snoring suddenly stopped.

Sam gasped as Thomas stirred and slowly regained consciousness.

Tucking the item behind her back, she slid the drawer closed, hustled to Thomas's side, and dropped the keys into the nook of the cushion. His eyes fluttered open just in time to watch her collect her handbag, where she had hidden the evidence in the macrame cavity.

"I'm sorry I dozed off," he apologized, still half-asleep. "It must have been the wine."

"Yes, the wine," Sam agreed.

"It's not too late to head to the bedroom," he murmured, gaze weakly trailing up and down her body.

"As enticing as that sounds, I'm going to head out. I want to beat the storm home." It wasn't all a lie. "And I'm sorry,

Thomas."

"Sorry for what?" he asked.

"I'm just sorry… for everything." She had no idea how true that would prove to be.

Then Sam Stanton left Thomas Cook feeling something he had never experienced before: utterly powerless and insanely infatuated.

Chapter 18

"This is gold!" Mr. Getty exclaimed after Sam dropped a leather book on his desk with the word *Accounting* in gilded print on the front.

Late into the previous night, with Fido's muzzle resting on her shoulder, Sam had sprawled out across her sofa reading line after line of handwritten words and corresponding numbers throughout the ledger.

Within an hour Sam had compared the names to ones listed in the phonebook, then broken down the list into doctor last names and drug identifiers. The numbers seemed to apply a sum payment based on the drug dosage. A little common sense and math led Sam to her final conclusion:

Thomas Cook had been paying off doctors, recording in his own handwriting the payouts prescribers received for each script. The bigger the dosage, the higher the payment. It was all the proof she needed and then some to show that Cook Pharmaceuticals was corrupt, paying doctors to prescribe everything from the Pill to Valium to pain medicine. And specifically listed among the prescriptions: Nosartin.

It was the very same heart medicine that had killed her father. Even more, the very same doctor who had prescribed her father the drug was inked on an entry for February 17, 1965— the very same date printed on the prescription bottle that Sam clutched in her hand as she read Thomas's entry with a quick breath. Same, same, same.

In short, her father's doctor got paid to kill him.

This meant war.

Morning couldn't come fast enough. Sam could barely wait to get to the office to show Mr. Getty her proof when she rushed out of her house an hour earlier than usual, oblivious to the newest *For Sale* sign that popped up on her street.

After rushing to the office to deliver the good news, the wait to see Mr. Getty was excruciating.

Sam had spent the morning enduring Mel's publicly unrestrained snide comments about her brownnosing the boss. During the afternoon she watched helplessly as the secretaries iced her out at lunch in the break room. Even the sole female research aid Mr. Getty had promoted from the mailroom cancelled their usual midday water cooler chat. So Sam slurped down her homemade roasted purple potato soup alone at her desk while the office staff giggled from the break room, throwing her a resentful glance over their shoulders when they passed by.

Sam lost hope as her deadline drew near. He'd pushed their meeting from 9:30 to 11:15, then postponed again until 2:45. It was now ten minutes to five, closing time, which gave Sam mere minutes to hand over her evidence and plead her case to keep her advice column.

Lately it felt like the whole world stood against her, pitying her for being a doormat, then hating her when she stood up for herself. She was considered either weird or fanatical, and neither of those attributes were attractive in a friend, colleague, or even, Sam hated to admit, a daughter.

When Mr. Getty's voice boomed across the bullpen calling her to his office, she nearly tripped over her own feet as she ran. With nine minutes left before the office closed for the night, she rushed through a summarized explanation of what she had found, then handed him the ledger.

"Absolute gold!" Mr. Getty repeated.

"You think so?" Sam beamed at the first compliment she had ever received from her boss.

"You definitely earned your advice column, Samantha," Mr. Getty praised while leafing through the best book—and possibly only book—he had ever read.

Mr. Getty didn't like to read, which made him the most un-ideal candidate for the job of magazine editor-in-chief. But he was a man with connections, so that was all that mattered.

"I delivered on my end, so I can write what I want?" Sam confirmed. "Including alternative medicine therapies?"

"After seeing this, you could write about the *Apollo 11* moon landing last year not being staged and I'd approve it. Heck, you may have earned yourself a raise."

"A raise?" she asked, nearly crying tears of joy.

"Well, don't get ahead of yourself. Let's see what we can do with this first."

We meant *he*. Sam wondered what kind of *something* Mr. Getty planned to do. Blackmail? Bribery?

"But, and this is important," Mr. Getty looked up for the first time since she'd handed the ledger to him, "this information *has* to stay between you and me. Do not tell a single soul, you hear? I don't want this leaking to the public. At least not yet, and not without me curating the narrative."

And there it was. He planned to steal her credit for exposing one of the biggest medical conspiracies in the nation. What Mr. Getty meant to say, but thought Sam too dumb to realize, was that *he* wanted control of this story. This was the kind of feature that launched an unknown women's magazine editor-in-chief into pulling rank as a lead journalist at *Newsbreak*.

Only because Sam had no interest in being rejected by *Newsbreak*—so far they had only one woman junior writer on staff, only because her boss had tired of covering fashion—did she allow Mr. Getty to have his prized ledger and all of the fame that would soon follow when the story broke.

"I think we're done here," Mr. Getty concluded. "I'm busy."

Busy listening to Myron Cope announce Steelers football stats from a brand new radio console in the corner that Sam was pretty sure the accounting department turned a blind eye to. Mr. Getty noticed her gaze and proudly stood up.

"This," he grandstanded, "is a cassette deck. It plays cassette tapes."

"What is a cassette tape?" Whatever it was, it looked expensive.

"It's like an 8-track, but smaller. It plays music."

Sam had heard of cartridge tapes, mainly used for recording and play-back purposes. But one that played music? Who came up with these newfangled inventions?

"Can you play a song?"

Mr. Getty shrugged. "I don't have one yet. The only cassette albums available are Nina Simone, Eartha Kitt, and Beatlemania. But mark my words, cassette tapes are the wave of the future, Samantha."

"You would know."

Mr. Getty shooed Sam toward the door. "Anything else you

need to bother me with?"

"You're the one that called me to your office, sir," Sam reminded him.

"Oh, right. I'm done with you. Now get back to work!"

A rap on the open office door dragged Mr. Getty's attention from his prized stereo to a crystal vase full of red roses. Hidden behind the mass of flowers Betty Number Five peeked out. "These came for you."

Mr. Getty's face scrunched. "What would I want flowers for?"

"No, sir, they're for *her*." Betty's eyes narrowed into a glare as she thrust the flowers in Sam's direction. With the sun-kissed fingers of a girl who spent all her weekends baby oiling and laying out at the community pool, Betty held out a tiny card in a tiny envelope, already opened and Sam's privacy breached. "It's from a Dr. Thomas Cook," she added coldly.

"For me?" Sam was shocked, having already written off Thomas Cook as a bridge burned.

"Thomas Cook sent *you* flowers?" Mr. Getty's jaw dropped.

Sam was mildly offended that her boss found it so ludicrous, so abhorrent, that any man would send her flowers.

"In a Lalique vase, no less!" Betty exclaimed, eyeing the vase covetously, then Sam with disdain.

Neither Sam nor Mr. Getty understood the significance of Betty's statement.

The poverty-level secretary who was intimately familiar with every wealthy label and brand scoffed. "It's a very expensive French vase. Do you know nothing about housewares, Samantha?"

"A vase is a vase," Sam answered.

Taking the card and flowers, she inhaled the sweet fragrance, already mentally cataloging a recipe that used rose petals for witch hazel.

Betty clicked her tongue. "That vase is worth more than you and I make in a year... combined."

"Do you want it?" Sam offered.

Instantly Betty warmed up to her. "Really? You'd give it to... me? After what I said about you?"

"What did you say about me?" Sam inquired, her mind filling with at least half a dozen close guesses.

"Oh." Betty stuttered, then quickly regained her composure while she quickly threw some pleasant-sounding words together. "Just that it was surprising you took the columnist job from Mel... and I was... speculating to the others what you had... done to achieve it, that's all."

"I didn't *take* it, I earned it," Sam clarified, "without sleeping with anyone. Anyway, I have no need for this nice of a vase, and you'll appreciate it more than I would. I'll find something else to put the flowers in and give it to you on my way out."

"Wow, that's really forgiving of you. Thank you!"

Then a thought occurred to Sam. It would be nice if she had at least one woman in the office on her side. "I have one request in exchange for this vase that's worth more than our salaries combined."

"A new hairstyle? I can definitely help you with that."

"No, my hair's fine." Sam absentmindedly fluffed her short 'do that was growing out and did actually need a trim. "If I ever need a favor from you in the future, will you help me out? Friend to friend?"

Friend to friend was a stretch for all the gossip Betty passed around at Sam's expense, but Sam *was* giving her a priceless vase, so the least Betty could offer was short-term friendship.

"You have a deal."

Betty's bronzed cheeks blushed. Most likely with embarrassment that she had judged Sam so harshly. For what, Betty couldn't even remember. No one liked *Mouthy Mel*—a nickname acquired from years of foul-mouthed venom he spat at any woman who rejected him. While *Malicious Mel* was more fitting, no one could manage to whisper it without drawing Mel's attention as he thought he overheard them calling him *Luscious Mel,* and considered it an invitation to flirt. It was a true wonder that any woman in the office would side with him.

"I never would have taken you for the kind of girl to lure a man like Thomas Cook, but some people surprise you," Mr. Getty muttered under his breath.

The phone rang, interrupting the gathering. "Go for Getty," Mr. Getty answered, then shooed Sam and Betty off.

Sam left his office carrying the roses into the bullpen and found Mel circling her desk like a vulture. He paused just long enough to gawk at the bouquet.

"I guess congratulations are in order," he said.

Word had spread fast through Mr. Getty's open office door that Sam broke a huge story. "Thanks. But according to Mr. Getty, mum's the word."

"Every person in this office already knows, Samantha."

"About the ledger?" Sam would be sure to tell Mr. Getty that she was not the one who mentioned it. She knew how to keep her lips sealed, not that she had any friends to tell anyway.

"No, I'm talking about you sleeping with Mr. Getty. It

finally paid off, huh?"

"Why would you think that?" Just imagining Mr. Getty naked and caressing her made her stomach churn.

"You got the column. *My* column. And I overheard something about a raise? How else could you have stolen it from me if you weren't blackmailing the boss?"

That would explain the looks Sam got from all the women in the bullpen. Sam should have known Mel wouldn't come bearing congratulations without cruelty. He could have given Miss Posey a run for her money in the passive-aggressive Olympics. But the fact was, Mel was the self-absorbed type who would never come to terms with the real reason his column *Tell Mel* needed to be euthanized.

Tell Mel's last words of advice spoke everything about its author that one needed to know, and it was the exact reason Sam desperately wanted to overthrow the modern notion that women had no valuable advice to give:

Q: Dear Tell Mel,

I desperately need your advice. The other morning, as I was heading home after driving my children to school, my car got a flat tire. My best friend lives only a couple houses away from where I had pulled over, so I walked there and noticed my husband's car parked in her driveway. When I knocked, no one answered, but I could hear them from the other side of the door. They were clearly having sex—she even screamed his name!

My husband and I have two children and have been married for fifteen years, but he refuses to acknowledge what he did or go to marriage counseling with me to restore what's broken.

Please help!
Horny-Husband Hater

A: Dear Horny-Husband Hater,

Luckily what's broken can always be fixed.

In order to replace a flat tire, you need to first loosen the lug nuts on the tire, then find the car jack, which you should always have handy in your trunk. Once you jack up the car, remove the lug nuts and slide the flat tire off. Your spare tire should be in the Continental tire kit on the back of the car, attached to the trunk above the bumper.

Simply remove the cover and spare tire, attach the new tire, and replace the lug nuts. Once this is done, you may lower the car jack and off you go! If all else fails, have your husband show you how to do it so that you might never find yourself in this predicament again.

Good luck!
Tell Mel

Women's House Magazine June 1970 Issue

SAMANTHA SAYS...

Q: Dear Samantha,

Boy, do I have a conundrum for you.

I have been working at my job for about six months, and it has become intolerable. I was even prescribed Valium to curb the anxiety. Here's the backstory:

I am single with no higher education, so my career options are pretty slim. I found this job through a friend, but now I'm regretting it. After months of dealing with an over-touchy, insufferable, married boss, he threatened my job if I wouldn't sleep with him. To protect my job, I caved... and now I'm pregnant. If I could have legally gotten the Pill I would have, but as you know, it can only be prescribed to married women.

Needless to say, my boss used my pregnancy to legally fire me. As a single pregnant woman, I have no legal repercussions and am now unwed, pregnant, and penniless.

I have been silent long enough. How do I speak up, and what do I say?

Sincerely,
Pregnant Patty

A: Dear Pregnant Patty,

Congratulations on taking the first step toward speaking up. You wrote me! And now hundreds of other women will be reading your story, seeing firsthand what they may one day be up against. We, as unified women, must prepare.

How do we prepare? By changing the laws. Legally, you have no way to get back your job or force him to take responsibility for the baby. Even with the latest paternity test that compares blood types, 90 percent of cases are easily disputed, leaving it your word against his, and a man's word always wins over ours. So when the system breaks you, you must break the system.

To any readers who want to take a stand to help Pregnant Patty, write to me and we'll work together to right this wrong. There are plenty of ways to do that—by exposing the men who do this, suing the companies that endorse this, and pushing back against the courts that allow this. Join me in the fight for our rights, ladies!

Considering you're pregnant, Patty, I would advise against taking Valium and steer clear of internal medicines that could harm the baby. Instead try acupuncture, an ancient Eastern practice that stimulates endorphin release and triggers the autonomic nervous system to lower stress without the side effects of prescription medicine.

Let today be the day your words gel into anger, your anger crystallizes into action, and your action solidifies into change.

Sincerely,
Samantha

Chapter 19

One thousand two hundred and fifteen. Sam had counted each and every letter in response to her fledgling column, and it amassed to 1,215 women who wanted to help Pregnant Patty, and who also wanted change. An impressive four digits, considering the magazine's circulation numbers weren't much more than that.

Mr. Getty had dumped the first mail sack on Sam's desk a week after the June 1970 issue hit newsstands, the canvas bag brimming with letters upon letters from readers who wanted to share their stories or share their solutions.

"You've only written two columns and already you're more popular than The Beatles," Mr. Getty had proclaimed as he read the cover headline: WILL THE BEATLES' BREAKUP LAST? After Paul McCartney left the band, it was all anyone could talk about... until now. Now Sam's column was the talk of the town. Or at least the talk of the bullpen.

A second bag arrived days later, stuffed and overflowing with more letters. The third bag was dropped off by a courier at her home, left on her front porch, which Raul nearly tripped over as he stepped onto the concrete stoop.

"What's all this about?" Raul asked the courier, staring down at the bag at his feet.

"According to a Mister..." the delivery man glanced down

at his form, "Franklin Getty, who instructed I drop these off at this address, they are, and I quote, '*madness that must be stopped.*'"

Raul laughed and hefted the mail bag over his shoulder and let himself into Sam's house with a Ricky Ricardo-accented, "Honey, I'm home!"

But when Raul wandered into the living room, finding two more half-empty mail bags with the contents splayed across the floor, the counters, and the tables, he realized whatever Sam had done had gotten a lot of attention. Perhaps too much attention.

"It looks like *someone* is popular," he commented, dropping the bag next to the others.

"It's all fan mail responding to my latest column."

Sam smiled up at him from where she knelt on the floor separating the letters by topic: anxiety, depression, motherhood, abusive husband, job woes, loneliness, aging… and that had only skimmed the surface. Women carried the weight of the world on very slim shoulders that were never supposed to hold that burden alone. As a result, it was crushing them one by one. But Sam hoped to help each and every one.

"No death threats, I hope?" Raul was well aware of the many fanatical readers out there, biding their time for the perfect moment to unleash their crazy on an unsuspecting celebrity. And with 1,215 pieces of fan mail, Sam was darn near close to celebrity status.

"None that I know of… yet." Sam's brain was fatigued and eyes blurry from reading.

"What was the column about? The issue was sold out at every corner before I could grab a copy!"

"A woman got pregnant from her married boss after he gave

her the ultimatum to either have sex with him or lose her job."

"What did you advise her to do?"

"There's not much a woman can do in a he-said-she-said situation like this." Sam sighed wearily. "I want this column to change that, though."

"How?" Raul asked.

"By changing the laws." Sam glanced at the letters, admiring the courage of all the women brave enough to reach out for help. "But if it was me in that situation? I'd sue the boss who coerced me. Then go after the company who hired him and refused to stand behind the victim. And then demand the doctors make birth control not just available to married women, but any women who also want access to it."

"That's a lot of wants."

"No, it's a lot of needs. Generations of women are unable to thrive in a world we helped build. How is that fair? It's time to change that."

"How are you supposed to do that, Sam?" Raul admired the goal, but he was also a realist. "You're one woman against a whole system."

"No, it's 1,215 women against a system. And I'm sure there are more out there. If this is how many women I can bring together with one brand-new no-name column, imagine if this made headlines on a bigger scale. Women could change the world!"

"If anyone could do it, it's you."

Fido whinnied at the front door, and Sam stood to her feet.

"Want to take Fido for a walk with me?" she asked, desperate for fresh air and sunshine.

Instead she would get steel mill smog and gray clouds, but

beggars couldn't be choosers.

Raul clipped on Fido's halter and lead rope as Sam threw on her floral gymsuit and loafers, opting not to wear the collared Danksin leotard her mother insisted was more on-trend because Sam didn't want the entire neighborhood—or Raul—to see every nook and cranny of her body.

Miss Posey tut-tutted from her front yard as they headed onto the street. "I hope you plan to marry that fellow," she warned.

"Why is that?" Sam dared to ask.

"So that you can move out of here, of course. Rumor has it your new next-door neighbors are a fright. Truly terrible people, I tell you."

"You've mentioned this before, but you never told me what makes them so awful."

"I heard one of them was," her voice dropped to a conspiratorial whisper, "incarcerated for violence. Or drugs. Or maybe it was both!"

Raul turned to Sam as they kept walking. "Did you hear that? Your very own neighborhood violent, drug-dealing villain!" As a journalist, Raul knew how a rumor could twist the truth until it was unrecognizable.

"Maybe I'll finally get bumped down the villain list," Sam said with a shrug.

As they passed the next-door neighbor's yard, the front door was painted in angry words slashed across the white door:

Criminal!

Go away!

Die!

"Wow, what did your neighbor do? Work for Hitler?" Raul

asked.

"I wish I knew."

"Be careful, Sam." Raul vividly remembered covering the story of the Boston Strangler, and only last year investigating the Ypsilanti Ripper. Both *"nice guys"* who could *"never have done such violent crimes."* After years of lingering so close to the underbelly of society, Raul knew the horrors mankind was capable of. "Obviously people know something about them that you don't."

"That's exactly the problem—I don't know anything about them. What if everyone else is wrong? Just because someone believes something is good doesn't make it good, and just because someone believes something is bad doesn't make it bad."

"You've just switched topics to Cook Pharmaceuticals now, haven't you?"

"You know me so well," Sam said, clucking Fido to pick up his pace as he stopped every couple feet to graze. "Just because a large group thinks something is safe doesn't make it safe. The group mentality can be dangerous, Raul. You of all people should know this, considering you've been writing against sheep mentality for years, trying to get people to see the facts over their feelings."

They continued walking, Fido nibbling on patches of summer-drought-beige grass as they went, until they reached the end of the street, where another *For Sale* sign stuck up out of a fresh patch of dirt. Before long the neighborhood would become a ghost town. Whoever Sam's new next-door neighbor was, it was certainly scaring everyone away.

They turned the corner, making their way around the block

where the plague of emptying houses hadn't seemed to hit yet. Everything on this street was fine and dandy. For now.

Sam fiddled with the necklace her father had given her. A gold heart on a gold chain—ironically, the same thing that failed him was the thing he had gifted her with.

"Can I ask you something, Raul?"

"Of course."

"Do you ever think about your dad?"

"The one who left my mom to raise me alone?" Raul shook his head. "No. He's dead to me."

"Are you sure you got all the facts? You know how important facts are," Sam reminded him.

"I got all the facts I needed when he never looked me up all these years, never reached out. I'm the kid, he's the dad. It's his job to prove his love, not mine."

"Don't you want to know why he left? If there's more to the story?"

"Well, my mom's dead, so there's really no way for me to find out, is there?"

If Sam had learned anything from Raul, it was that there was always a way to find out the truth. "If you want, I could help you. I could look through old obituaries, or see if he's listed in the phonebook. Anything you can think of that can help me track him down. I'd do anything for you, Raul."

Raul's pace slowed, and Sam's matched his. "I know, Sam, and that's exactly why I don't want to know more. Because I'm afraid to find out he is not worth the effort." Raul reached across the space separating them and wrapped her in a hug. "But I appreciate the offer."

When Raul told her he had no desire to meet his father, he

only meant it in that way that any abandoned child does. Meaning he wanted his father to find him, not the other way around. Raul often dreamed of the day a knock on the door would reveal his father on the other side, who had overcome every obstacle to be reunited with the son he had crossed seas and climbed mountains to meet.

No matter how convincing Raul sounded that he didn't care, his father was always waiting on the outskirts of his mind. Plenty of people had let Raul down in his life, but only one of them mattered. And that one person hadn't found Raul yet, and Raul doubted he ever would.

Only one document, one picture, and Raul's blood proved that Raul's father ever existed. The single page had given the stranger a name, though Raul had only a vague memory of the man claimed on his birth certificate: Gabriel Smothers.

It was a faded memorial of a time when Raul was too young to fully remember but old enough to cling to the pieces. The details were scraps of an incomplete picture. The black and white tile bathroom floor of his childhood home. The yelling—his mother at his father, his father at his mother, the shouted words unclear. Raul gripping the glass doorknob, turning, finding the door locked. No escape. Just like his mother had been unable to escape Gabriel. When the lock finally clicked and the door opened, Lilith Smothers stood on the other side, arms open, smile comforting, and promise flooding his ears:

"He's gone, Raul. You're safe now."

Raul couldn't remember anything before that day, like his father's atrocities that Lilith later confided to him, or the reason his father one day picked up and left, leaving no forwarding address. All Raul knew was that his father was there, then he wasn't. And he never heard from him since.

The picture Raul kept in his wallet was a yellowed newspaper clipping of a child-version Raul standing next to his adult-version duplicate who could only be his dad. The man wore a newsboy hat and was plainly dressed, none of which fit with the severe New York City skyline. His face was kindly looking, which didn't match the narrative Raul had created in his head of his ruthless, runaway father. The article headline from the clipping read:

SMOTHERS SMOTHERED THE COMPETITION IN LOCAL
NEWSWRITING CONTEST

The article went on to explain that Gabriel Smothers, husband and father, won a local newswriting competition for the *New York Herald Tribune* in their search for the next great news writer. His piece covered the polio epidemic of 1952, and the promising work on a vaccine. A curious irony, as Raul would unknowingly follow in his news-writing footsteps.

Raul clung to that lone memory along with the lasting grudge against the man who had helped give him life, but in the end was dead to him. Over the years Raul asked his mother about the man who abandoned them, the husband who turned her cold, and the father who turned Raul competitive. If his father could win an award for news writing, Raul would win two. Even beyond the proverbial grave Gabriel still drove Raul to succeed.

"When's Daddy coming back?" Raul had begged his mother the day his father left, wanting more than anything to know why, what Raul had done to push him away.

"He's never returning, honey," Lilith had replied simply, turning away to look out the window.

That day, Raul trudged slowly to his bedroom, watching his father hail a taxi, which a moment later drove away. For endless nights afterward he conjured ways to make his father return. He first tried acts of deviance—talking back at school, playing hooky, smoking cigarettes—which only earned him beatings. Then he tried his hand at overachieving, which barely caught his mother's notice but at least served him well in life.

It was biological, a parent's impulse to care for their young. If nature abounded with examples of this instinctive phenomenon, wasn't humankind even more so inclined? But the only way his father ever showed up was on the front page of the newspaper, his name printed in ink, his stories covering everything from Rosa Parks' unjust arrest to the threat of a nuclear holocaust.

Raul devoured each of his father's stories as if they were his sustenance, filling his soul with the same words his father tapped into, until one day the articles stopped, and his father disappeared.

When Raul was sixteen, he had looked his father up. Found his address listed in the directory. Then he took one trolley, two buses, and walked six blocks to his father's apartment. When he arrived outside the building, his father was walking out... holding the hand of a young boy. And so Raul was forced to accept that not only had his father ended one story—the one with Raul in it—but he had written a whole new story with a whole new ending, replacing Raul with a whole new family.

By this point Raul, Sam, and a grass-nibbling Fido had made two more left turns and were briskly walking back to

Sam's house. An unfamiliar car sat in her driveway, and an unfamiliar man waited on her porch.

"Who's that?" Raul asked with the slightest hint of jealousy that Sam hadn't detected.

"I don't know, but I'm about to find out." Sam marched up to the porch, eyeing the man dressed in head-to-toe burgundy, wearing a messenger boy cap. "Can I help you?"

The man glanced down at a paper in his hand. "Are you Samantha Stanton?"

"Yes."

"I'm from Western Union and I have a special delivery for you." A moment later he began swaying and snapping a beat before belting out an offkey version of "Be My Baby" by The Ronettes. He had just finished the first verse in a pitchy crescendo and was fumbling into an eardrum-agitating chorus when Sam cut him off.

"That's enough, thank you," Sam interjected, glancing over at Raul for an explanation. He was the only man Sam could think of who would send her a singing telegram about love… and even that was a stretch.

Raul shrugged. "Don't look at me. I didn't hire him."

"Shall I continue?" the messenger offered with a sway and a snap.

"No, thank you. I'm sorry, but who sent you?" Sam asked.

"Dr. Thomas Cook sends his regards, ma'am."

Sam's cheeks blushed. Raul's mouth dropped. And the messenger noted an instantly tense vibe.

"If that's all, I'm going to skedaddle," he said, making a beeline for his car.

When their vocalist was out of earshot, Raul turned on Sam.

"So you did it. You got to Thomas Cook, and now you are *dating* him?" Raul glared at her with unmistakable possessiveness smothering every syllable, which this time Sam definitely picked up on.

"I most certainly am not dating him. I don't know why he's sending me flowers and chocolates and balloons and... love songs."

"Wait—there was more before this?" Raul gestured to the vacant space where the messenger had just been standing. "I thought I told you to stay away from him. He's dangerous!"

"Whoa there. I don't follow your orders, Raul. And besides, he's harmless."

"You're the one who claims he's responsible for your dad's death. How is that harmless?"

"Why do you care so much what I do?" Sam stormed into the house, letting the metal screen door slam behind her.

Raul followed her inside, wanting to tell her everything yet knowing he couldn't. If Sam found out what Raul knew of her father's death... No, there could be no *if*. Sam could never find out, but dating Thomas Cook would most certainly push her closer to that horrible, awful truth.

"I don't want you getting hurt. Especially if you start digging too deep."

"What does that even mean? What do you know, Raul?"

"I know this man is clearly obsessed with you, and I'd like to know why you're leading him on."

"I'm not leading him on."

"Then what are you doing, Sam?"

"Well, it's a long story," Sam stuttered.

But it was not a long story. It was in fact a short enough

story that Sam could fit into approximately two minutes of explanation about the night she met Thomas Cook and stole his ledger, somehow wooing him in the process. But none if it seemed to quell Raul's heartache or his worry, no matter how much Sam tried.

Chapter 20

During the weeks following their first—and only—encounter, Thomas Cook had sent Sam a bouquet of red roses to her office, paid a delivery boy to leave a box of dark chocolates on her desk, tasked his secretary with tying a dozen balloons to her car door handle, and ordered a Western Union singing telegram to perform on Sam's front porch. For a girl who had up until this point never received a single flower from a romantic interest, it was terrifying and, more than that, complete torture.

Attention like this from someone like Thomas Cook was not without its own special breed of aftermath. It impacted every area of Sam's life—both personal and professional.

Ever since the singing telegram, Raul had left her in a dark silent treatment. Sam's mother rambled daily messages on the answering machine offering everything from makeup tips to dating advice, hoping to secure the rich and successful son-in-law of her dreams. Even Sam's co-workers couldn't resist the urge to make her job more isolating—and thus more miserable—than ever.

The typists in the bullpen assumed Sam was dating Thomas Cook for the promotion. The research aids suspected Sam was putting out. The nice girls called her a gold-digger behind her back, while the not-so-nice girls gossiped in front of her face. Mel called her a slut. And Mr. Getty called her his golden goose.

Never in a million years would anyone have guessed that Thomas Cook's taste in women was as plain as vanilla yogurt, and most other vanilla yogurt women would have jumped at a shot with the big-wig with the big house and big bank account to match. But not Sam.

The truth of the matter was simple: Sam had loftier goals than marrying a millionaire.

"We're not dating," Sam would have answered if someone asked. But no one asked. Not even Thomas Cook, it would seem.

Had anyone asked him, Thomas would have said that Sam was as good at "playing hard to get" as she was at writing columns, which he now voraciously read. And enjoyed, by golly! As far as he was concerned, Sam was the perfect medicine for the disease he had: his chronic inability to be challenged.

It had started when he was young. There was no math equation he couldn't solve. No chemistry calculation he couldn't deduce. He was unable to be stumped, which made him unable to be stopped. Eventually finding success so easily became boring. Predictable. No fun at all.

Until finally he met a challenge he could not easily overcome—and she came in the form of a plain-faced, average-intellect woman who against all odds remained firmly out of reach.

Thomas didn't care that she was unoriginally unattractive, wore too much weight on her midsection yet could barely fill a training bra, had terrible taste in clothes, and sported a short shag haircut that did nothing to compliment her features. None of that mattered to him.

It was her mind that satiated him, an insatiable man, and it was her quirky apathy that intrigued him, having never met a woman who was apathetic toward him. Women usually draped themselves all over him, and yet Samantha Stanton could care less. It was the most addictive feeling in the world. Yes, to Thomas Cook, the richest and most desirable eligible bachelor in town, she was indeed the perfect drug.

And this made everyone hate her.

Which made Sam hate Thomas Cook.

Perhaps *hate* was a strong word, but the man was responsible for Sam's father's death, so *hate* wasn't a far stretch from what she felt. But she still did not want to send mixed signals or break hearts, no matter how cold and hardened Thomas's heart was in its natural state.

Not wishing to drag Thomas through the ringer another day, Sam selected the perfect consolation prize for her final goodbye and good riddance. Nothing said *I'm no good for you* like a five-foot-tall poisonous oleander shrub.

Poking up from the back seat of her convertible, the plant had lost most of its bright pink flowers to the gushing wind by the time Sam crookedly parallel parked in the first available spot she could find, which was three blocks away from Cook Pharmaceuticals' downtown building. Lugging the heavy planter the near quarter mile from her parked car to the US Steel Tower entrance, she finally arrived at the foot of the skyscraper, dreading the thirty-minute climb to his office.

The main first-floor lobby was empty and still closed to the public—unless you had enough money to buy early admission—with not a soul in sight. She glanced at the elevators, the blinking numbers of which appeared to be in working order, then kept walking past them and headed straight for the stairwell. There was no way Sam was going to risk being stuck on an elevator alone in a vacant building.

The pot Sam carried up countless floors, for Sam's claustrophobia simply could not endure the tight space of an elevator, weighed almost as much as Fido, but the oleander bush would be a perfect addition to Thomas Cook's office, with its sparse flowers and poisonous leaves potent enough to kill a grown man. Only Sam could appreciate the symbolism.

She arrived at the Cook Pharmaceuticals floor panting and winded. When she peeked around the shrub and announced herself to Thomas's nail-filing receptionist, she was shocked to hear that he had been expecting her. Then the secretary set down her manicure set and ushered Sam into his office, where he stood with a huge grin.

"You finally came!" Thomas declared. "I figured the singing telegram would do the trick."

"I brought you a thank-you gift," Sam replied, dropping the pot onto the floor and scattering soil in a rim around the carpet. She nudged the sun-loving plant closer to the wall of windows overlooking the city. From here she could see her own skyscraping building across town.

"What is this?" Thomas asked.

"An oleander shrub. It's the least I could do after the flowers, chocolates, and balloons you sent. But the singing telegram, well, that was too much."

"So you bring me a tree—and you don't think this is a bit... too much as well?"

"It was the best way I could think to thank you."

Feeling parched, she headed to a drink cart where a

sparkling water machine sat, one of the newest must-have household appliances, thanks to the jingle "Get jizzy with the fizzy!" It didn't hurt that since the 1850s consumers had been duped into believing spring water could remedy everything from sea sickness, fever, and ague, to curing dyspepsia, liver, and kidney complaints. Now homes across America were taking their toxic Cook Pharmaceutical medicines with a gulp of imported Perrier bottled water that could do nothing to save them.

After pouring a glass, she gulped a sip then headed to the window and dumped the remaining water onto the plant.

"It's been forty-eight days since I've seen you," Thomas commented. "What took you so long to reply?"

Thomas had been counting the days since their first meeting? This was worse than Sam thought.

"Technically it's been fifty," Sam corrected, which she only knew because she had a memory for anything to do with numbers.

"Not if you count the day we met and today," Thomas countered.

"I didn't realize you were keeping track."

"You still haven't told me why you took so long to get back to me. No one has ever made me wait so long, Samantha. It's a good thing I'm a patient man."

Sam doubted that.

"If a woman makes you wait fifty—sorry, *forty-eight*—days for a reply, it usually means she's not interested."

Thomas laughed, because never had a woman not been interested. Sure, he knew he wasn't the finest-looking man, and he could be incorrigible to deal with, but wealth and power went a long way in hiding those flaws.

"Look, I don't want to lead you on or drag this out. This plant was intended to be a parting gift."

"A parting gift? Are you saying you don't want to see me again?"

One date with Thomas Cook was plenty for Sam. She couldn't imagine enduring his lecherous gaze, or his ego-inflated spoken poetry, or his drunken touches another night. There was no good way to explain that she had only been using him to secure her column. But even if she had found him remotely good-looking, which she didn't, or enjoyed his conversation and company, which she found repulsive, they still would have been doomed from the start. Because Sam was in love with Raul, and if no handsome conversationalist could change that fact, certainly no mediocre one could.

"I'm not really a dating type of girl," she replied. Which was a lie wrapped in a truth, because Sam simply hadn't found a man worth dating... yet.

Men baffled Sam in general, their one-track brains constantly warring between sex, sports, and power. And Thomas Cook—so brilliant in science and yet so dumb in common sense—specifically left her dumbfounded.

"But why not give me a chance? You'd be the envy of every woman in Pittsburgh." He met her at the window and ran a fingertip down her bare arm. The feel of it sent a row of goosebumps popping along her skin, the kind of goosebumps that shot the hairs up in warning.

"I don't want to be the envy of anyone."

"But every woman wants to be the envy of everyone."

"Not me," Sam stated. "I prefer anonymity and simplicity."

Thomas threw his arms up with an anguished moan. "And this is why I must have you, Samantha Stanton! You defy every expectation. You renounce conventionality. You're stuck in my brain, and I can't think, I can't sleep, I can't eat... and I keep hearing a ringing sound..."

Though to Sam he appeared plenty refreshed and well-fed, no matter how much sleep deprivation and starvation he claimed she was putting him through. Though now that she was looking at him, truly scrutinizing him, Thomas Cook didn't look well at all. In fact, he was sweating like a woman in the throes of menopausal hot flashes.

"Are you okay, Thomas? Your eyes are dilated... and you're... swaying."

"I am?" Thomas asked, vacillating so far to the left that he nearly toppled over.

Sam guided him to a chair and sat him down. Resting her hands on his shoulders, she felt the muscles popping and twitching. "What the—? Thomas, did you ingest something out of the ordinary today?"

He shook his head, but Sam suspected otherwise. When he leaned forward to catch his breath, Sam noticed a damp stain all over the back of his oxford shirt. Lifting up the hem of the shirt over his head, his skin was sticky with residue.

"Thomas, what's on your back? Is this..." she sniffed it, examining the viscosity, "lidocaine?"

"Oh yeah, that. I applied it to my sore muscles."

"Sore from what?"

"I started lifting weights... to impress you."

"I'd be more impressed if you donated your wealth to the poor." A rash had spread across his back in angry pink blotches.

"Anyway, I think you OD'd."

He chuckled weakly. "You can't OD on lidocaine... can you?"

"You most certainly can. And you most certainly did."

Sam scurried to the water cart and grabbed a glass, along with a handful of cocktail napkins. She poured it all over Thomas's back, wiping off the lidocaine and carefully watching Thomas for any improvement.

Within a few minutes the rash subtly lightened, his breathing started to normalize, and the twitching stopped.

"How are you feeling?" Sam asked.

"You were right. I guess I did OD on lidocaine. I feel a lot better, thanks to you. I can't believe you—" Thomas turned his watery gaze up to meet hers, his voice choking with tearful gratitude, "you saved my life. Thank you."

"Happy to help," Sam tried her best to sound nurturing, awkwardly patting his soaked back.

"I could have died."

"Well, I highly doubt lidocaine toxicity would have killed you."

"And you saved me."

"I simply tossed some water on you."

Thomas grabbed her hands, full with wadded up soaked cocktail napkins, and fell to his knees before her. "Give me one chance to prove I'm worth it."

"Worth what?"

"A date. Friday night." He rose to his feet, pressing her hands to his heart. "It's one of the last baseball games the Pirates will play at Forbes Field before they move to the new stadium."

"I don't think I should..."

"Maybe I'll surprise you."

"I don't like surprises."

In fact, Sam hated surprises, for they were rarely, if ever, good. The last surprise she had gotten was a phone call from her grandmother telling her she had a surprise waiting at the house for her. Sam showed up, thrilled to accept this mysterious gift, then entered the house to find her grandmother keeled over in her knitting chair, clutching a wrapped box.

Only after the funeral did Sam build up the courage to open it and found a handkerchief with *Samantha Stanton* embroidered across the corner. She could never look at that hanky again without conjuring the gray face of her dead grandmother, and she distrusted all surprises ever since.

"Maybe this will change your mind." Thomas paused, closed his eyes, released her hands, and crossed his palms over his heart.

For a moment Sam thought he was going to pour something eloquent from his soul. Instead he proclaimed something much, much worse:

"You saved my life, it's true.
And so I must thank you.
Let me rebuild your faith in me
like the fans rebuilt their faith in thee,
America's greatest pastime sport.
And let me woo you enough to court.
Goodbye to crumbling walls I say
And begin a life with me this day."

Thomas paused, opening his eyes and watching her for a

reaction. "I just now wrote that for you, Samantha. And I meant every word."

"I truly believe that. It's quite... original," was all she could muster.

"If I can't convince you to give me a chance by the end of our evening together, I'll walk away and never contact you again. With no hard feelings."

But Sam also knew men tended to break promises. "I really, really don't think it's a good idea, Thomas."

He exhaled heavily. "Don't make me do this, Samantha."

"Do what?"

"I really think you should reconsider."

"Why?"

"Because I know what you did."

Her heart skipped a beat then felt like it had gone a full stop. He knew *what* exactly?

"Ah, you didn't think I'd find out or piece it together? I'm smarter than I look." Thomas turned to the window, his reflection catching the shadows of his tensing jaw and narrowing eyes. "My ledger, I know you took it. And I'll simply ask for it back and forget all about your thievery—if you give me my one request. If you can't, then I will be forced to go to the police about your sticky fingers."

This was the thanks she got for saving his life, a terrible choice to make: Another night in the slammer, or another night with Thomas Cook? It seemed like both options were unequivocally a dead end.

Chapter 21

For the first time in her life, Sam appreciated a crowd. She was grateful for the 30,000 bodies crammed into Forbes Field's stadium seating. Happy for the loud yells of fanatics heckling the other team—Sam couldn't for the life of her remember their mascot, only that she was rooting for the players dressed in black and yellow—thundering in her ears. Approving of the sweaty stench of overzealous enthusiasm soaked into the #17 Dock Ellis baseball jersey Thomas had handed her when he picked her up in his Rolls Royce Silver Shadow, then instructed her to wear over her blouse. Because as long as the sounds drowned out Thomas Cook, she could avoid the conversation he was so eager to have.

Shoving a mouth full of crackerjack that Thomas insisted she eat during *American's favorite pastime*, Sam watched as the player whose number she wore pitched a ball over the home plate.

At this point Sam had picked up on the basics, like the endless length of each *inning,* the long wait to get three *outs,* and how infrequent the players got *runs.* How anyone *enjoyed* stretching out an entire evening to fill nine of these innings was baffling.

"Isn't this great? That's Dock Ellis, one of the greatest pitchers of all time," Thomas explained as the din of the stadium died out momentarily. "Last week he pitched a no-hitter against the Padres. Someone said he was on LSD at the time, but who cares, right? I'll take a no-hitter any way it comes!"

Sam didn't know what a no-hitter was, and she was about to ask, just to avoid the inevitable dreaded relationship conversation. But Thomas shifted gears, lurching her into unwanted territory.

"So I know you're as eager to discuss this as I am," Thomas went on, oblivious to the painful wince wrinkling Sam's brow. "I think it's time."

"Time for what?" Sam dared to ask.

"Time for us to, you know"—he paused, then crowded her with the thought he had been antsy to bring up all evening—"make-it-official," he rushed to say.

Sam's forced grin hung crooked and stiff. "But I don't even know you, Thomas."

"Sure you do. Haven't you read the papers? They're always talking about me."

"Not the *real* you."

"Okay. What do you want to know?"

In the six innings Sam had suffered through, they had talked about almost everything—her column, his new drug, her house pony, his housekeeper, even their shared dislike of creamed corn. There was only one obvious exception to the conversational rotation: their relationship status.

It hadn't been intentional—not at first, anyway, as Thomas tirelessly educated Sam on the *art of baseball*, which Sam felt held as much *art* as Thomas's spoken poetry. But by the seventh inning stretch it became clear it was now or never.

It's not to say that Sam wasn't mildly intrigued by *the* Dr.

Thomas Cook. Who wouldn't want to wade into the shallow end of the self-made millionaire's childhood and meet the cast responsible for creating him—perhaps a brilliant but misunderstood mother. Or a competitive brother who drove him to work harder. Maybe even an eccentric wealthy benefactor who funded medical school. But the topic of *family* was intimate, and Sam barricaded off intimacy like it belonged in the polio isolation ward.

Sam had already dipped a toe in and detected that Thomas tried desperately to hide his Boston accent, and someone in his family encouraged the arts—even if it was poorly written spontaneous poetry. But other than the obvious symptoms of a child who grew up constantly being told how wonderful he was, she had no desire to wander in too far.

"Tell me something you've never told anyone else," Sam suggested. "Something real. Personal."

Thomas knew this could be dangerous, sharing something so private with a woman who could later use it against him. She *had* stolen his ledger, after all, and he still didn't know why. But something about Sam felt honest. Safe.

"Hm. Okay. You ever heard of Clark Stanley?"

Sam thought for a moment. "The snake oil salesman?"

"The one and only."

"You're related to the Rattlesnake King?"

Thomas chuckled. "Oh, no, but my grandfather is the reason Stanley became the Rattlesnake King. It was my grandfather, a Boston druggist, who helped Stanley market his tincture as a painkilling snake oil, and distributed it to drugstores all over the country. After word got out that it was just turpentine and mineral oil, my grandfather lost his job and my family became the laughingstock of Boston. It's why my father moved us to Pittsburgh, because our family became a pariah and we needed a fresh start."

"Is that why you went into medicine—*real* medicine, that is? As a way to save face?"

"You could say that. Plus I wanted to get rich, and I knew medicine was the best way to do that. Everyone gets sick. It's the one commodity that people will pay any price for—health."

"Why is being rich so important to you?" she asked.

"Have you ever been poor?" His voice was flat. "I'm talking empty pantry, no electricity, ice-cold house in winter poor."

She considered the handful of times she had overheard her parents arguing over a pricey grocery bill here, or a late mortgage payment there. But never had their pantry gone empty, their lights flickered out, or their rooms grown frigid in the dead of winter.

"No, I guess not."

"Then nothing I say will help you understand why it's so important to me that I never go through that again," he said bluntly.

"I'm sorry," she said, taking his hand in hers.

It was the first time she'd seen a soft side of him, and for the first time since meeting him, she actually felt something for him. Pity. Sorrow. It was hard to differentiate which.

"I understand why you don't like me." His voice was reedy as he turned to her with a glum expression. "I'm sure you have all kinds of predispositions about me. But I'm wagering only half of them are factual."

"And the other half?"

"Mildly accurate."

"Such as?" Sam asked as the crowd surged to their feet. She looked around, trying to figure out what all the commotion was about, then noticed the Pirates' score climb by one point.

"My mother was a genius. And perfect in every way. Though my father made sure to keep her in her place. It's why she took her life."

While Sam's maternal genius speculation was accurate, she would have never guessed Thomas had suffered such a significant loss to suicide.

"How heartbreaking." She paused, uncertain if it was appropriate to ask the question nagging her. "Do you agree with your father—that *her place* was to hide her brilliance?"

"If it meant she didn't make my father look like a fool, yes."

Sam sat on that for a long moment before asking, "How old were you?"

"I had just graduated high school. Then my father took his life a few months later."

"That's terrible."

She wanted to ask how it happened, but his tone—so dark and low and strange—warned her to go no further.

He shrugged. "It was a long time ago. I've learned since then that we can never understand someone else's experience. All we can do is harden our hearts to others and it doesn't hurt so much."

"Do you really believe that?"

The truth was that Sam could relate. As tragedy after tragedy struck her family, she had learned not to dare dream for anything good in life, because the price for it was usually too high. In Thomas's case he learned not to dare love anyone, because the aftermath was usually heartbreak. We all had our hang-ups.

"That's why I was a womanizer," he said matter-of-factly. "Past tense."

"Oh?"

"Not anymore. Because of you," he added. "Something about you, Samantha—"

"Sam—" she corrected. If he was going to profess his love for her, he might as well use her preferred name.

"Sam," he said abruptly. "You inspire me. You make me believe in something greater than sex."

It almost sounded like he thought she was the opposite of sexy, which made her laugh because she genuinely didn't care what he thought of her. It was liberating.

"Should I be thanking you for that?"

"I mean that in a good way. You challenge my mind, Sam. No woman has ever done that before, only you and my mother. Maybe that's why I like you so much—you remind me of her."

"You must not know very many women then. There are a lot of us who are deeper than we appear and more intuitive than you assume."

For example, upon first glance at Sam's mother, one might assume she was a simple woman who loved makeup and could cook a killer chicken a la king (no pun intended). But the reality was that Minnie Stanton was an artist who could recontour a face with a handful of simple ingredients and few simple strokes of a brush.

Or take Miss Posey, a woman who rarely left her house and was famous for her gossip. But Sam saw beneath that and discovered she was quite the weather geek, inventing an anemometer from soup cans and a hygrometer from milk bottles.

"I don't know about that. You're not like most women," he said, then added, "and by the way, you should smile more. You're more attractive when you smile."

Sam didn't like when people lumped all women into one mold, and she hated when people told her to smile, as if her teeth were purely for their entertainment.

"Your turn," he said, his voice wooden in stark contrast to the rising emotions around them. "Tell me about your parents."

"Must I?" She dreaded telling her own story.

"It's only fair."

"Well, my father died a few years ago, and my mother visits too often and sells Avon and makes women beautiful for a living."

"You're kidding! And she raised… you?" Thomas almost shouted, shocked that this plain woman sitting next to him could have any relation to someone so closely tied to the beauty profession.

Sam paused, as if she might have missed something. "Why is that so surprising?"

"Because you don't seem to care a thing about makeup. There's a living in that?"

She turned her head toward him. "Oh, yes."

He grinned, trying to imagine a motherly type forcing beauty on a younger, littler Sam.

"Anyway," she said, "obviously the beauty regimens didn't take."

"You're beautiful in your own way, Sam."

"Not that I care what you think," Sam said, appreciating his proper use of her name. Maybe she *did* care what he thought.

174

"But my mother's talent for time traveling makes her stand out."

"Wait. What's this about time travel?"

"She's able to shave years off a woman's face with just a few skin regimens," she said, reverting to her passion for nature. "Did you know apple skins contain phloridzin, which is why they stay ripe for so long? When extracted and applied to your skin, it can reduce wrinkles and fight aging." She grinned proudly. "After I told my mom that tidbit of information we went through apples like they were going out of style."

"Is that what got you interested in homeopathy?" he asked in wonder.

"I guess it is." Sam had always credited her father for her interest, but upon further reflection, her mother had been the catalyst. "I should thank her for that. I had always thought it was my father."

"Why so?"

"Because he died," was all Sam said, because she couldn't tell Thomas the truth, that it was his medicine that killed him.

For a fleeting moment she wished she could be truly honest with Thomas. As Sam had her fair share of death, she never considered that someone else might have more than her share.

"Oh." Thomas sighed a compassionate sound. For so long he thought he was the only one, but Sam had suffered too. "Who took care of you and your mother after your dad... passed?"

"We did, of course!"

"But... how? You're women!"

"You act like it's impossible for a woman to be resourceful and smart and talented. That kind of thinking is exactly why I said you clearly don't know very many women, Thomas."

"What if I told you it's only you I want to know."

Sam still couldn't understand his interest in her when there were so many other potential victims.

"I want the truth, Thomas. Why are you so determined to have me? I've read the tabloids. I know I'm not your usual type."

He paused as if searching for an honest answer to this obscenely simple question. Thomas picked up her hand, weaving his fingers through hers.

"Because I love you," he finally said, his voice so low she barely heard him.

"But what if I don't love you back?" Sam asked, barely above a whisper. "Will you still turn me in for taking your ledger—which I don't have, by the way."

His hand tightened, squeezing hers until it hurt. "Stealing is a crime, Samantha."

"But we had a deal, Thomas. One date and you'd let me off the hook." She slipped her hand free of his grip, scared of the strength she felt in it.

"That deal is no longer on the table. Instead I have a new deal for you."

Certain it would be just as bad or worse, Sam dreaded hearing this one. It would probably require her to sleep with him... or, God forbid, listen to more of his spoken poetry.

"Okay?"

"I need that ledger back, period."

"Like I said, I don't have it."

"Well, then I suggest you give me a chance—and officially be my girlfriend."

"How does that fix things with the ledger?" Sam could not for the life of her understand his logic.

"I can easily discredit anyone who tries to use the ledger against me. When you have enough money, you own the media. But the only way you can make it up to me is if we're dating."

"And if I say no?"

He stared at her with a dark look that held a deadly threat.

"Trust me, you don't want to find out what a man with power can do to a woman with just a single word."

Women's House Magazine
July 1970 Issue

Q: Dear Samantha,

I grew up in the Hill District but was recently displaced from our home when the city bulldozed over our neighborhood to put in the new Civic Auditorium. While sports fans might love the state-of-the-art retractable-roof dome with its view of the sky, it made my family homeless.

So we moved into a suburban neighborhood, but within days of my family's arrival, houses were being vacated left and right. My front door was vandalized. My toddler was targeted by bullies. Before even meeting me, the neighborhood hated me.

My husband claims I'm worrying about things I can't change. But I can't accept that this is how it will always be. As the Reverend once said, "Change does not roll in on the wheels of inevitability, but comes through continuous struggle."

Your column speaks of women solidarity. Where

is the solidarity when I'm an outcast from the very women who pledge to fight for one another? I refuse to believe my worry is in vain, or that the struggle won't one day bring change. What can you suggest I take to alleviate my worry?

Sincerely,
Worrywart Wanda

A: Dear Worrywart Wanda,

I cannot offer anything to alleviate your worry, nor should I. That is not worry you feel—it is a willingness to change things.

Already you have greater understanding of what it takes for women to rise up than most. Why do women compete with one another? Why do we spread hatred amongst our feminine community when together we could do so much for our greater good?

While I can't offer a quick solution, I can suggest something that may help give you a sense of peace. The active ingredient is a friend, and the dosage is two cups of Russian Friendship Tea, composed of lemon, cinnamon, and cloves. The lemon contains antioxidants for better immune system health, the cinnamon lowers blood sugar, and cloves provide gut health. With a supportive friend, a healthy body, and a will to change things, your "worry"— but more so your willingness—can make a difference in this world.

Don't give up on those who are too blind to see.

TAKE YOUR MEDICINE

One day unity will be ours.

    Sincerely,
    Samantha

Chapter 22

In the twilight, when the world was just awakening, Fido had already pooped once in his manure bag, trotted from the bedroom to the kitchen, nibbled two green onion plants down to the root, and was now nuzzling Sam awake. When he finally decided to whinny at the window, Sam could no longer ignore him.

"Go back to bed, Fido!" Sam shoved her head under her pillow, but it did little to mute Fido's neighs. She hadn't slept soundly and wanted nothing other than to hide under her covers from the world.

The baseball game had run late into the night, but the adrenaline from the game wasn't what kept Sam's brain buzzing until dawn broke. And while Thomas Cook's profession of love had spiked her anxiety, that wasn't what sapped her sleep either.

The sleep thief was Thomas's threat that she either reciprocate his feelings and return the stolen ledger, or face the consequences. And while demanding the ledger from Mr. Getty sounded impossible, and losing her column once and for all felt heartbreaking, going to jail for theft was the worst possible outcome. It wouldn't only be a slap on the wrist and a single night behind bars this time.

When Fido let out a louder neigh, coupled with a sneeze that sprayed the bed, Sam threw her covers off and forced herself up and over to the bedroom window where Fido paced. Outside a group of kids were already gathering, standing and staring at the house next to hers.

What now? The rumor mill had been churning out new stories every day, to the point where the children were obsessed with the *"villainous masterminds"* living next-door. Sam decided then and there that it was time to put this big mystery to rest once and for all. If her neighbor was indeed a former prison resident, at least Sam could find out what he was in for. And if he wasn't, she could clear his name and redirect the flight pattern of the fearful neighbors.

Not usually one to feel anxious, especially over a little gossip, Sam wondered where the public concern had originated. There was usually a morsel of truth found in every fictional tale, which didn't bode well. The words *criminal* and *threat* had been flung around too much to ignore, especially if these mystery neighbors endangered the growing crowd of elementary-aged looky-loos.

Sam turned from the window, hoping some coffee would clear her muddled head, until a *rat-tat-tat* filled the air, loud enough to send Fido into a trot, ears up, eyes wide. While Sam had never heard an actual gunshot before, this sound was the closest she could imagine to it. She peeked outside, watching the kids scamper. Had the neighbor shot at them?

Throwing off her nightgown and stepping into a shift dress, Sam ran outside, gaze darting as she gauged the situation. The kids had all scattered in different directions, but no one appeared hurt.

This community crisis had to end. Now.

She crossed her lawn and headed next-door. Sam knocked

until the front door of the neighbor's house, freshly painted with a gray clean slate, swung open. A little Black boy stood on the other side of the screen door, young enough that his eyes barely peeked above the aluminum bottom. The whistling and honking sound of cartoons blared in the background.

The moment he waved and greeted her with, "Hi, I'm Awonzo Junow!" Sam wondered what kind of *criminal* family raised friendly toddlers who watched cartoons.

Sam knelt on the concrete stoop. "Hi, Awonzo Junow. My name is Sam. I live next door. Is your mommy home?"

The little boy wordlessly nodded, his smile a row of chiclet-white baby teeth, then he pointed into the dark interior of the house. His tiny, dimpled fingers fiddled with the locked handle until it turned, then he pushed the door open for Sam.

Sam lifted her foot to step inside, then she hesitated, knowing nothing other than what the neighborhood had warned her: *Dangerous criminals. Violent thieves.* Then she walked right in behind the little boy, letting the screen door slam shut behind her.

"Hello?" Sam called out.

A moment later a woman came scurrying into the living room, hands clutching a towel.

"Who are you, and how did you get in my house?" the woman demanded.

Sam held out her hand. "Hi, I'm Sam Stanton. I live next door and your son let me in."

The woman glared at Sam's outstretched hand. "What do you want?"

"I heard a sound... it sounded like gunshots. I just wanted to make sure everyone was okay."

The woman seemed to soften, only slightly. "Those were firecrackers that the neighbor kids threw at our house. Again. And yeah, we're okay, so you can leave now."

But Sam, not all that good at reading irritated verbal cues, didn't budge.

"Why were they throwing firecrackers at your house?" Sam asked, oblivious to the way the Black woman inched toward her, pressing in on Sam, subliminally urging this strange white woman to leave.

"Isn't it obvious?"

"No. Should it be?"

"Uh, I'm Black. And I just moved into a white old-lady neighborhood."

"And…?" Sam asked, genuinely confused.

"Are you serious right now?" the woman asked, uncertain if Sam was actually that stupid or just playing dumb and exceedingly good at it.

"I'm sorry. Am I missing something?" Sam could sense she was a beat behind, as she usually was when it came to reading people and situations, but this felt like she was singing a whole different tune.

Shifting to the wood-encased black-and-white television console, the woman turned down the obnoxious sounds of *Looney Tunes*. She propped her hands on her hips.

"Your uppity neighborhood wants me out because of the color of my skin."

"No, that's ridiculous. While I admit I've gotten my own fair share of judgement for being a single woman and owning a pony, the people here are harmless. Truly."

"Maybe for you, but you're like them."

"I'm nothing like them."

"I meant you *look* like them, honey. You fit in."

"I've never fit in. Anywhere. But isn't that what makes us exceptional?"

The woman cracked a slight smile. "Exceptionally good at standing out."

"You just made my point. We stand out. Who wants to fit in when you could stand out?"

"Those who don't want a target on their back," the woman exclaimed, growing exasperated at explaining something that Sam would never deeply understand.

"A target means you've made waves," Sam said. "I'd much rather spend my life making waves than drowning in them."

"Then I guess we understand each other, don't we?" At this point the woman gave up trying to make Sam leave and decided maybe it wouldn't be so bad if she stayed. "So why are you standing in my living room?"

"As I said, I heard what I thought were gunshots, which now I know were firecrackers, so I guess I'm still standing here to offer friendship. Woman to woman. Target to target."

Only now did the woman accept Sam's still extended hand, which she shook slowly, as if waiting for the punchline, or for Sam to zap her with a hand buzzer.

"Okay, then it's nice to meet you, Sam Stanton. I'm Bernadette Breedlove. And this," she pulled the child who couldn't be much older than four, to her hip, "is Alonzo Junior."

"And all this time I was calling you Awonzo Junow and you didn't correct me," Sam teased him with a light poke to his rib, which made him giggle. "Breedlove. Any relation to Sarah Breedlove?"

Bernadette's jaw stiffened as she remembered what the neighborhood kids had painted across her front door. She wasn't used to people recognizing her husband's family name, especially not a white person. "You've heard of my husband's grandaunt?"

"Who doesn't know of her? She was the first woman self-made millionaire! And her hair care products were all natural, which was unprecedented for the era." Sam recalled when she had first come across Madam CJ Walker's Wonderful Hair Grower at the five-and-dime store. Using plant-based ingredients, Sarah Breedlove had discovered a way to regrow her hair after going nearly bald from stress.

From that brief moment in the drugstore hair aisle, Sam realized plants were so much bigger than just food. They could restore, they could heal.

"Her understanding of the way to use nature to care for the body was innovative. In fact, her work inspired me to pursue homeopathy."

"Most people don't recognize her by her maiden name Breedlove. They only recognize her business name—Madam CJ Walker—but no one ever seems to know what she's famous for."

"Oh, well, I do. She was brilliant. And an incredible philanthropist. I can't believe you're related to her. She used to have a beauty parlor in the Hill District."

"I know. That's where I'm from."

While something in Sam's brain clicked, Bernadette nodded, wondering what this odd woman was actually here for and if she could trust her. Part of her wanted to believe this was a genuine friendship budding, but that required a special brand of faith that she wasn't sure she had left.

"Thanks for checking on the noise. I'm sure I'll see you around." Bernadette considered inviting Sam to stay and chat over family-favorite oven-fresh biscuits and gravy. But the memory of the firecrackers and vandalism and *For Sale* signs erupting after she'd moved in stopped her short.

"Of course we will. We live next to each other," Sam stated, unmoving.

"Well, have a nice day," Bernadette wavered, a little disheartened that her dreams of a friendly neighbor were expiring so quickly.

As neither woman moved, it would seem as if they were not quite ready to part ways, as both felt the same tug for companionship.

"Do you happen to like tea?" Sam asked. "Perhaps Russian Friendship Tea?"

An hour later, Alonzo Jr. sat watching *Captain Kangaroo* while Sam and Bernadette had circled around several topics, including which topping tasted best on a biscuit, what it was like for Bernadette being married to a police officer, and how Sam had come to commandeer the art of botany. They had finally segued into chatting book club selections—with Bernadette sharing her book club read, *The Bluest Eye,* while Sam lamented falling behind on her book club read, *The Godfather*, followed by Bernadette's shock at discovering that the current bestselling romance novel, *Naked Came the Stranger,* was in fact a hoax.

"The book was a social experiment," Sam went on to tell her. "The author wasn't a woman but a group of male journalists who wrote the most sexual, vulgar literature they could come up with to poke fun of women's literary culture. Their theory was that modern women's literature was so base that if enough sex was thrown into the plot—regardless of terrible prose quality—it could be a bestseller. Maybe they were right, since here we are a year later and it's still at the top of the bestseller charts."

Bernadette laughed, her voice boisterous for the first time in the months since moving onto this street. "Sometimes a woman wants Italian gangsta crime," she said, "and sometimes she wants cheap smut. That doesn't make us any more disreputable than a man!"

"Exactly. The same could be said for men and their movies. Throw in a bunch of six-shooters, horses, and cowboys and it's an instant box-office hit."

"Nothing could be truer," Bernadette agreed. No one had ever spoken the exact words she was thinking before. She felt an instant kinship to this quirky stranger.

"Look," Sam added sharply as she set down her teacup. "I need to come clean."

"Come clean about what?" Bernadette had been unknowingly waiting for this moment. It always came.

"About you," Sam said firmly, gesturing first to Alonzo Jr. then to Bernadette. "And something I need to confess."

"I knew it."

"Knew what?"

"That the color of my skin was going to be an issue. Just like it's been an issue in this neighborhood since day one."

"Oh, that's not what I was coming clean about." Sam now had second thoughts bringing it up, lest she crumble their fragile foundation. "Never mind."

"No, spit it out, Sam."

"I…" Sam waved her hand uncertainly, then looked off into

the distance.

Bernadette exhaled, and folding her arms across her dress, she waited for the rebuff she knew was coming. In the last couple weeks, she had gotten death threats left in her mailbox, her door painted with vulgar words, accused of scaring the good neighbors away, and firecrackers thrown at her son. While moving to the picket-fence suburbs was supposed to be *living the dream*, it was quickly becoming a nightmare she could not escape. The dream because segregation was behind them, schools were integrating, her husband was promoted to patrol unit, and the neighborhood was safe. But the reality? No one wanted her here.

"Okay, here goes," Sam began. "I'm a columnist for *Women's House Magazine*, and I recently had a woman write in about a situation very similar to yours. I'm hoping perhaps you can help me understand her."

Bernadette's mouth dropped open. Her eyebrows arched with surprise. Then she inhaled a steadying breath.

"Then I, too, have a confession to make," Bernadette finally replied. "I'm Worrywart Wanda."

Chapter 23

"Absolutely, unequivocally, under no condition can I do that," Mr. Getty replied when Sam turned up at his office Monday morning begging for the ledger back. "You really are a thorn in my side, Miss Stanton. Are we done here?"

"Well, no, sir. We still haven't resolved the issue about the ledger—"

A phone that Sam couldn't find rang, interrupting her as Mr. Getty shushed her. When he lifted the lid of an ornate wooden box sitting on the corner of his desk, Sam saw the telephone receiver and dial pad hidden inside.

"Go for Getty," he grumbled into the receiver. Sam couldn't hear the rabble on the other line, but whatever it was seemed to be bad news as concern wrinkled Getty's brow. "Yes, sir. Understood, sir." He hung up and closed the lid of the fancy phone box.

"Another new contraption?" Sam wondered how on earth the newspaper budget afforded the growing number of luxuries cluttering her boss's office.

"Are you admiring my Deco-Tel hidden executive box telephone?"

"Not really, sir."

"I got it for a steal."

Unless he actually stole it, Sam was pretty certain that her boss was single-handedly using up *Women's House Magazine* entire staff budget on his latest gadgets.

Mr. Getty lifted his chin and yelled to the open door, "Betty, coffee me!"

Sam's palm itched to slap him for the way he treated his secretary, like a dog fetching his newspaper, but she kept her mouth shut. As Mr. Getty's "thorn in the side," she was better off staying as still as possible unless she wanted to be ripped out and tossed.

Rustling into the room came Betty Number Five carrying a fresh cup of Nescafe—definitely not the burnt stuff from the office carafe—along with today's newspaper. Mr. Getty sloshed the coffee over the desk as he grabbed it and slurped.

"So what do you want me to do about the ledger *now*?" he said.

"The ledger is stolen property. I simply want to return it to Thomas Cook."

"No can do, Samantha."

"But I could go to jail for taking it—which means you could go to jail for forcing me to do it."

"Forcing you? Did I hold a gun to your head and demand you steal it?"

He might as well have, Sam thought to herself. He did threaten her job, after all. Sam was pretty sure that fit somewhere in the crime of coercion.

"You know what I mean. You were going to fire me if I didn't."

"No, what I told you to do was get creative in getting me dirt on Cook Pharmaceuticals." Mr. Getty crossed his arms. "I have no recall of ever telling you to steal anything. The theft, my dear, is all on you. Besides, it's too late to do anything about it now. It's already out of my hands."

"Out of your hands? What do you mean?"

He handed her today's copy of the *Pittsburgh Post*. Splashed across the front page was the headline:

COOK PHARMACEUTICALS: SAFE OR SCANDALOUS?

"What is this?" She already had a hunch of what it was. A quick read confirmed Sam's worst-case scenario: Mr. Getty had exposed the ledger to the world, and now Thomas Cook was going to come after her. As she skimmed the article, her very own name popped out at her. "You credited me personally for exposing the ledger?" she yelped.

"You're famous now. I thought you'd be happy for the investigative journalism credit," Mr. Getty scoffed.

"Why would I be happy? I now have a target on my back! And my entrance into journalism will be marred by the fact that I'll probably end up *dead* from this! Or at the very least I'll be writing my column from a jail cell!"

"Unfortunately we have a strict no-convict hiring policy, so you'll be fired, Samantha. But at least you'll have free room and board."

While Mr. Getty seemed to take pleasure in envisioning Sam's future sentencing, she found nothing entertaining about the prospect.

"What am I supposed to do now?"

"Too little, too late, I'm afraid. What's done is done. I suggest you prepare yourself for the slew of reporters that will be contacting you soon…"

Mel took this moment to pop his head in around the doorjamb. "Did I hear something about Samantha being fired?"

"Were you eavesdropping in on our conversation?" Sam asked.

"No. I just happened to be passing by." But Mel, loitering just outside the office doorway, seemed in no hurry to get to wherever he was going. "So about my previous columnist position..."

"Don't you have somewhere to be?" Sam grumbled at Mel, shooing him away. Then a light-bulb moment occurred. "What if we print a retraction, Mr. Getty?"

"It's too late to retract the article. What's published is published."

Except Sam knew as well as he did that it was the entire point of retractions—to *take back* false information.

"You should have never published that story."

"Like I said, it's done. You want my advice?"

Sam had never wanted anything less.

"Consider relocating to a new zip code, because you're about to get very popular."

Sam could have sworn she heard Mel snicker under his breath right outside the office door.

Chapter 24

Across the city, in Morewood Heights, where the yards were so manicured they looked like tv show sets, and the streets clean enough to eat off of, Thomas Cook sat at his usual morning spot on the veranda overlooking his million-dollar neighborhood, sipping his rich espresso, and picked up today's copy of the *Pittsburgh Post*. Within five minutes of opening the paper to page one, he jumped up from his seat, spat out his drink, and threw the paper down on the wicker table.

"Guadalupe!" he screamed to the closed front doors, where the lion's-head knocker glared back at him.

Moments later, attuned to Thomas's voice even through brick walls and closed doors, Guadalupe rushed to his side, still clutching the July 1970 copy of *Women's House Magazine* she had been reading over sangria. If only Dr. Cook understood *real* problems, like the one she had been reading about Worrywart Wanda and the discrimination she was experiencing. Men like Thomas Cook were above such trite snags in life.

Her summer sky blue maid's uniform rode dangerously high. Why men insisted a woman wear a miniskirt to handle housekeeping work was beyond her, for instead of bending over to pick up something, she had to cumbersomely lower herself to avoid showing the entire house staff her bloomers. And instead of having the free mobility to reach up to grab something off a high shelf, lest she once again expose her rear, she had to waste precious minutes retrieving a stepstool upon which to carefully step up on. It was ridiculous that even a maid could be sexualized, as if she needed to be debased any more than she already was.

"Yes, sir?" she asked, fingering the peter pan collar of her dress.

Then she glanced at the spatter of coffee on the patio floor, the newspaper thrown down, and the red blotches across her boss's cheeks.

Thomas had just read today's front-page headline:

COOK PHARMACEUTICALS: SAFE OR SCANDALOUS?

And for some reason he had beckoned her for what? To clean up his mess? To threaten the paper's editor-in-chief? To break the journalist's kneecaps? Some days she felt like his subservient, and others she felt like his mother, God rest her soul.

"Can you believe this?" He gestured to the paper, which Guadalupe picked up.

Below the headline was a photograph of his ledger displaying all the evidence they needed to shut Cook Pharmaceuticals down. At least temporarily, until Cook's lawyers paid off the right people.

"I'm sure you can fight this," Guadalupe consoled, knowing nothing about the situation, or if it was even fightable. Though she knew quite a bit about personal injury law, her breadth didn't extend to corporate law.

"You wouldn't understand the ramifications of this. You're

just a simple-minded, illegal Mexican—"

"Actually, I'm not Mexican. And I'm legally here," Guadalupe corrected. Not that it mattered to Thomas, if the labor was cheap enough. "I'm named after my Spanish ancestors who immigrated to the Caribbean island of—"

But Thomas was too busy plotting how to deal with the woman he once loved—but now hated—to hear a thing Guadalupe said.

"If I'm being honest," Thomas rambled over her, "it's not her exposing the ledger that I'm most upset about. It's about losing the woman who broke my heart."

"I'm sorry, sir, but I'm not following. What does the ledger have to do with a… love interest?" Certainly no woman was behind the hugest story to hit newspaper stands since the *Apollo 13* explosion. And since when did Thomas Cook have a heart?

"Samantha Stanton, the one who got away," he lamented.

Guadalupe almost detected a tear in his eye before his face went stoic and his jaw clenched. The name rang a bell, but it was too distant and faint to grab hold of.

"She did this. She rejected me after she made me fall in love with her." Then he turned to Guadalupe with earnest, gripping her hand. "Where did I go wrong with Samantha? What can I do to win her back?"

"I can't imagine you did anything wrong." Guadalupe could easily imagine a dozen offensive things he had done. "Perhaps some nice jewelry would work?"

Diamonds were indeed the best friends of the women Thomas usually went for, but Guadalupe doubted it would work on this *one that got away*… and hopefully stayed away.

Then Thomas did something he had never done before. He

hugged Guadalupe. Like a son hugged a mother… if the son was a grown man who treated his mother like a housekeeper. Which was pretty much most men.

Her hand moved up and down in a clumsy pat, reiterating her role as makeshift mother when it came to Thomas Cook's love life.

"I am sure she will want you back," she continued, fairly confident the young lady would not, "but whether or not Ms. Stanton reciprocated the feelings, there are plenty of gold-digging women who would do anything for your affection."

"But I don't want them. I want Samantha. I've never met a woman with a mind like hers. She was like a man wrapped in a woman's body."

Guadalupe wasn't sure exactly how to interpret that, but she continued to soothe him nonetheless. "What was so special about her?"

"She saved my life. And she was just… different. She knew a lot about medicine, for starters. And had talent as a writer." He exhaled against her shoulder, remembering Sam's mediocre poem in response to his much better one. "A little feminist for my tastes, but I could stifle that eventually."

Knowledgeable about medicine? A writer? And a feminist? Certainly it couldn't be… Guadalupe glanced at the latest *Samantha Says* column and suddenly realized it had to be *her*. The woman who had shown up on this same doorstep where she awkwardly held Dr. Cook.

Thomas stiffened and let go of Guadalupe. "But now she's dead to me."

If truth be told, their love had been doomed from the beginning. It was no surprise that when Thomas proposed the incredibly generous offer to be exclusive to Sam—as far as she would ever know—even he had his doubts. First, he wasn't the exclusive type. Second, Samantha wasn't even that pretty. What would people think when they saw them together in public? But third, and most important, Sam worked for the very magazine he already had plans to shut down.

Thomas Cook wasn't just a pharmaceutical mogul. He also dabbled in publishing. And Cook Media had taken ownership of the dying rag with the intention of dismembering it and shifting gears to something more national—like a hunting or fishing magazine. Everyone liked hunting and fishing! And more than actually hunting and fishing, people liked reading about others hunting and fishing. Thomas believed he was tapping into a goldmine.

He had kept this secret to himself while he whittled away at Sam's resolve not to date him. But now all bets were off. Not just because Sam stole his ledger, or because she went public with it, and definitely not because she betrayed his heart. Bottom line, she was a powerless woman who needed to be put in her place. He no longer loved Samantha Stanton. She was plain looking, overly opinionated, and worst of all had terrible taste in men.

What better way was there to control a woman than taking everything she loved? After he made sure Sam's writing career ended in a train wreck, he'd next go after her reputation. But women like her didn't mind a little public judgement. So the final attack would hit her where it hurt: siphon any lingering passion from her un-Thomas-loving heart.

He couldn't wait to give her a taste of her own medicine.

Chapter 25

Miss Posey shivered from her front porch, arms folded against the October chill, hair in curlers, tut-tutting Sam's every step.

"It's only downhill from here," she yelled across her yard at Sam, waving the latest *Pittsburgh Post*. "You've made the papers. *Again*."

This wasn't the first time someone had approached Sam about the latest media frenzy dragging her against her will into the limelight with her Big Pharma exposé. For the past couple months the tabloids had merely tainted Sam's personal life as a "scorned ex-lover seeking vengeance," but it was only a matter of time before Thomas Cook countered with something that would destroy her professionally.

When that day finally came, and it inevitably did, Sam's mass destruction showed up on the cover of *Newsbreak*. They accused her of falsifying documents in a vendetta against Thomas Cook after he dumped her in order to push her "dangerous homeopathic quackery."

Of course everyone took his word over hers. She was just a woman scorned, a tree-hugging fraud trying to sell empty promises. He was a reputable doctor, an honest businessman trying to save lives.

"You should be ashamed of yourself." A woman in the produce section of the grocery store stopped sniffing a pomegranate to turn and stare at Sam, who was searching for an in-season fall fruit she could pass out for Halloween and that wouldn't get her house egged.

"Excuse me?" Sam asked.

"I recognize you from the papers."

Sam glanced at the fruit the woman had stopped scrutinizing in exchange for scrutinizing Sam instead.

"Based on the skin color, that pomegranate is overripe. It shouldn't have dark spots," Sam offered, hoping to distract the woman from piecing together Sam's face with the photo on the front page. But the woman was relentless.

"You're the girl trying to discredit poor Dr. Cook because he broke up with you."

"Wouldn't you be a little upset if a man proposed to you, got you pregnant, and then suddenly up and left?" Sam said innocently as she rubbed her belly gently.

It was the third time that week someone felt compelled to inform her of how horrible she was, and since she couldn't put the rumors to rest, she figured she'd just create some more.

"You're pregnant with his child? Out of wedlock?"

"It's either that or I've got a bad case of gas."

For a split second, the woman's eyes widened in shock, then instantly narrowed. "No one likes a smart-aleck, missy," she gruffed.

"And no one likes a rotten pomegranate," Sam replied, then whispered to herself, "Or a rotten woman."

An hour later a wiry-haired attendant shook his head at Sam as if she were a traitor to her country. "I hope you're proud of yourself," he commented as Sam pulled up to the gas pump. "You deserve jail for such slander."

Ten minutes later Sam barely made it home as she cruised up her driveway on fumes. A blue Pontiac sat out front of her house, and leaning on the hood of the car was Raul. As she parked, he walked up to her car door and opened it, holding out a small paper bag.

"I brought chipped ham sandwiches for dinner."

She glanced at his other hand, which held today's newspaper.

"With a side dish of bad news?" Sam asked.

"I had to make sure you were okay," he said, following her up to her house.

"I'm fine."

"You can't possibly be fine after reading what they wrote about you."

"Which is why I didn't read it."

She opened up the front door and entered, dropping her purse and grocery bag to the floor as she squatted to plant kisses all over Fido's dirt-covered nose. She spotted the pot of mutilated kale Fido had gotten into.

"Are you my hungry boy?" she cooed as the pony's muzzle smeared potting soil all over Sam's cheeks.

"Sam, you can't just pretend this isn't happening," Raul persisted.

"I'm not pretending anything," she countered.

"Fine, *ignoring*."

"I'm not ignoring it either."

"You just said you didn't read the latest article dedicated to bad-mouthing and discrediting you."

"In which paper? There are so many to choose from these days."

"*Newsbreak.*"

"Oh, then no, I didn't." She glanced up at Raul while Fido rubbed his neck all over her, demanding the massage she was too distracted to give.

"What about the *Pittsburgh Post*?"

"Not that one either."

"Any of them?"

Sam stood, looking so ridiculous with dirt all over her face while Fido rubbed around her legs like a cat that Raul couldn't help but grin.

"Why would I want to read any of that garbage?"

"Oh, I don't know, so maybe you could demand a retraction for the theft accusations. Point out Thomas Cook's lies."

"But I *did* steal the ledger. Technically they aren't lying. So there's nothing I can do about it."

Raul hated how defeatist Sam was being, as if she had already lost. "Sam, you have to take this seriously! You're being accused of two different things: theft and falsifying documents. It's either one or the other. It can't be both."

"Don't you think I know that?" Sam shot back. "I'm not an idiot, Raul."

"You sure are acting like one," Raul yelled, wanting Sam to at least fight for herself. "You could go to jail for theft. But if *Newsbreak* is reporting that you falsified documents, you need to lean into that. At least then you will stay out of jail. And the worst you can get charged with is slander... and that's a big *if*. At the very least you should give your side of the story."

"I don't have a side. And it's not a story. It's fake news, Raul." She leaned over, grabbed her purse, and hung it on the coat rack before heading to the kitchen to grab plates for the sandwich she wasn't hungry for anymore.

"But the reporters and readers don't know that. You need to clear your name of the theft and redirect the story."

"Why bother? No one will believe me."

"You have a column that thousands of women read—all of them are your supporters." He waved to the endless stacks of letters still covering a large corner of the living room. "Use that to prove your innocence."

"What *innocence* am I supposed to prove, Raul? Like I said, I *did* steal his ledger, and I'm not going to stoop to his level and lie that I made it all up. No matter what I do, I'm either made out to be a thief or a liar. Neither looks good on me. And even if the smoke does clear, what will I be left with? Worst-case I'll end up in jail, and best-case I lose my job, my home, everything."

Only now could Raul understand Sam's inaction, her silence. "No matter what happens, you'll still have me, Sam. You'll always have me."

But Sam couldn't give him the response he wanted.

"And how long will that last when you're visiting me at Allegheny County Jail?" Sam could already imagine the fateful walk across the Bridge of Sighs that connected the courthouse to the jail.

From personal experience, Raul had felt that tight spot between the rock and hard place where Sam now found herself stuck. He'd had his fair share of obstacles in his career, but he always managed to wiggle his way out of them. Why? Because he was a man. Sam didn't have that luxury, considering her boss was just as eager to throw her to the wolves as Thomas Cook was.

"You're not going to jail, Sam. I'll find a way to clear your name."

"Even you, with all your media connections, can't promise that, Raul. If there's one thing I know—especially as a woman—it's better to do nothing at all. Trying to force my will doesn't work. It only ends in regret."

He nodded as if he understood, but he didn't and not just about the ledger. Because this felt like a conversational shift into something else: *them*.

Raul had been dreaming about the day they went from *Sam and Raul* to *SamRaul*. So badly he wanted it that he was certain he wore it on his face, in the way he looked at her, the way he waited for her calls. Other people noticed it too, like the man on the sidewalk outside of Raul's building who stopped to comment on them last week. Sam had showed up at his apartment, eagerly chattering about the sales record the magazine had just passed. Excited as an eager beaver, she grabbed his hand, and he twirled her around under a cascade of crisp burnt orange leaves while every part of him wanted to swoop her in his arms. As she danced with him across the concrete pads, satiated on the anticipation of snuggling by bonfires and sipping hot cocoa, the stranger had approached them.

"You make a beautiful couple," he said out of the blue. "You both deserve a wonderful life together."

When Sam didn't correct the stranger, Raul's heart floated. And yet still Sam resisted him. Raul could always tell. And so he resisted himself too.

Each time they'd seen each other over the past seven months, despite his urge to cup her perfect face in his hands, he exerted every effort to vibe nothing but friendship. Wasn't that what she still wanted? So he avoided anything remotely romantic when he'd taken her out to lunch—since dinner implied something more intimate—and even let her pay. He never told her she looked pretty when she clearly went the extra effort to apply lip gloss or the occasional barrette. His intention was to make this whole friendship label easier on them both, but it was only becoming more excruciating by the day.

"Enough about the ledger," Sam said, eager to move on. "Let's focus on happier things, like death and ghosts."

Sam busily emptied the grocery bags on the kitchen counter, pulling out mandarin oranges and celery.

"Uh, what are those for?" Raul asked.

"We're going to peel these and turn them into little mandarin orange pumpkins! Watch." She proceeded to peel one, sliced the celery into a thin sliver, then pushed the green stick into the middle of the orange, which effectively gave the appearance of a tiny pumpkin.

Raul smiled, thinking it was cute but deadly. No child would accept this in lieu of candy without a fight to the death.

"Great idea, right?"

"Sure," he answered dully, thinking of how hard it would be to clean a dozen eggs off her siding.

"And I put together costumes for you, me, and Fido. Here is yours."

She handed him a button-up dress shirt, thin black tie, sticky thin gray mustache, and black-rimmed eyeglasses.

"Who am I supposed to be?"

"You're Walter Cronkite reporting the assassination of President Kennedy, obviously." Then she dumped several bags of cotton balls on the counter beside a bottle of glue.

"And you are?"

"A puff piece, get it? I'm going to glue the puffs all over my shirt. Hilarious, right?"

Raul smiled, enjoying Sam's trick-or-treating enthusiasm. "What about the pony?"

"Since he's already black and white, his was pretty simple. I'm going to put red washable paint on him."

"I don't get it. A murder victim?"

She took a step back, surprised by his ignorance. "What's black and white, and *read* all over?" Sam nudged Raul's ribs with her elbow, the tips of her ears reddening. "A newspaper!"

Raul could only laugh at how awful the joke was, since Sam was awfully adorable.

"You're going to make a great mother someday," he blurted out, realizing too late that it was the completely wrong thing to say and the wrong moment to say it.

Even though Sam had claimed she didn't want marriage or children, as far as he could tell, she did. She was a natural at it! Who planned a themed Halloween costume with a man unless there was some kind of romantic interest? And who cared about ensuring kids got a healthy snack unless she had a maternal bone in her body? As a hot-blooded man familiar with women's signals—as well as their disgust—he knew how it worked. And he knew what made Sam tick. Sam wanted marriage and children; she just didn't know it yet.

"Do you think we should skip the costumes?" Sam fished.

Watching Raul carefully, she noticed his mild confusion over the outfits. How much clearer could she be with her intentions? No one planned matching costumes unless they were children trick-or-treating together or a married couple… but it seemed Raul wasn't getting the hint one bit. Or maybe he did and was trying to let her down easily. She wondered if perhaps his feelings had changed. After all, the countless lunches he took her to, and then made her pay her own way?

Either chivalry was dead or Raul's feelings were deader. And yet each time they were together, she felt an urge to kiss him. When their time together concluded—which she often ended prematurely because she was afraid she *would* kiss him— she felt lonelier than ever.

"It's up to you, Sam," Raul answered with a sigh.

So he didn't want to dress up and play house with her, she concluded. "Let's just forget the costumes. Well, I should probably get the pumpkin oranges ready."

"And I'll run to Woolworths to get backup candy," he offered.

But neither of them moved, instead avoiding each other and searching for someone to intercept this awkward moment in Sam's kitchen.

"Do you really think the kids won't like fruit?" she finally ventured.

"Of course they will," he lied. "It's just a good idea to have a sugary backup."

"Right. In case we run out," she said, nodding.

Then she turned and began peeling, while he turned and headed for the front door.

She glanced over her shoulder and watched him walk away. Raul wasn't stupid. He knew no one gave sex appeal vibes like Walter Cronkite. And wordplay was the ultimate love language. What a dork she was, thinking the holiday of horror could finally bring them together.

He probably assumed she was only after his help dealing with Thomas Cook anyway. Because why else would a woman play dress-up on Halloween over chipped ham sandwiches while the vibrant orange sun burned the sky, carrying the autumn scent of freshly fallen leaves, unless it was all part of a ploy to get rid of her archnemesis? That was the only reason anyone would go through all of this effort celebrating a holiday she didn't even care for.

Except that he had just told her that she'd make a great mother. Did he mean the mother of *his* children?

He was already opening the door when she shouted uncertainly, "Raul?"

She took a step toward him.

He turned and shut the door when he answered hopefully, "Sam?"

He took a step toward her.

They stared at each other in heavy silence, weighted with all the things they wanted to say but were afraid to utter, lest they lose their hold on this perfect moment. Sam lost herself in Raul's brown eyes sparked with flecks of gold, while Raul found himself in Sam's green eyes sparkling with adoration.

Then the urge to cup her cheek came over Raul, the feeling he had every time he saw her. And the urge to kiss him came over Sam, the feeling she had every time she was in his presence. But this time they acted on it, Raul reaching out with both hands to draw her face to his, and Sam leaning up on tiptoes to invite his lips to hers.

A breath later, their first kiss inked a story that even two professional wordsmiths could not put words to.

Women's House Magazine November 1970 Issue

Samantha Says...

Q: Dear Samantha,

I've been married for over twenty years, and I've stood by my husband through his mood swings, his drinking, his affairs. I silently and steadfastly carried out my duties as a wife while he criticized my housekeeping, complained about my cooking, and told me how terrible I was in bed. But now he has done something I simply can no longer abide.

Last night he made me drink my supper.

According to him, I had overcooked the chicken and undercooked the pasta, so he threw it all in a blender, poured it into a cup, and handed it to me. When at first I refused, he threatened to hit me. So I drank it... and I would have thrown up if I didn't think he would have made me re-drink that too.

I may be making my husband sound like a monster, but he's got Warren Beatty good looks and a high-paying job to his credit. But I can no longer play Bonnie to his Clyde as his moods have gotten darker. I don't know how to appease this stranger in our home. Please help, before I do something I will truly regret.

Sincerely,
Supper Sipper Sally

A: Dear Supper Sipper Sally,

I can't imagine why you would want to give this man another chance rather than divorcing him on the spot, but I understand the reality of the predicament. I'm assuming you've always been a homemaker, so perhaps you don't think you have any job skills. Maybe you're afraid of doing life alone. Sometimes we grow comfortable in the discomfort. While I hope you'll find the courage to leave, in the meantime I can suggest a medicinal remedy that might make life more tolerable.

Nux vomica seeds—also known as the "poison nut"—while in their natural state are highly toxic, when they are treated by soaking and boiling them in milk, this process removes the poison and has a safe and proven mellowing effect. Sprinkle a handful on his next dinner dish and kick your feet up and relax together the rest of the evening. But don't forget to pre-treat the seeds or it could be fatal!

Sincerely,
Samantha

Chapter 26

"Delivery for Samantha Stanton!" a voice echoed throughout the *Women's House Magazine* bullpen where glittery remnants of the New Year's party from two weeks ago still draped across the walls.

After several men groaned, "This is a place of business, not romance," and a spattering of women seethed, "Look who is showing off again," all eyes turned to Sam sitting at her small metal desk in the corner, where gold ribbon and a few stray balloons had been piled up for Sam to clean up. Then their attention pivoted back to the delivery man dressed in snow-dusted drab gray wool at the other end of the bustling office.

It didn't make Sam proud that these deliveries kept happening. First Thomas Cook's gifts, then the heaping bags of reader mail, and now what? It was drawing unwanted attention that created enemies in the office, as if she needed anyone else to hate her right now.

When Sam heard a snickering erupt behind her, she turned to look. The delivery man dropped a dead plant at the foot of her chair and bid her a better end to her day. It was the dried, crispy, brown remains of the oleander bush Sam had given Thomas Cook. A hand delivered threat, if ever there was one.

A loud *pop!* startled Sam out of her seat. Behind her Mel approached, holding a deflated balloon, which he tossed at Sam.

"Finally you're getting what you deserve."

"And what is it I deserve, Mel? I'm dying to know."

"Your life crumbling before your eyes. It's what you get for overreaching, Samantha. Don't say we didn't warn you to stay in your lane."

Sam had always thought that writing about plants and natural remedies was her lane. Now she wasn't so sure.

Passing by her desk, Mr. Getty gave one look at the dead plant before he barked, "Get that thing out of this office. You can dump it in the Dumpster near the parking garage."

"But that's two blocks away," Sam said.

"And? Don't you have working legs?"

"This planter is pretty heavy, sir."

"I didn't hear the delivery man complaining. You want to be treated equal to men? Well, here's your chance!"

"But there's more than a foot of snow out there. Can't it wait until I leave for the day?"

"Absolutely not. I don't want leaves and dirt all over the floor. Are you trying to make the janitor's job more difficult?"

As if just because the plant sat here it would suddenly drop all of the five remaining leaves, and dirt would suddenly start pouring out of the pot.

"No, sir. I'll take care of it now." Sam lifted the significantly lighter pot than she remembered. Bone dry. Clearly Cook had murdered it.

Pausing at the elevator that could save her back and arms an inevitable muscle ache tonight, she glanced at the stairwell door to her right. Then Sam headed right, cursing her claustrophobia. She had done it once before, carrying it up to Thomas's much higher office floor; she could handle the much safer downward stairs again.

Lugging it down the several flights to the lobby, where the receptionist watched her with pity, Sam made the two-block trek through the snow to the Dumpster and set the pot next to it. She would grab it on her way home, in case there was any chance she could revive it. Worst case, she could repurpose the planter.

As she trekked back to the building, a reporter standing between the two bronze-framed revolving doors spotted her.

"Hey! You!" he called, instantly recognizing the plain-looking woman with the bad haircut that had made the front page of every local newspaper and many national papers too. He ran toward her, bounding over a three-foot-tall snow bank. "You're Samantha Stanton, aren't you?"

Not again. Not another one. And then Raul's words came to mind: *Give your side of the story.*

"Who's asking and why?"

"Floyd Jameson with *Newsbreak*." He followed her under the massive stone portico, which gave little protection from the bitter wind. His nose was bright red and lips chapped and peeling. "I'd love your version of the Samantha Stanton Scandal." Not that he had any actual interest in her version unless it was juicier than the one he had composed in his head.

"Are you willing to represent the facts?" she dared ask.

"Of course!" he replied, a flap of dry lip skin dangling. "Does that mean you're willing to go on the record?"

He salivated at the thought of being the first one to interview the elusive Samantha Stanton, girlfriend—scratch that, *mistress*—of the wealthy—scratch that again, *esteemed*—Thomas Cook.

"Okay, I'll give you the lowdown," she agreed.

"Is it true that you were dating Thomas Cook?" he began.

"Dating implies seeing someone regularly. We only went out twice."

He scribbled out *mistress* and replaced it with *one-night-stand*. "Did you sleep with him in order to steal his ledger?"

"No way! I—"

Sam had meant to correct him about the sex part, not the ledger part, but the reporter continued to bulldoze right over the rest of her reply.

"And my understanding is that now you're pregnant with his baby?"

"How on earth could I get pregnant if I didn't sleep with him?"

"So whose baby is it, then?"

"Wait—what baby?"

"The baby you're carrying. For goodness's sake, how many men on average do you sleep with, Ms. Stanton?"

"First of all, that's none of your business if I *was* sleeping with someone. And second of all, I've slept with none!"

"Ever?" the man scoffed.

Sam rolled her eyes and headed for the revolving door. "No further comment. What kind of interview is this, anyway?"

Returning to his notepad, he trailed her, asking, "Can you clarify why you came up with the idea to fake a ledger against Thomas Cook? Was it so that you could bring Cook Pharmaceuticals down for the death of your father?"

Sam stopped, her fingers clutching the bronze door handle. Her heart felt like it had stopped too. "How did you know about my father's death?"

"I'm a journalist, dear. Digging up dirt is what I do. Can you answer the question?"

Her mother. Of course. A woman in need accepted what she could get, even if they were scraps.

A week earlier, this very man had paid Minnie Stanton a meager sum for any information on why her daughter would be caught up in a forged ledger scandal. Desperate for money and naïve when it came to journalists, the clueless widow spilled everything about her husband's heart condition, the Nosartin he was taking, even what he had for breakfast that morning.

"Well, no, that's not exactly how it happened—"

"And didn't your father enjoy a grapefruit each morning with his cup of coffee," he glanced down at his notes, "with two sugars and a splash of cream?"

"I don't see how that's relevant."

"Oh. Of course you don't. That's because you're not a *real* doctor, are you?" He shook his head. "If you want to play with the big boys, maybe you should read more of this," he handed her that month's January 1971 issue of *American Scientist*, "and less gardening books, Ms. Stanton."

How dare he! Sam wanted to shout at him everything about the corruption she had uncovered, but she knew this man had no intention of reporting on the facts, or helping her expose Big Pharma. All he cared about was making her look bad.

She skimmed the cover of the magazine, staring curiously at a picture of a grapefruit next to a prescription bottle. When she opened up the magazine to the page number associated with the article, she gasped, horrified.

"The truth hurts, doesn't it?" He was watching her as she pieced together a whole new story. A story that made her the worst villain of all.

How could she have missed it?

Without another word Sam turned and marched through the revolving door into the Art Deco lobby, partly because she was done with this farce of an interview, and partly because she didn't want this cruel, ruthless, but very shrewd reporter to see her cry after discovering what she had done.

Chapter 27

"It's my fault my father died, Raul." The words vomited out thick and toxic.

The *American Scientist* magazine sat on Sam's lap while she wept on Raul's shoulder as he comforted her the following day. She had told him about the vulturous reporter, but she had been too ashamed to bring up the grapefruit. But Raul had a way of drawing the awful truth out of her, no matter how hard it was to face. She wondered if her mother knew.

"How can you say that? It was the medicine, Sam. We both know that."

"No," she said through tears. "I've been blaming Cook Pharmaceuticals and Nosartin all this time, but it was me."

Raul's face screwed up in a question he was afraid to ask. "What are you talking about?"

The guilt pressed heavy on Sam's chest like a swollen balloon. If only she could pop it. "I told Dad to eat grapefruit to help lower his blood pressure."

"Oh, Sam..." Raul had dreaded this day for years. He hugged her tighter. "I had hoped you would never find out."

Leaning away from him, she looked up at him and gasped. "You knew?"

Raul nodded. "I figured it out when I started researching Cook Pharmaceuticals years ago. I had cornered Thomas Cook for an interview right after your dad's death, telling him I was going to expose the deadly side effects of his heart medicine. That's when he told me to do better research—that 3% of the patient deaths related to Nosartin were all connected to grapefruit. I guess you weren't the only one who discovered the health benefits of the fruit. It was the new rage. Anyway, as soon as he told me that, I remembered you mentioning grapefruit in your dad's diet as part of your health plan to get him better, so I dropped my investigation."

"Why didn't you say something sooner?"

"I didn't want you to blame yourself."

Raul remembered all too vividly how dedicated Sam was to helping her dad get better. But this kind of revelation—finding out your best intentions ended up killing the person you were trying to save—was the type to crush a person, heart and soul. Raul knew firsthand how devastating personal blame for losing a parent could be.

"I *do* deserve the blame. I should have known that grapefruit makes it harder for medicine to metabolize! If I would have done even the tiniest bit of research, I would have known that scientists were already studying the effects of grapefruit on medicine absorption. They published all of these findings right here!"

She tossed the copy of *American Scientist* on the coffee table.

"Dad probably overdosed on the heart medicine without realizing it because the medicine was staying in his system too long, building up—all because of the grapefruit! How could I be so reckless?"

Noticing the grapefruit on the magazine cover, Raul picked

it up and scanned the article. His gaze flicked over facts and figures, dates and data.

"Sam, this study only *began* a year ago."

"So?"

"So—so your dad died years before any of this information came to light. And the research isn't even definitive yet. Those were only their preliminary findings. Besides, you can't possibly know everything there is to know about this stuff." Raul turned her question on its head, hoping to redirect her blame from herself.

It didn't work, however.

"Thomas Cook apparently made the connection."

"Only because he was trying to save his ass. He saw the liability of the heart medicine and preemptively looked for a way to redirect responsibility. It just so happened that 3% of those victims were eating grapefruit. That's not your fault your dad happened to be one of them."

"I'm his daughter! I'm supposed to be a health expert! I should have known, or at least looked into it first. I'm the one who told him to eat it. How can I help others when I basically murdered my dad with my so-called expertise?"

Raul pulled her to him, holding her while she let the internal balloon deflate, soaking his shirt with her tears.

"Sam, I think it's time to let it all go. The ledger, the medicine, the grapefruit... all this guilt... it's been six years since your dad died. It's time to stop faulting yourself, stop going after Thomas Cook, and move on."

Sam sniffled, wiped her snot on Raul's sleeve, and straightened up. She was utterly exhausted. More than she had ever felt before.

"You know what? You're right. It's time to give up."

Raul had never been accused of being right before, at least not by Sam, but for the first time since this whole Thomas Cook drama had started escalating, he felt relieved.

"Good. Now how about we get some fresh air and take Fido for a walk?"

Sam nodded silently, calling Fido over to put his halter on. As she snapped his lead rope onto the strap, Raul stood at the front door, looking at the snow-covered street where a group of people stood yelling at the house next-door. Among them was Miss Posey. In the side yard Bernadette stood under her porch's short striped eave, bent over a frosted metal tub, washing her clothes and rolling the handle of the wringer.

"What's going on out there?" Raul asked Sam.

"Bernadette is washing clothes in the cold. I need to go help her."

"No, I'm talking about them." He pointed to the growing group of looky-loos.

"Oh, they're just the friendly neighborhood welcoming committee. They don't like that Bernadette's family moved here, so they want to make sure she knows it."

"Did the family do something to deserve it?"

"Why would anyone deserve being treated like that?"

"Certainly they must have done something wrong." As a former reporter he assumed there were always two sides to every story, and as always, his assumption was correct. In this particular story, there were two sides: the white one, and then the "wrong" one.

"You mean other than being born with a darker complexion? And you know what the worst part is? The husband is a police officer. He spends his life serving and protecting the same people that vandalize his home and intimidate his family." Sam handed Raul the lead rope. "Here, you take Fido for his walk while I go check on Bernadette."

"Okay." Raul's brain began popping and fizzing, as it often did when an idea—a possibly brilliant, or possibly dangerous idea—began to form. "The husband is a cop, you said?"

"Yes. Why?"

"No reason. Just something came to mind..." Raul's ambiguity only held Sam's attention so long before Fido started huffing an urgency to get outside.

While Raul took Fido in one direction, his mind working overtime, Sam walked across the yard in the other direction, offering Bernadette as forced a smile as she could manage after finding out she had killed her own father.

"Hello, neighbor. Ignore the impromptu town meeting out there."

"You mean the meeting about me in particular, and which I wasn't even invited to?" Bernadette grumbled.

"They're just bored, lonely people. Here, let me help you with this."

Bernadette glanced at the group of gray-haired terrorists whose complaints could be heard across the yard, then she grinned stiffly and grabbed the basket full of wet, frozen clothes.

"I'm actually done. Want to come inside?"

"Definitely." Sam emptied the wash tub, then followed Bernadette's trail of footsteps through the dusting of snow, across the ice-slicked porch, and into the warm kitchen. "With a family of three, why don't you have an electric washing machine? Washing by hand must take forever."

"The seller took the one that was here with her when we bought the house, so we're saving up for a new one. It's just been tight financially…"

Bernadette, Sam, and every family in the suburbs felt the same pinch. Prices across America had skyrocketed since inflation had squeezed every last penny out of America's middle-class pockets. While the laundry hung to dry, Sam set down two plates of shortbread cookies and two cups of tea from a special blend she had given to Bernadette.

"Why do you think they're starting this up again?" Sam asked.

It had been quiet on the block over the winter holidays, but suddenly the volatility was picking back up and Sam couldn't figure out why.

"Because it's the anniversary of the Reverend's birthday. In honor of him, our family celebrates his legacy and mourns his death. And those people out there hate it."

It had been just shy of three years since Dr. Martin Luther King Jr.'s assassination, yet to Bernadette it still felt like yesterday.

"I don't know if I can bring another child into this environment of hate," Bernadette said pensively.

"Another child? Are you saying…"

"Yes, I'm pregnant," Bernadette confirmed.

Bernadette vividly remembered the day she knew she was pregnant with Alonzo Junior. It was in the middle of teaching her kindergarten class their ABC's.

She had gotten to the letter N when the nausea hit. By O, oh how she made a mad dash for the tiny bathroom connected to her classroom! By the letter P she was puking, while little girls peeked under the stall door wondering if their teacher was dying.

That evening she emptied what was left of her stomach contents and couldn't keep down a morsel for two straight days, until she finally went straight to the doctor's office with the same symptoms. She hoped he had something to help with this stomach flu bug that simply would not let up. Half of the elementary school she taught at was perpetually sick with something, so it seemed a logical conclusion. Rather than offering her a quick remedy of Pepto-Bismol to put the symptoms behind her, he instead confirmed a long road ahead of her:

"You're expecting!" he had declared.

"Expecting what?" she asked dumbly, unaware of the *pregnancy brain* that would only worsen.

"A baby, of course!"

By the time her baby bump grew the size of a *grapefruit*—the doctor had compared it to—Bernadette swiftly lost her teaching job, since obviously a pregnant woman was incapable of caring for children. Along with the job went their second income that allowed them to afford a proper home to raise their growing family in. But that wasn't all Bernadette lost. Next went her entire wardrobe, shoes that fit, handfuls of her hair, and sleeping through the night without umpteen pit stops to the bathroom.

Like Sam, the word *grapefruit* held a whole new meaning.

Bits of Bernadette's sanity continued leaving as she cleaned marker off the walls during Alonzo Jr.'s terrible twos, demonstrated toilet training on his wooden potty chair during the tedious threes, and recently learned just how opinionated he could be during his feisty fours. Some days she wasn't sure they would make it to the fantastic fives that her mother assured her waited around the corner.

"How can you be so sure you're pregnant? We have been eating a lot of carbohydrates lately." Sam bit into her third shortbread cookie, only now noticing how her own skirt waist felt a little snugger than usual.

"I just know."

"It could be indigestion."

"It could also be a baby."

Having never been pregnant herself, Sam had no real idea of the changes—the varied alarm bells that rang and whistled, announcing *Intruder Alert! Terrorist Attack!*—a woman's body went through the moment those tiny cells took hold. If she knew how powerful a singular cell could be, how a pea-sized cluster could topple an entity a thousand times bigger, make her sob at the slightest offense or sprint for the bathroom at the faintest smell, Sam would have never asked the question, because when a woman knew, she *knew*.

"I'm two weeks late, and I'm already feeling the morning sickness, so I'm pretty certain."

"You could always pee on wheat and barley," Sam suggested with a mischievous grin.

"I'm sorry, what?" Bernadette asked, laughing.

Sam was full of weird facts and unusual humor that few understood, with Raul and Bernadette, and maybe even Thomas Cook had he been given the opportunity, being the only exceptions. Such as how in ancient Egypt, medical professionals asked potentially pregnant women to urinate on bags of wheat and barley. They believed that germination of the grain indicated not only pregnancy, but gender: wheat for a boy and barley for a girl. Surprisingly, this method was 70% accurate when scientists tested this theory in 1963.

"Just some bad homeopathy humor." Sam chuckled. "But joking aside, I've got just the thing to help with the morning sickness." And then Sam remembered her father and the grapefruit, and decided it was best to leave the health advice to a *real* health expert. "On second thought, you should let your doctor take care of you."

"Actually, I'm thinking of using a midwife this time around."

"A midwife? Why?"

"When I was pregnant with Alonzo Jr., my doctor prescribed me something called DES to prevent miscarriage, claiming I had low estrogen. I never felt right when I took it... but the doctor insisted I keep taking it. And if I didn't? Judgement and condemnation and a list of reasons how I was going to fail my baby."

During her Nosartin research, Sam had come across a study done on DES, the complicatedly long drug name that Bernadette was referring to that treated low estrogen. For almost twenty years, since as far back as 1953, trials unequivocally showed that the drug wasn't effective, in fact possibly dangerous for the baby, and yet Bernadette's doctor still prescribed it?

"I didn't know they were still prescribing that..."

"And don't get me started on how the doctor tuckered out a few hours into *my* labor and tried demanding I get a C-section in order to speed things along so that he didn't miss his golf tee time. I just want to have the kind of pregnancy and birthing experience that I feel most comfortable with, you know? And ever since you told me about your dad's heart medicine and the pharmaceutical scandal, I just don't know what to think anymore."

"Well, there's something I haven't told you about my father's death..." Sam began, afraid that being honest with her friend would completely discredit everything else she told her about DES, Thomas Cook, or anything health related. But if there was one thing Sam valued most, it was integrity, so she shared her darkest secret with her closest friend. "My father's medicine was not the cause of his death. I wrongly blamed the pharmaceutical company for something I actually did wrong."

"Sam." Bernadette cocked her head as she always did when making a most important observation. "Trust your instincts. You sniff something's not on the up and up? Follow that trail. I love you, honey, but you need to believe in yourself more."

"It's hard to trust myself when I made a terrible mistake."

"We all make mistakes. It's an unintentional consequence of life. But you *know* Cook was paying doctors to prescribe things—which is unethical. Even if the medicine didn't cause your dad's death, the conflict of interest and kickbacks are illegal and still need to be exposed."

By now Alonzo Jr. was jumping up and down at the living room window, exclaiming that there was a strange man stealing Sam's pony and making his way up their front yard.

"That must be Raul with Fido."

"Ooh, does this mean I get to finally meet your boyfriend?"

Bernadette was dying to meet the man who stole Sam's heart, even if he did look a bit disturbing as his gaze darted to and fro like a paranoid pothead.

"Is he okay?"

They both noted the odd way Raul paced, holding the lead rope to the infamous pet that dethroned Bernadette as the village villain and placed Sam at the top of the hit list.

"He's probably just deep in thought," Sam rationalized. Though on second glance, something definitely looked off.

"So what's the deal with Fido the House Pony, anyway?" Bernadette asked, gazing out the frosted window at the thigh-high mini-horse whose velvety lips rummaged through the snow in search of grass.

"There's not much of a story there. It was a year after my dad died, and I was driving through the country and saw him, skinnier than the rails that fenced him in a pasture of dirt, with no water. He looked like he was on death's doorstep, so I simply trespassed onto the property, opened his gate, and led him out to my car by tying my scarf around his neck."

"You're kidding!"

"I managed to entice him into my convertible with an apple I had on hand, put the top down on that freezing winter day, and drove him home with me—perilously slow, I might add. I'm pretty sure the wind chill was in the negatives that day, but Fido didn't seem to mind. I think he'd rather freeze to death in my car than starve to death on that farm. So when I finally got him home, he headed straight into the house! I realized then and there he wasn't a pony but in fact a dog. So I named him Fido and it stuck."

As Sam finished her story, a bang on the door was followed by Raul yelling, "Sam! You need to come out here urgently! It's bad—really bad!"

Chapter 28

Sam cracked opened Bernadette's front door to find Raul panicked and breathing heavily, while Fido tried to push his way inside the house. Sliding through the gap, Sam met them on the porch, shutting their conversation outside to avoid dragging Bernadette into whatever new drama had wormed its way into her life. This was not how she wanted her best friend to meet her boyfriend for the first time.

"What's wrong, Raul?"

"I was about to take Fido home when I saw cop cars turn onto your street. When they pulled up in front of your house, I hurried over here. The cops are at your front door, Sam!"

Sam glanced down the road, noting not one but two police vehicles parked in front of her house, lights flashing.

"What? Why?"

"I have a hunch this is why."

Raul handed her that morning's newspaper, which he must have found buried under the snow in the yard and she had failed yet to read:

SWINDLER STANTON AT IT AGAIN

"What's it say?" Sam skimmed through the article, scouring for as many facts as she could while Raul elaborated.

"The media originally accused you of stealing the ledger, but the story's changing. Now they think you faked the accounting numbers. And somehow rumors are spreading that you slandered Cook with a false pregnancy claim."

Oops. Sam really regretted making that joke to the lady in the supermarket.

"So what? I already knew all this."

"It gets worse." Raul sighed. "It sounds like they're trying to turn it into a legal double-whammy. And Thomas Cook is officially pressing charges against you now."

"For what crime, exactly?"

"For theft."

"I thought I was being accused of forgery."

"Let's hope so!" Raul exclaimed.

"Hope so? Why would you say that?"

"Because theft is a way worse charge than forgery, Sam."

When Sam read the byline, she instantly recognized the journalist's name as the one she had met only yesterday outside of her office building in three feet of snow: Floyd Jameson. He had wasted no time running with his version of the story!

In his article he painted a picture of a victimized Dr. Thomas Cook, orphaned CEO of Cook Pharmaceuticals and casualty of slanderer Samantha Stanton. According to Jameson's anonymous resources, Sam had stolen Cook's empty accounting book, then she filled it out, masterfully faking his handwriting, all in an effort to launch a personal attack after a pregnancy scare. Long story short, this could easily convince readers that Sam was public enemy number one.

"What am I going to do if they end up pressing both charges—larceny and forgery?"

"Don't forget slander," Raul added.

"But it's all a lie!" Sam yelled as Raul placed a hand on Sam's trembling shoulders.

"I'm so sorry, Sam. I'll do what I can to fix this, but Thomas Cook is determined to get the last word. I tried to warn you..."

But it was not the time for an I-told-you-so, and Raul remembered this a moment too late. Sam sucked in a steadying breath, grabbed Fido's lead rope, and without a goodbye slowly trudged across the yard toward the greenhouse she had spent six months saving up for and one month building with her own two hands.

Once inside the only place she felt herself these days, she rummaged through a metal box hidden under a shelf, pulling out an envelope with the words *In Case of Emergency* penned across the front.

Calmly making her way to her back porch and through the house, she found Raul in the front yard arguing with the police. She released Fido, planted a kiss on his forelock, and told him to behave while she was gone. Then she gave one last long look at the home she would leave behind.

She approached the officers and handed Raul the envelope. "Get this to Mr. Getty at *Women's House Magazine* and insist he run it. Don't take no for an answer."

"What is it?" Raul asked as a policeman read Sam her rights while handcuffing her.

"I'm taking back the last word, Raul."

Leaving Raul with a final kiss, she was led down her sidewalk while Miss Posey tut-tutted and gawked at her. Sam was jailed two hours later.

Chapter 29

When Sam was ten, after a scolding for stealing a tube of Avon Double Dare Red lipstick from her mother's vanity and using it to color Valentine cards for her parents, she packed her Captain Kangaroo Tasket Basket with the pet frog her parents didn't know she kept in her bedroom. Then she wrapped herself in her favorite handknitted blanket, stuffed a sleeve of Saltines in her pocket, and slipped out the back door, determined to run away forever.

Sam had run almost a mile in the February cold before she looked back to find her father before he slunk into the bushes, barely out of sight but eyes locked on her. Half a mile later she stopped, turned around, and ran into her father's open—and shivering—arms.

She knew in that moment she would never truly be alone; her father would always watch over her, no matter how far she strayed. Sitting rigidly in the police department interrogation room, all she could wonder was what her father was thinking as he watched her from above. Knowing what she knew now, a single sentence kept echoing in her mind:

I should have kept running.

"Do you understand the charges, Miss Stanton?" the detective was asking her.

A vent in the ceiling of the interrogation room blasted

lukewarm air that did nothing to temper the chill. The coffee he had offered her tasted bitter and almost as lukewarm as the air.

"No, sir, I don't."

"You're being charged with theft."

"Theft? I thought it was forgery."

"Do you want me to add forgery to the list?" he asked with an upward tug of his sliding-down pants that looked two sizes too small for his potbelly waist.

"And what about the slander?"

"Slander on top of the theft and forgery? You really know how to go all the way, lady."

"Who is pressing the charges?" Sam sighed wearily.

Her brain buzzed from being overloaded with police jargon, and her rear ached from sitting in the metal chair for too long.

"It says here Thomas Cook is pressing charges for theft. As for the forgery, I don't know about that. Probably the district attorney."

"So there are two different charges from two different people?"

"That's correct, ma'am."

"Let me get this straight: Cook formally accused me of stealing his top-secret ledger. And someone else backtracked and accused me of forging that same ledger?"

The detective's face screwed up. "Yes, that's also correct."

"Is there any evidence of either crime?"

"Well, no. Only his word against yours. And you admitted to stealing it."

"Exactly! I'm pleading guilty to larceny, which is a worse crime than forgery. So then how can both be correct? I either stole it or I falsified it! Which one is it?"

"I… I… I'm going to get my boss to talk to you, ma'am."

But the police corporal above him, and the lieutenant above him didn't seem to know anything more as each one couldn't tell Sam exactly what she was being arrested for. To Sam it didn't seem as if anyone knew what they were charging her with, who was leading the charge, or why.

"First my name is smeared all over the media for stealing a ledger that exposes Cook Pharmaceuticals paying off doctors to prescribe drugs to patients. Only after that did someone else come out saying the ledger is in fact fake. But why would I have stolen a blank ledger when I could have easily bought one? And how would I have known how to fill it out? None of this makes any sense."

"You're telling me," the officer agreed.

"At the least you should be looking into both sides, since his crime of bribery is far worse than mine. So why isn't he sitting in this room being interrogated as well?"

"We already questioned him and he said he's innocent."

"And that worked?" Sam shook her head sadly. "So you think that I'm so brilliant that I could procure hundreds of dates, doctor names, prescription drugs, dosage amounts, and payments all on my own, all perfectly imitating Thomas Cook's handwriting of course. Because I bet if you look into each of those payments, they'll match an exact prescription made by the exact doctor named for the exact date listed. That data is not lying; Thomas Cook is!"

Any intelligent person could see the flaws in their presumptions, except for them. So Sam decided to take the simple tactic that would almost certainly meet their standard of logic.

"Sir, do you really think someone like me, an ordinary, uneducated young woman, would be capable of outsmarting the smartest man in the world?"

"She has a point," the detective agreed.

"Look at her haircut. There's clearly something wrong with her in the head," the corporal added.

"So please explain to me why I'm being charged with a crime I simply am not smart enough to pull off."

The detective stammered, the corporal shook his head, and the lieutenant huffed as they all searched for a logical answer that simply didn't exist.

Women's House Magazine
February 1971 Issue

Q: Dear Samantha,

I recently read an article calling you a thief and claiming you falsified a ledger in order to discredit Cook Pharmaceuticals. As readers who have supported your column, I feel like you owe us an explanation of what really happened and who you truly are. All we want is the truth... are you the real deal or a gal who'd steal?

If you are in fact not a hack, can you recommend any healthy advice for weight loss? My best friend thinks I should shed a few pounds, and she swore by the black beauty pills, until she started hallucinating. I'd prefer to avoid that route, since at Woodstock I experienced enough hallucinations to last a lifetime.

Sincerely,
Must-know Maggie

A: Dear Must-know Maggie,

If you are reading this, I have either been thrown in jail or murdered for exposing the scam behind one of the country's biggest prescription drug companies. I wrote this letter before I was incarcerated—or killed—with the intention of it being published in the event of my disappearance. I do hope it's the former, not the latter, but in either case, I also hope it's not in vain.

To the countless questions my readers are probably wondering, yes, the ledger is in fact real. Just like the payments it records Cook Pharmaceuticals paying doctors to prescribe drugs are real. Ask your own doctor if he's ever made money off of writing you a script. I can only assume he'd be honest about it, since he lives by the Hippocratic Oath to do no harm... right? Unless that harm goes against his pocketbook.

You may be wondering why I dared speak out if it put a target on my back. If you've noticed the running theme in my column, it is a constant public plea for all women to learn their value. To not to let others bulldoze over your dreams. To take responsibility for what is yours—your body, your health, your relationships, your future, your happiness. It is not up to others to dictate who you are or what you're worth or what will make you happy. If you're too skinny or too fat. If you're beautiful or ugly. If you're smart or dumb. We must hold ourselves accountable for what we accept, and I chose not to accept the norms society sells us. Or the lies Big Pharma feeds us.

Today I chose to use my words to expose the lies and dig for truth. Even to the point of jail. Or death. In which case, I cordially invite you to my funeral.

We are not called Women's House Magazine for nothing. This world is our house too, and we must take it back.

Sincerely,
Samantha

Chapter 30

"You're being released, Miss Stanton," the guard announced as he approached Sam's cell. "You can thank Officer Alonzo Breedlove for stickin' his neck out for you."

Bernadette and Alonzo would be getting the thank-you gift of a lifetime. Sam debated between planting them an herb garden or gifting them with a mountain of Fido's manure. Either would certainly be chronicled in the annals of Best Gift Ever!

It had only been two days behind bars, but it felt like forty-eight hours. Each minute tick-tick-ticked slowly down to some terrible fate Sam anticipated with horror, as she kept one eye on her crafty long-fingernailed bunkmate carving a shiv out of the soap bar, and the other eye on the cell door, hoping a guard could hear her screams when her bunkmate finished whittling and murdered her in the cleanest stabbing in history.

The keys rattled in the lock as the guard grabbed and pulled open the cell door. Sam bid her roommate good luck with the soap knife sculpture and nearly ran into the guard's bulky arms.

Side by side, the guard thundered and Sam tiptoed down the long corridor passing rows of jail cells where inmates eyed her with jealous disdain. As they neared the end and stepped into the release processing room, Sam felt close enough to the exit to dare ask why they were letting her go.

"Cook Pharmaceuticals dropped their charges against you,"

he said. "Apparently Thomas Cook grew a conscience and decided to retract his statement."

Sam couldn't help but wonder why. A man of his power and influence didn't just wake up one day with an angel on his shoulder where the devil used to live.

"And between you and me, they were unfounded allegations. You might have taken the ledger as evidence of a crime, but faking an entire accounting book full of doctor's names, drug abbreviations, and transactions? It's too easy to prove with one look into Cook's accounting."

"Thank you, sir. Finally someone gets it!" Sam exclaimed.

"There's no way any jury would buy their lies or want to punish you for exposing their death toll due to their criminal practices. I hope you take Thomas Cook and his evil empire down."

"I hate to break it to you, but I'm done with that battle. I think it's best I retire and go back to being a typist."

The guard stopped dead in his tracks, turning Sam around by her arm. "Why are you giving up?"

"Because I'm not who everyone thinks I am. I thought I was helping people, but it turns out I'm responsible for my father's death—not Thomas Cook. I blamed him when it wasn't his fault."

"Oh, the grapefruit, huh?" The guard frowned empathetically.

"You heard about it too? Is there nothing private about my life anymore?"

He rested his meaty palms on Sam's narrow shoulders where the itchy gray prison uniform rubbed her skin raw.

"Maybe your dad was part of that 3% of grapefruit-related

deaths, but there are still 97% of them who weren't—those who died due to medicinal complications are the ones you are fighting for."

Sam pressed her lips defiantly. "*Were* fighting for. Past tense."

"Cook deserves payback for what he did, and you're the only one who can do it. What else can you possibly lose?"

"Not much," Sam hated to admit.

"Even my physician brother wants to see you succeed."

"A physician who actually agrees with me?" After all of the negative publicity, Sam had assumed every doctor hated her almost as much as Thomas Cook did.

"Sure. There are plenty of doctors who promote healthy lifestyles for their patients, only suggesting medication when appropriate and necessary. Not all of them throw a prescription at every malady, or are on Cook's payroll. All of us are rooting for you. Don't give up on your message… or your column."

"You know about my column?"

"Of course. I have every copy of the last ten issues since you started writing."

"Wow, tell your wife thank you for reading my column."

"Wife? No, I'm not married."

"Wait—*you* read my column?" Sam asked, surprised that any man other than Raul, let alone a single, giant, muscly one at that, cared what *Women's House Magazine* had to say about anything.

"You've got fans of all kinds, Miss Stanton. Don't assume all men are women-hating jerks out to get you. Just like not all doctors are pill-distributing sell-outs, and not all prison guards think their inmate wards are guilty. Some of us actually want to support the work you're doing in the name of women's progress."

"I write about health, sir, not women's rights."

He laughed at that, his belly jiggling. "You actually believe that's all you're doing?"

"Yes, offering alternative medicine and general advice."

"Oh, Miss Stanton, if only you knew! You're giving readers much more than that. For the first time in a long time, someone is prescribing hope. Don't you see what you're *actually* doing?"

It was four months later when her best friend asked her the same exact question after Sam had gotten herself stuck in the biggest heap of trouble she'd ever stepped in.

Chapter 31

"Don't you see what you're *actually* doing?" Bernadette proposed as Sam set a spiny potted plant on a table beneath her open living room window that let in a warm June breeze.

"No, I can't see anything. The plant is blocking my view."

Sam had been running errands all day with this plant sitting in her back seat along for the ride. First to the nickel-and-dime store, then to K-B Toys when she hadn't quite found what she wanted. She didn't plan to stay long, seeing as poor Fido couldn't hold his gallon-sized bladder forever, and cleaning up after him required at least an entire roll of paper towels that Sam couldn't afford to waste.

"I'm not talking about the plant, Sam. And this isn't a joke. You've got to stop digging for dirt against Thomas Cook. You're putting yourself in his crosshairs. The media is painting you as the antihero, and readers are starting to buy into it."

As winter had come to an end, Sam and Bernadette bonded over baking and tea since Bernadette had cut back on coffee at Sam's suggestion. When spring shot colors across their yards full of flowers, so too did their friendship blossom even more. But as summer slid in hot and heavy, Bernadette felt every bit of it as her belly felt heavier than ever, while Sam's reinvigorated investigation into Thomas Cook was making Bernadette sweat.

Their friendship had grown to a new level of honesty. They were not quite at the place where Bernadette could tell Sam she needed to grow out her hair and attempt a more modern, flattering style. At what point in a friendship would that conversation ever be ready to navigate, just like the proverbial wife asking her husband *does this make me look fat*? But at least she now felt the freedom to urge her friend to stay out of trouble. Unfortunately, Sam was just as stubborn as Bernadette.

Ever since Sam befriended her, Bernadette realized Sam tended to attract as much trouble as her Black family moving into a white neighborhood. Perhaps that's what made them such a perfect pair: neither backed down, no matter how much their friends and family tried to sway them otherwise. While Bernadette begged Sam to walk away from her investigation, Bernadette's own mother had begged her to return to her inner-city home. In typical willful-woman fashion, Sam persisted her whistle-blowing, and Bernadette had just installed a new washing machine. Neither of them would budge.

"No matter what readers believe, at least I'm giving people the truth," Sam pointed out. "I refuse to compromise that."

"I get it, honey. I really do. I just don't want to see you lose everything."

Lately Sam was getting more hate mail than fan mail, and the readership numbers were starting a slow decline as the media fed lie after lie about Sam's *"underhanded attempts to discredit Cook Pharmaceuticals"*—their words, not hers. If it kept going at this rate, Sam would be out of readers—and out of a job—before her twenty-fourth issue, per her agreement with Mr. Getty. But there were those pesky nagging ethics telling Sam not to give up.

"I can't ignore the facts, Bernadette. I read the medical journal reports on the effectiveness of at least two drugs that Cook Pharmaceuticals manufacturers. The results don't line up. He's hiding something... big."

"Well, ask your boy toy to look into it for you. You shouldn't get involved," Bernadette warned.

"Enough worrying about me. You have a growing baby to worry about."

"If it grows any bigger I'm gonna' split wide open," Bernadette groused.

While Bernadette continued pointing out all of the merits of not being a media target, Alonzo Jr. approached the plant Sam had brought, eying its spikes suspiciously.

"Don't worry, it won't bite," Sam assured him. "Though you can safely bite it."

Alonzo Jr. laughed, then leaned forward with his mouth open.

"No, Alonzo Jr., she's kidding." Bernadette eyed Sam. "Right?"

"Actually, aloe is perfectly safe to eat."

Bernadette examined the glossy ceramic floral pot that didn't match her décor one bit. "So explain this to me. You brought me a plant, Sam?"

"And I have another one in my greenhouse for you—spinach. It's packed with zinc and folate, and you can get your daily serving by nibbling a few leaves each day," Sam explained, forgetting that Bernadette was a grown woman and not a house pony.

Sam knew little to nothing about the needs of a pregnant woman, other than that growing babies and their mothers required plenty of zinc and folate to aid in fetal brain development. Sam wondered how much more of society would have better common sense if they weren't folate deficient.

"As if I need something else to take care of?"

"Aloe plants are very low maintenance. Ignore it and it will thrive. But they're one of the best plants for purifying the air. Living in a steel town, our houses are full of benzene, which can cause headaches and red blood cell depletion. The cleaner your air, the better it is for you and the baby. Oh, and the aloe from its fleshy leaves can be used for skin and haircare."

Bernadette smiled, loving her friend all the more for just how thoughtful she actually was, even if she had old-fashioned style.

"Then thank you for this, Sam. You know, you'll make a great mother someday."

Sam scoffed at the now second time someone had told her this. "Me, a mother? No. I don't plan on having children."

"Why not?"

"I'm too disorganized," she said, rooting through her purse for the K-B Toys bag she could have sworn she put in there. "And children are so opinionated," she added with certainty, though she had very little real-world experience with any other than Alonzo Jr. "And the trouble they get into…" she concluded as she made a mental note to thank her jail guard for the kind fan mail he had written her recently.

"It sounds like you're afraid of raising a child just like you, but you turned out pretty good, don't you think?"

"That's still up for debate, according to my mother. I *did* go to jail… twice. And piss off a powerful man who could easily put a hit on me."

Tucked beside the plant, Sam found the bag she had been searching for and handed it to Alonzo Jr., the top overflowing with the latest, greatest toys according to every television commercial that summer of 1971.

"You brought me presents?" Alonzo Jr. exclaimed, pulling out a Nerf ball first.

"And you say you're not maternal," Bernadette uttered.

"I got you that so you can practice your throwing while sparing the windows!" Sam exclaimed.

"Okay, maybe I take it back," Bernadette withdrew. "Alonzo Jr., I don't care what Miss Sam says, no throwing balls in the house."

Next Alonzo Jr. pulled out a small round figure made of plastic. "What's this?"

"I hear it's called a Weeble. According to the advertisements, *Weebles wobble but they don't fall down.* You can try it out for yourself."

Sam glanced at her watch, realizing Fido still needed to be let out, and her tuna casserole was about to be mush.

"Oh, shoot. I have to book it. I forgot dinner was in the crockpot, and my mother and Raul are coming over tonight." Sam dreaded the fact that lately her lonely mother felt the need to chaperone her not-so-romantic evenings with Raul. "Gimme some skin, Alonzo Jr." Sam held out her hand for a low high-five, which he excitedly slapped.

"Sam," Bernadette said, pulling her into a hug, "do me a solid and please stop pushing Cook's buttons. You're like a dog with a bone, and I know you just want to make things right, but that's not always how the world works."

"I'll try," Sam halfheartedly agreed, though she had no

plans of the kind to stop. As her mother often said when Sam was a child, she was a professional at pushing others' buttons.

Thinking some fresh salad could make up for the tuna slop, Sam headed straight toward the backyard fence, stopping abruptly at the open gate. The yard was a disheveled mess, and her glass greenhouse didn't look right. In fact, it looked completely wrong. Upside-down, and sideways all at the same time.

The hanging plants were buried under the germination pots. The shelf for vegetables was cracked in half and tossed where the fruit trees used to be. And where were the fruit trees, anyway? Windows were smashed, the roof punched through, the door crooked on one remaining hinge... the entire structure shattered, her entire life gone.

She ran across the yard, stepping on glass shards that were scattered across the grass, and all of her seedlings and shoots trampled. She knelt down, tenderly picking up a crushed remnant of spinach with the hope she could revive it for Bernadette as the urge to cry wretched her chest.

"Sam? What happened?"

Unable to turn around to answer Raul, she kept her back to him as he stood on the porch holding a bottle of celebratory wine at his latest news for their not-so-romantic evening. He had planned to tell her something that could change everything between them, but the moment was as destroyed as her yard.

"It's... it's gone," she whispered, choking down the heartbreak. "All my work. My plants. My everything... gone."

Raul didn't know what to say, so he said what came naturally to him. "I'll fix it, Sam. I promise."

Sam turned around to face him, anger pouring from her.

Anger at the destruction of her dreams. At the man she didn't want to be rescued by. At the fact that she even needed to be rescued. Again.

"How, Raul? I don't have the money to replace all of this on the pittance I make. I can barely afford to feed myself and Fido. And now he's probably peed all over the house and I can't even afford the paper towels to clean it up!" she wailed.

Raul ran down to the yard, pulling her into a hug.

"Hey, it's okay. I'll take care of it. I'll pay for the materials and we'll rebuild it together."

Sam stiffened and pulled away. "So that Thomas Cook can just come back and destroy it all over again? It will never end until I give up. Bernadette is right. I put a target on my back and now I'm going to lose everything over that man."

She stomped into the house, bringing the wilting spinach with her, wondering if anything in the former greenhouse, now garbage heap, was salvageable. She yanked the lid off her crockpot, the casserole having achieved an unusual crispy burned outer layer with mush in the middle, just as Minnie arrived carrying her mail.

"Oh, honey, that's not what we're eating for supper, is it?"

Minnie scooped a spoonful of tuna mush, chewing a small bite of what tasted more like rubber than food. Apparently the only edible thing in Sam's kitchen was a sliver of sad-looking spinach. When Sam didn't crack a grin or spit out a retort, her maternal instinct kicked in. Something was wrong.

"What happened? Why so glum, chum?"

"I'm just tired," Sam answered moodily.

"Do you need a Valium? I'm sure I have one in my purse…" Minnie was already digging through her handbag searching for what she called her *pep pills*, advertised as such because they put some pep in her step.

"No, Mom…"

"Her greenhouse was vandalized," Raul cut in.

"Not vandalized. *Destroyed*," Sam corrected.

"Was it those new neighbors of yours? I heard they're a terror, Sam. You need to move home and live with me for your own safety."

"It wasn't Bernadette. It was someone else. I'm pretty sure Thomas Cook sent whoever did it. As if unleashing the entire media army on me wasn't enough."

"Maybe you shouldn't open this then," Minnie warned, holding up an envelope. "Just in case it's not fan mail."

She set it aside on Sam's counter, but the name above the New York return address written neatly on the front startled Sam out of her self-absorbed misery. She instinctively yanked the letter off the counter and tucked it into her pocket. It couldn't be. Of all the letters in all the world… it couldn't be *him*.

An extremely important message waited inside that envelope, and whatever it was, it was too heavy to deal with on an empty stomach. And certainly not with her mother—and Raul—present, monitoring her like she belonged in an institution. As Sam gazed out at her junk heap of a greenhouse, and felt the crisp edge of the mysterious letter, being whisked away to an institution sounded like exactly what Sam needed.

Chapter 32

The day after Sam's father died, her mother said something that would stick in her memory like Grandma's dumplings stuck to her ribs:

"Our family is cursed."

Sam had never been the superstitious type, until example after example seemed to prove her mother right. Generations of Stantons befell tragedy shortly after achieving success, the first known case dating back to Sam's great-great-grandfather. He and his family had barely escaped the potato blight of Ireland, survived the four-week treacherous journey on a "coffin ship" to the land of the free and the brave, only to step foot on Lady Liberty's shore and contract typhoid fever a few days after his arrival, which left his penniless, pregnant wife all alone in a new country with not a soul to help her.

With grit and perseverance, the Stantons overcame. Until one fateful day in 1885, Sam's great-grandmother beckoned the midwife to the birth of her firstborn, which she had been anticipating with great joy, as she was already edging woefully past her reproductive prime at the old age of twenty. It would be her final joy, however, as she took her last breath the moment the midwife placed her healthy pink baby boy, which would become Sam's Grandpa Stanton, in her arms.

History would prove the curse again and again as four

generations of Stantons had finally achieved their lifelong goals, only to have them ripped from their cold, dead hands.

Sam once read that among families with generational curses, 70 percent of them lasted more than four generations. Sam would be the fifth. The article had used the Kennedy family as proof of theory, but Sam wondered if that only applied to noteworthy families worth documenting. And what about the non-noteworthy families—what percentage of curses lasted more than four generations? Statistically speaking, Sam's own familial curse seemed to be out to get her. And it was making great progress through the efforts of Thomas Cook.

As Sam considered the Kennedy curse, she felt a regretful kinship to their tragedy.

The Kennedy curse began stalking Edward Kennedy, marking the family with loss, scandal, and tragedy when, in 1941, his elder sister Rosemary underwent a lobotomy that resulted in permanent institutionalization. Three years later his eldest brother died in a plane crash during the second world war. By 1948 his sister perished in yet another plane crash. Why any Kennedy would ever step foot on a plane after that was beyond Sam, but clearly the Kennedys weren't done testing those odds, because their curse didn't end there.

Sam would never forget the 1963 assassination of JFK as the presidential motorcade rolled through Dallas, Texas. Then a year later, Edward himself narrowly escaped death when his plane crashed in an apple orchard. By 1970, the Kennedys had lost another brother to an assassin, and Edward's car drove off a bridge into the water below. While it didn't kill him, his failure to report the accident for more than ten hours left a suspicious stain on his reputation.

Sam felt that same haunting over her own future, so tangible she could smell it. Like the sulfur lingering behind hell's gate, or the cigarette smoke wafting from Mr. Getty's open office door.

"I have good news for you, Miss Stanton," Mr. Getty announced as Sam walked in, coughing as the smoke invaded her virgin lungs. "Somehow your little stunt with Thomas Cook panned out."

Sam would have amended that it hadn't been a *stunt*. And she would have added that *Mr. Getty* had been the one to start the media frenzy in the first place when he went public with the ledger and attached her name to it. But her boss didn't give her the chance to speak as he rambled on.

"The fan mail has been off the charts, the magazine is selling at record numbers, and," he beamed as he stood up, "I'm getting promoted!"

Sam wasn't sure how that was good news for her, but she smiled nonetheless. "Congratulations, sir."

"Like I told you, there's no such thing as bad publicity."

"As always, you're right again."

"Anyway, since I'll be leaving the position of editor-in-chief open, it is up to me to promote someone to take my place…"

A breath caught in her chest, and her neck warmed as Sam's hopes and dreams ran ahead of her. She couldn't believe it. She was getting promoted! Everything she had worked so hard for finally was coming due, her efforts and successes at last noticed and acknowledged. Damn that family curse back to hell where it belonged!

"… and after a lot of deliberation…"

A little flutter in her stomach added to a nauseating thrilled sensation.

"… and all of the work you've put in to turn this magazine around…"

Blood rushed through her as her heartbeat quickened.

"… I've decided to give the promotion of editor-in-chief to…"

As for that breath she had been holding? Still tucked in her lungs, waiting for Mr. Getty's final proclamation:

"Mel."

And just like that her brain glitched and breath swooshed out in a disappointed syllable:

"No."

"Did you just tell me no?" Mr. Getty asked.

"I'm sorry, sir, but *Mouthy Mel*? Mel can't handle that kind of responsibility. Did you even consider me for the position?"

"Didn't you hear me? You're too busy turning the magazine around! You won't have time to run the whole thing."

"But you said there was good news for me…"

"Oh, yes, I almost forgot. You are inheriting the newest addition to my collection of gadgets: the Magnavox Odyssey!" When Sam didn't look impressed, he went on to explain, "It's a video game that is able to display up to three dots on a screen *and* a vertical line! Technically it doesn't come out on the market until next year, so you can't get this anywhere yet. Far out, right?"

"Sir, no offense, but if it doesn't type or cook for me, I have no use for it. What about the raise you promised me? Am I at least getting that?"

Mr. Getty seemed to deliberate. "How about fifty more

cents an hour?"

Sam had wanted $2 more an hour when she fought for the columnist position, which was still several dollars an hour lower than *Tell Mel* had earned for his failing column. But Sam knew arguing this point would get her nothing but a foot in the rear and thrown out the door, so she accepted it with a stiff grin. She'd accept the pointless video game and sell it to help pay for her greenhouse rebuild.

"How wonderful," Sam deadpanned. "Finally I can afford to eat something more than rice and beans. Maybe I can add a vegetable to it now. Perhaps cabbage."

"See? I told you it was good news. And one more surprise," Mr. Getty added with a flair. He dragged Sam over to a desk along the wall and pointed to a green case. "Open it."

Sam clicked open the glistening metal latches and lifted the top. The latest typewriter model on the market, and another huge waste of the magazine's budget that could have gone toward Sam's $2 more per hour raise.

"I already have a typewriter."

"Not this one! This is a portable Smith-Corona with features that make it faster than your old manual typewriter. It's got an all-electric carriage return. A space bar that repeats. Automatic paper advancement to the next line. You'll love it and can work faster than ever before!"

Mr. Getty's obsession with the latest fad gadgets and gizmos was becoming a serious problem. One that was stealing money out of the employees' pockets for his fleeting entertainment.

A light rap at the door turned Sam around to find Mel and Betty Number Five swooping in, with Mel wearing a crap-eating grin and Betty carrying a stack of papers.

"Congratulations on your huge accomplishment," Sam gave her best impression of sarcasm, which Mel couldn't hear over the raucous applause inside his head.

Mel could already imagine his hateful wife's overdue praise for him *finally* not being a total failure of a husband, for *finally* becoming the successful man her parents had forced her to marry. Not that she was any prize either, as he discovered ten years into their matching failure of a marriage.

When she wasn't wrecking his self-esteem with snide comments about her boredom in their bed, she was reminding him of every disappointment he left her with: His letdown of a job, their mediocre home, their childless extra bedrooms. If he couldn't give her children, at least he could now afford to give her a spa day.

"And I hear you got yourself a raise," Mel said, already plotting when he could demote the cheeky feminist who he assumed would justify his wife's cruelty in the name of women's rights to be a bitch.

"If you call fifty cents a raise," Sam replied.

"There's paperwork you have to fill out," Betty informed Sam, handing over a clipboard. The paper was as baffling as Mel's promotion: Husband's name. Husband's bank account. Husband's signature.

"Who's getting the raise here?" Sam asked. "Me or my nonexistent husband?"

"Which leads me to my new office rules, Miss Stanton," Mel interjected. "Rule number one: No snark in this office."

"You're telling me I can't have a personality now, Mel?"

"And rule number two, you must address me as *boss*."

After filling out the paperwork she couldn't even sign, Sam hauled her new typewriter to her old desk, realizing that having Mel as her boss simply was not going to work. For all of the advice she had given over the past year and half, Sam had a problem she didn't know how to solve.

Chapter 33

When Sam read the letter she had hidden from Raul, she felt surprised. And very few people could surprise Sam, because Sam avoided surprises at all costs. Experience had taught her to be wary of anything unexpected, but sometimes one simply could not anticipate or avoid it.

Like the day her greenhouse was destroyed, or on that same day when Sam had received the mysterious letter. It turned out not to be your average fan mail, though. A written correspondence from Gabriel Smothers, Raul's long-lost father.

That day she found herself genuinely surprised. And terribly stressed.

While she *disliked* surprises, she *hated* secrets. And now she was none other than a super-secret-keeper from the man she loved most. Five weeks of holding this secret had nearly killed her, and now she was piling more on.

After reading Gabriel's eloquent note—like father, like son—she could never tell Raul about their written exchange until she met with Gabriel face to face. So she wrote him back telling him exactly that. Only, it was easier said than done, and it took much longer than her impatience could endure. He lived a full state away, and each correspondence took over a week to receive, and then add on another week waiting for a reply.

Finally, five weeks from the day she first laid eyes on his

grammatically perfect letter and New York return address, she would tell off the man responsible for Raul's distrust of love. The man who had singlehandedly destroyed Raul's ability to lower his guard. And here he was, across a wobbly booth from her, in the flesh, both of them sweating in a stifling August heat that the single window air conditioning unit couldn't keep up with.

Sam had picked a nondescript diner that Raul would never frequent, in a nondescript part of Pittsburgh no one she knew ventured into. It was just outside of the newly erected projects where Blacks were cordoned into and whites fled from. Considering segregation was supposed to have been a thing of the past—since the Civil Rights Act of 1964 had made desegregation a law seven years ago—still whites found their loopholes to build walls that kept them "safe" from the scourge of a dark complexion.

"So," Sam began, nervous.

"So," Gabriel echoed, hopeful.

While her gaze flicked to a Muhammad Ali poster hanging on the wall beside their booth, his eyes remained locked on Sam. The same endless brown with sparks of gold as Raul's.

Under normal circumstances Sam would have asked Gabriel how his trip from New York City was, or where he was spending the night. She may have even offered her sofa, had she trusted him. But she didn't.

"You wrote. I answered. And now I've been forced to keep this secret from Raul for over a month. What gives?" Sam launched the conversation straight to the only point she cared about.

"I never asked you to keep it a secret from him. In fact, I

was hoping you might tell him so I might see him."

So maybe Gabriel wasn't fond of secrets either. At least they had that in common.

"Why haven't you contacted your son before now?"

Gabriel considered her question far too long for Sam's liking. "I don't want to badmouth his mother, but she had forbade it."

Of course he would throw blame on a woman who was too dead to defend herself, and it was a terrible excuse at that.

"Raul is a grown man, and his mother passed away. So try again, Mr. Smothers."

"Lilith... is gone?" Gabriel grabbed the metal edge of the cheap plastic table dividing him and Sam. It shifted on crooked legs as Sam propped her elbows on it to steady it.

"Yes, she passed in 1969. I don't know the details, since Raul doesn't like to talk about it."

"Wow..." he exhaled pensively. "Over two years she's been gone and I never knew. I'm sorry..."

"Don't apologize to me. Apologize to Raul."

"I've wanted to! Boy, how I wanted to. I just didn't know how."

"Easy. The same way you contacted me."

Sam wasn't buying Gabriel's remorseful act. A real father didn't just disappear on his child. A real father stuck by until the end... even if that end was a bitter retreat into death. It was the last thing her own dad had taught her.

"You don't understand, Sam. I have been watching Raul from afar for years. Did you know I clipped every single one of his articles since he became a journalist? But then suddenly they stopped, and I worried something had happened to him. Every day I searched the obituaries in a panic, worrying I would find his name. But nothing." He sighed, a mixture of relief and sadness.

"How did you find him then? All the way in Pittsburgh, no less."

"One day I couldn't stand another day of not knowing. So I drove down to the Library of Congress in Washington DC and searched the phone book records of every single state until I found Raul's name. Luckily there aren't more than a handful of Raul Smothers in the country. It took showing up at the wrong residence a couple times until I finally found my son. So, that's how I found out he had moved to Pittsburgh."

"Why didn't you introduce yourself then?"

"I tried. Once. Maybe you remember it? I showed up at the apartment listed in the directory and planned to introduce myself, but I saw him with you on the street. I instantly recognized him, you know. And for the first time in his life, he looked genuinely happy. You see, he wasn't a happy child, I'm afraid. But as a man, with you, he finally was. So I decided to go home and let him live his life the way he deserved."

"I was there?" Sam couldn't pull up this memory, no matter how hard she tried.

"You sure were. I never forget a face."

"You could have said something."

"I did—don't you remember? It was last fall. You two were dancing on the sidewalk." Gabriel's gaze clouded as if he was caught in the past. "Anyway, having a father resurface after all these years... I knew it would be painful for him. I figured it was best if I didn't stick around and disrupt everything."

"Oh, you're the man who told us we made a beautiful

couple, aren't you?" Sam recalled the day a stranger had approached them on the street. She hadn't thought anything of it at the time, but now it all made sense.

"Yes, that was me. While I was admiring you two, I overheard you both talking about your magazine column, so I grabbed a copy before I left to drive home. But I must say, I was genuinely inspired by your words. I truly wanted to support your efforts, even if it didn't lead me to Raul."

"For someone who abandoned his wife, I find it ironic you want to support women's rights. Is this an attempt at redemption? Because I can't offer you that."

"No, you have it all wrong, Sam. I never left Lilith. She left *me*."

Sam almost found that laughable, considering single motherhood was darn near impossible in a world where women couldn't open up a bank account, purchase a house, or get a decent-paying job. When pressed hard enough, sure, an abused wife might leave. But leaving a perfectly good man? Unheard of.

"It wasn't her fault, though. She was depressed. One doctor I had taken her to told me she had hysteria, but he couldn't offer any help. They just kept telling her it was temporary, that eventually she needed to settle into life in order to be a good wife and mother. Then one day I came home from work and she was gone. Without a trace. When I finally did track her down months later, she demanded that I leave her and Raul alone— that she could never be happy with me and for the good of our son I needed to stay away."

"I'm sorry to hear that. But if it's any consolation, I don't think she was any happier without you."

"Why do you think Raul was such a sad child? His heart is so big that he tries to siphon all the sadness out of the people he loves, but that only ends up spreading it more. I'm just glad he wasn't afflicted for life with it like she was."

It explained why Lilith had seemed so cruel. Sam had misjudged her terribly as a heartless mother when the woman's heart was struggling so hard just to beat.

"Did you ever start a new family?"

Raul had confessed that fear once to her as the driving force that kept him away from searching for his father.

"Not exactly. I never remarried, but I adopted a boy who had been abandoned by his parents. I always wanted a brother growing up, and when Raul was little he used to want one too. Maybe he can meet his brother someday…"

"Yeah, maybe."

Meeting an estranged father *and* a brother? Sam couldn't begin to guess how Raul would feel about all of this when she told him. *If* she told him. He had been so adamant about Sam leaving it alone, but how could she possibly keep all of this from him?

"I brought something for you to give Raul." Gabriel rummaged through a leather briefcase that sat at his feet, and he pulled out a worn book. He slid it across the table at Sam. "This is his mother's journal. She left it behind when she took off. I was hoping you might be willing to pass it along to Raul so he could understand better what his mother had gone through. I don't want him hating her. And while I'm sure he hates me and I can't change that fact, I want him to at least understand why I had to stay away."

Sam held the diary to her chest. "I'll give him this, but I also think you should tell him yourself. I don't want to be the messenger."

Gabriel heaved a long "uhhh," glancing away. "I don't know if that's a good idea. I'm pretty sure he will never forgive me."

"Don't you want to change that?" Sam challenged him.

"I don't know what I could say to make it better."

"Just tell Raul the truth and let him work it out. A hard truth is always better than a soft lie."

Sam opened the journal, reading the pristine penmanship of a woman who could barely control her life or emotions, and yet found a way to rein them in just long enough to write them down.

"Writing is healing," Sam's father had once praised her when she confessed her dream job of becoming a columnist. She had expressed doubt in her career aspirations, since who would listen to a silly woman when there were much smarter men out there? *"Every person has something worth saying, Sam. Don't stifle your gifts—your words could one day heal the world."* Sam had believed her dad back then, and she still believed him now.

"I have an idea…" Sam began tentatively. It was unconventional for sure, and it'd be breaching a fine line that could further hurt Raul more than help him, but at this point, anything was worth a shot. "I'd be willing to help you tell Raul in a way that I think would be easier for him to handle, but you might not like what I'm about to suggest…"

Gabriel straightened then leaned toward her. "I'm listening…"

And while Sam added yet another secret between her and

Raul, Raul was busy amassing an even bigger secret of his own.

Women's House Magazine
September 1971 Issue

Q: Dear Samantha,

It is a Saturday morning, normal in every way. My son has just turned one, and a fierce headache insinuates itself early on. By breakfast, the pain is piercing. This explains why I am skulking around with a futile remedy of my mother's: a soft cloth tied around my head smelling of Vick's Vapo-Rub to "draw out the pain." I wear it like a warrior headdress, while every muscle in my body tenses as if in a battle against self. In a way, I am.

I stand at the kitchen sink, looking out at a world in which I no longer relate. It feels like I've been standing here forever, rinsing dishes, wiping surfaces, my horizon full of fearful days and nights, falling like dominoes, one after the other in sluggish succession.

Desperate for normalcy, I have decided to start writing: diaries, letters, an unfinished book— anything to redirect my thoughts. When I'm not caring for my son, I bend my neck and with trembling hands jot, tittle, jot, tittle. Sometimes the words flow so beautifully that I think they're from a stranger, and other times I wonder if I'm doing a good job at anything, agonizing over every last detail until my mind is awash with self-doubt. Is my son's delayed speech because of me? Will I have enough milk to last the week? Must I venture in public to the store so soon? Am I a good enough wife? Am I a loving enough mother?

I push myself to maintain pristine housekeeping, to the point where I am maniacal in my need to set everything in order, endlessly folding doll-sized underwear, matching myriad socks one by one, searching far too long for the one missing its mate. Cleaning is always at the top of my list of mindless activities, probably to distract me from thinking of anything else. The house sparkles, every inch a Pledge-dusted sea of clean. My intense need to straighten, dust, sweep, mop, and wash exhausts me, but my hands and feet will not stop. As I stand back looking at missed spots, I internally punish myself.

When I am not sorting and cleaning, and my pen hasn't touched paper, I dwell. Nightly insomnia renders me useless most days, and overcompensating on my good days also drives me to exhaustion. My throat tightens when I eat, and food leaves me feeling empty. Who can swallow past what feels like a large rock wedged in my throat?

During my last doctor visit, I spoke to him of my problems, but mere words cannot describe this internal hell. When he turned to my husband, he made disconcerting tut-tutting noises.

"You're too thin," he observed.

"Yes, I can't eat," I explained, pleased finally someone noticed.

"You look haggard," he added.

"That's because I don't sleep," I offered as though I was handing him a menu of my ailments.

Looking over me, he studied something on the wall behind me, scribbled something in my chart, and shook his head at me. When I closed my purse with a click, my husband wrapped his arm around my bony shoulders, but it felt too heavy. The guilt of my wifely failures was too great. I was little more than a useless feral cat, slinking around the corners of life.

"Hysteria," the doctor declared pointedly.

No kidding! I wanted to scream at him. Instead I said nothing.

Today, my acrobatic heart goes on a rampage, turning somersaults in my chest, heartbeat thundering in my ears like a herd of horses. What plagues me most is the nightmarish restlessness, now extending down my arms, the back of my neck, my jaw. Terrified, I call to a neighbor through my open window. The rest is a blur, except for the worried, frightened face of my son.

Within a few minutes—or hours, or days, for they all feel the same to me now—a screaming ambulance rounds the corner, and after a cursory examination, two paramedics load me onto a stretcher and out I go, like a piece of furniture of no more use. In the ambulance, safe from the world, I cling to one thought and one thought only:

Wherever I'm going, I hope they keep me.

After a few hours, the ER doctor releases me to my concerned and perplexed husband with a diagnosis of "neurasthenia," a catch-all diagnosis for certain female maladies when a wife is unable to function due to strange, unexplainable symptoms.

I return home to the scene of the crime and cry for several days. My husband, good and kind in every way, is clumsy in his efforts to soothe. He stands nearby watching helplessly.

Hours and days pass and then slowly, guilt begins to pull me from the bed, lifting me up, bit by bit and at last, I rise. And so, the business of living returns. I have broken down but have no choice now but to get up. Get up! You have a war to win and a husband, a son who needs you.

My throat-lump has grown bigger, along with new more terrifying symptoms: a buzzing under my tongue shoots through me like electricity. My lips are numb one day, and on another day my arms tremble uncontrollably. My legs twitch, my heart flutters. Everything that was supposed to feel normal now feels dangerous. And still I keep putting one foot in front of the other. I have lost the ability to save myself. Surely, there must be someone, somewhere who can help me. Then I realize no one can. My husband tirelessly tries, but I only chain him by my sheer existence.

So I leave, taking my son, perhaps the only one who can save me, in order to free us all.

Please forgive me.

Sincerely,

Low-spirited Lilith

A: Dear Low-spirited Lilith,

You will never read this, for you have passed since you first wrote this diary entry years ago, not for me, but for someone dear to me. No one heard your cries back then, but I hope they hear them now. And I hope they will not be in vain. So this reply is not just for you but for the many women who share in your heavy burden.

Maybe you have trouble leaving the house, walking to the mailbox, driving to the grocery store. And yet somehow you do it again each day with heavy footsteps.

Maybe you can't be left alone, wait in lines, cross a bridge, swallow food. And yet somehow you press on with a fake smile.

Maybe your husband can't understand you, your doctor can't help you, medicine only numbs you. Maybe you feel like you're part of a tribe of troubled people, your own unique breed of brokenness.

Don't lose hope that one day you'll grab a piece of toast, bite, and realize it's the first time in months you've swallowed food without thinking. Recovery will happen minute by minute, hour by hour—small gains some days, a step backward on others.

You may have a battle on your hands, a war you fight every day just to feel normal. We women go to war in our own ways, with no basic training whatsoever. We often fight alone, brave as a decorated soldier there in the trenches of our own kitchens.

They may think we're worthless. But every day we must take our medicine—the sheer will to open our eyes to morning sun and remind ourselves of the immense worth our lives truly hold.

Sincerely,
Samantha

Chapter 34

Sam had never felt nerves like this. Spazzing and sparking and buzzing.

Even under the most dire of circumstances her heart usually remained at a steadfast rhythmic treble, but when Raul called on a random Wednesday night, a working middle-of-the-week night, asking to meet her for dinner, with something important to discuss, she knew. She knew he had read his mother Lilith's letter in her column and he had pieced her web of omissions together.

Sam had intended to make it as clear as day for him, that she had met his father and published his mother's diary, but she hadn't considered the fallout of his discovery. Not until now.

"What is this?"

With Muhammad Ali looking over his shoulder, Raul sat across from Sam at the same restaurant Sam had met his father, in the same wobbly booth. She had suggested this place for Raul, so he might perhaps feel the lingering of his father's presence in the very seat where he sat. Perhaps it would help soften the blow.

"Uh, well…" Sam stuttered.

"Explain why this sounds a lot like my mother. In fact, the writer even has her same name!" He slid the magazine across the table at her, and she realized perhaps she had made a terrible mistake in judgement.

As an avid truth teller, Sam spit it out as quickly and efficiently as she could. "Because it is your mother. It was your mother's cry for help long ago. It's the reason she left your father."

Raul's thoughts spun as he took this shocking revelation in. The man who chased scoops had missed the biggest story of his life! And the girl he loved was the one who kept it from him. It was too much all at once.

His face warmed, and his eyes swelled. His throat dried, and his nose dripped. Before he could stop what society would have considered an abomination to the male species, Raul cried. Not just cried, but sobbed. Sam skirted around the table, sitting on the booth beside him, holding him, rocking him, feeling every bit of the heartbreak with him.

"I'm so sorry, Raul."

"How do you have this?" he sputtered, tears slipping down his cheeks.

"I met your father Gabriel. He sat right there where you're sitting."

Raul placed his hands on the table, still crooked, still wobbling, and ran his palms down across the plastic booth, his fingertips drawing life from the cold, stiff fabric.

"I don't understand. How did you find him?"

"He found me. He looked you up and came to see you once. After that, he wrote my advice column a couple months ago, and I recognized his name from the return address and wrote him back. That's when he hoped to meet you, but first he wanted you to understand why he stayed away."

Raul sat silent, as if waiting for the moral of the story.

"And?"

"And your mother was the one who left him because she wasn't mentally well. He didn't want to make it worse for you, so he let her take you away from him, thinking she would be happier without him."

"And you thought it would be better for me to find all of that out on a public forum like this?"

Sam had her quandaries about it, but when she really thought about it, Raul's heart always leaned toward the benefit of mankind. If his mother's story could help other women, she thought he would appreciate that their shared suffering wasn't futile. That his mother wasn't the sum of the darkness he knew, rather she was simply a light hidden. It was this compassion for others that made them so compatible, because Raul would always strive for the greater good. Even if it cost him much.

"I'm sorry, Raul. I thought maybe reading of her brokenness might first help you understand her… only after that could you talk about it, maybe even forgive her. And your dad too. I didn't mean to make a headline out of your pain. I can see now that I made a grave blunder."

Raul dried his eyes and sat stoic for a long moment. "Do you have his contact information?"

"I can give you his phone number and home address," Sam offered, returning to her seat to find the contact information she had scribbled down and stuck in her purse. "He lives in New York, outside of the city. And I should tell you now that you also have a brother. Your dad adopted him."

"Wow, I have a brother? So my dad was a pretty good guy, huh? At least that's what my mom said about him in that journal entry."

"Yes, he seemed genuine when I met him too. He sincerely wanted to make amends, Raul." Sam handed him the yellow square Post-It note with his father's address.

Reaching across their plates, Raul intertwined his fingers with hers as the table trembled below their elbows. "Sam, how do you know me so well?"

"Because I love you. When you love someone, you make the effort to know them."

"Did you just tell me you *love* me?"

The ever-thinking Sam didn't even need to think about it. "Yes, I did. And yes, I do."

"I love you too."

"Even after I lied to you? And kept your father a secret from you? Because I certainly wouldn't love me if I did that to myself."

"Good thing I'm a lot more forgiving than you are." Raul released her hands, got up, and moved to her side of the booth. "I need to ask you a favor."

"Anything."

"I want you to quit, Sam."

"Quit what?"

"The magazine, the feud with Thomas Cook, all of it."

Minnie Stanton could attest to one of Sam's greatest flaws: Sam never quit. When her mother begged her to put aside her botany course and pick up beauty school instead, it only made Sam add on an agriculture class. And when Minnie took away her garden tools and handed her ballet slippers, it only forced Sam to start using serving spoons as shovels and forks as tillers. The point was, Raul should have known never to ask Sam to quit. It only made her more determined to press on.

PAMELA CRANE

"Why do you want me to quit now? I've come so far."

"For the first time in my life I see something amazing up ahead. You and me together. Me and my dad reunited. And having a brother! I've never had a real family before, Sam, and it's all right there. Right in front of me! But if I lose you… it's gone. Thomas Cook attacked you personally. He destroyed your greenhouse, got you arrested, is launching a public smear campaign against you… and I'm worried about you. I'm worried he's going to take it too far. He's going to take you away from me."

"He's a three-piece-suited coward, Raul. He may fight dirty, but it's not like he would hire a hitman to come after me."

Even as Sam said it, she wasn't so certain it was true. Thomas Cook showed zero conviction for the death toll his medicines caused.

"Come work with me for Fred Rogers. You'd love the guy! He's all about kindness and understanding and all the principles you care so much about."

"I don't know…" Sam wavered. "My dreams are finally happening. My own advice column. A successful magazine. I even got a raise! Sure, it came with Mel as my boss, but I can't have it all." She paused. "You can't ask me to give up when I finally did something no one else in my family could do."

"What's that?"

"For the first time in four generations, I survived the curse."

Chapter 35

Sam should have known better.

Dreams always ended in disaster. Life had taught her this lesson again and again, but blinded by love and consumed by happiness, Sam had momentarily forgotten. For several months she lived off of Raul's kisses, her new promotion, and the magazine's growing numbers, all thanks to her hard work.

Until now.

It was at the office Easter party when Mr. Getty made a surprise visit with a surprise announcement. Everyone was already boozy from Betty Number Five's famous purple punch, and the snack table was mostly empty except for a few crumbs. Sam had been forced to dress up in a bunny suit, which she actually didn't mind as she played the part well, handing out dyed hard-boiled eggs that she reminded everyone to eat for their daily dose of lean protein and calcium. But when Mr. Getty showed up, his mouth turned down in a glum frown, he ordered Sam to remove the bunny head and called the room to attention.

"Mr. Getty has some news!" Sam yelled over the din, but no one paid her any heed.

"As you all know," Mr. Getty followed up with, and the room fell to an instant hush. Mel stood at his side in the bullpen surrounded by wavering writers, tipsy typists, and soused supervisors. "There have been some changes at *Women's House*

Magazine. Mel became my right-hand man as editor-in-chief when I got promoted to vice president of Cook Media. But over the past few months I was faced with some very difficult decisions. One of which is going to be especially hard to share with you today."

Murmurs spread across the room as everyone speculated about the news. Mel's face turned a pale shade of gray, and Sam felt her stomach drop.

"The owner of *Women's House Magazine* has decided to shut us down by summer."

The room erupted.

"May 1972 will be our final issue."

"But our sales have been off the charts!" the marketing manager yelled.

"And our reader base has quadrupled!" the mailroom supervision added.

"I know, I'm as shocked as all of you are," Mr. Getty said. "But that gives us three issues to give our readers our best work yet before we close up for good."

"Why should we even bother?" Mel asked.

"Because that's not all the news I have for you. For those who would like to relocate, the powers that be have offered jobs for all of you to work for the sister magazine *Ladies Home Journal* in New York City. So anyone who wants a job will automatically have one starting in September. Of course, they'll be expecting stellar results like you've brought to our little rag, so bring your A game, people."

"But why are they shutting us down?" Sam asked. "I did what you told me to do—proved that we could increase sales with our new content. Readers love us. The fan mail has been unprecedented. I don't understand the logic when we're profitable and growing. Why would they shut us down when we're doing so well?"

"You can blame yourself, Samantha," Mel grumbled.

"Me? Why is this my fault?"

"Do you know who owns our magazine? Cook Media, that's who. And who owns Cook Media? None other than Thomas Cook. You sparked the fire that burned us all down."

The company Cook Media had started out accidentally on purpose. When Thomas first started dabbling in media, he had no idea of the massive amounts of profit that all things publishing and television could tap into. He had only wanted to get his poems published, and no reputable publishing house or magazine would print them. So what does a rich man do whose heart is set on sharing his lyrical gift with the world, despite rejection after rejection? Does he work on refining his craft? Certainly not! Instead, he buys the publisher and then forces them to print his collection of poems.

But that's not enough to tame that ego hungry for more. So he then goes on to place a bookstore order of 10,000 copies to ensure his little book of poems hits the *New York Times* bestseller list, even after a three-week newspaper strike. Despite the critics calling it "juvenile prose" and "barely worthy of my five-year-old daughter's talents," it wouldn't matter because he had won. Thomas Cook was in the business of winning, and he was remarkably good at it.

When owning the media meant owning a woman's magazine, he had scoffed and proposed a hunting and fishing magazine to replace it. Until his accountant pointed out how profitable vanity literature—especially smut aimed at women—

could be. Give them their fashion magazines and romance novels and soap operas. It was a gold mine that Thomas accidentally tapped into, and planned to keep tapping as long as it brought in his prized cash cow.

Like any livestock owner, eventually the dying cows were sent to slaughter. That's what *Women's House Magazine* had been—a dying cow needing a good butcher to cut off of the rotting part and keep the filets. The plan to shut it down had been in the works for years, but then Sam happened. She resuscitated that dead cow beyond everyone's expectations.

And then she had to go and ruin it all.

Despite her rejection of him, he couldn't punish her by leaving her jobless, no matter how much she deserved it. He wasn't that cruel, even though he did have her greenhouse destroyed and reputation ruined by a stint in jail. But when Sam made it clear he had no chance in heaven or hell with her, he decided maybe he *should* be heartless. It was better than suffering a broken one. And so he proceeded with shutting down the magazine.

"Well, Sam is not exactly to blame," Mr. Getty shockingly came to her defense, which Sam surmised would probably revive the rumors that she had slept her way into her advice column after all. Not that it mattered anymore, considering she would no longer be working here in three months.

"What do you mean?" Mel probed.

"Apparently Cook had planned to shut down the magazine a long time ago due to..." he paused, choosing his words carefully, "budget issues."

Sam knew exactly what kind of *budget issues* they were— the new console radio, the cassette tape stereo, the hidden telephone box, the video game, the state-of-the-art typewriters… No wonder they were being shut down when Mr. Getty had the fiscal responsibility worthy of the United States Government.

"He only kept the magazine up and running because of Miss Stanton…"

"You couldn't take one for the team and sleep with him, could you?" Mel accused.

Usually scandals revolved around a woman sleeping with a man, not avoiding him like the bubonic plague. And yet here Sam was, caught in a scandal of Cook's own making and paying the price for not being a slut. You were shamed for being loose, and shamed for not being loose enough. Women could never win, could they?

The following Monday morning Mel summoned Sam into his disaster of an office that smelled like rotten eggs, as there was no room in the budget for the janitor anymore. A new hire sat in one chair and Sam sat in the empty one beside him.

"I'm sure you saw this coming, Samantha," Mel cut to the chase, "but you're fired."

"Fired? I still have until May, don't I?" Sam had been relying on those last months of paychecks to cover her bills until she found something else. Something completely unrelated to journalism or holistic medicine, as both had caused her nothing but problems.

"No, it's effective immediately."

Obviously Sam had to go, the sooner the better. For Mel, that is. Mel had standards, no matter how low they were, as evidenced by the fact that he married a woman who daily reminded him why she hated him, and he stayed in a job beneath him. Sam was the reason the magazine was getting shut down because she couldn't open her legs like any other woman who wanted to climb the ranks. But if Sam were to go, where did that leave him with *Ladies Home Journal*? Back to the grind with his mediocre column, that's where. His promotion had only been due to his tight grip on Sam's column's coattails. Mediocre columnists didn't inspire much in the way of climbing up the editor-in-chief ladder.

Mel hated to admit it, but Samantha was the key to their success. Publicly unrecognized, of course, but she acted as if she knew. Not a day went by when the mail staff didn't drop a heaping bag of letters on her desk—along with a complaint from the typists who were forced to help sort them and bring Sam *tea*, as if Sam were better than them! What was she—British? Opinionated, feminist, tea-drinking Sam, the bane of their existence. And yet the magazine had only hung around for as long as it did because of her.

Fortunately, Mel had been studying Sam's work, so he sent for copies of every column she'd written straightaway. *Ladies Home Journal* needed assurance that Sam's so-called innovative approach could be mimicked without her. But as soon as the magazines were dropped on Mel's desk, he knew he was in trouble. He didn't know a darn thing about women.

So he sought out his next-best journalists. One reluctantly conceded that Sam had a completely unique approach to health that he knew nothing about. Another overachiever assured Mel he could reproduce something as good—if not better—by the end of the week. Make that the end of the day! But when he turned over a column advising the advice-seeker that the best cure for suicidal thoughts was to stash them away, dab on some makeup, and get busy in the kitchen, Mel realized he was in the presence of a misogynistic idiot. Publishing was rife with them. And the new hire sitting in front of him now? He couldn't even spell *advis colum*. But Mel was determined to get rid of Sam no matter what.

"I'm confused. Our magazine is shutting down and you're firing me, but you hired a new guy? Why? On what grounds am I being fired?"

"I think you know."

"Enlighten me," she said, leaning forward, her hands clasped together in a tight mass. She wasn't sure from where her composure came, but she was determined to keep it.

Standing next to his desk was Betty Number Five, who was busy taking notes. And probably including details in case a police report was needed for Mel's imminent murder by Sam's hand.

"You stole Thomas Cook's ledger," Mel said. "I can't keep a thief on staff."

"Those charges were dropped. So according to the justice system, I am innocent of any wrongdoing."

"Innocent of wrongdoing?" he choked. "That's bold coming from the woman who attacked the reputation of the owner of our magazine!"

"I never attacked Thomas Cook. I simply pointed out a curious accounting phenomenon in his ledger. What does that have to do with my work?" She folded and unfolded her hands, keeping them busy lest she reach for the letter opener on Mel's desk and stab him with it.

"You have a lot of nerve even showing up here after the stunt you pulled. You know very well women know nothing about accounting, and to run with that story... what you did was disgraceful."

"Women are actually quite good with numbers. Is your wife in charge of the checkbook?"

"What's that have to do with anything?"

"You just claimed women know nothing about accounting, but you must trust your wife enough to manage the checkbook, don't you?"

"How dare you," he said, his voice rising. "A woman telling me how to run my household. Who do you think you are?"

She seemed surprised by the question. "A woman who knows basic accounting."

"Miss Stanton," Betty Number Five stated, her hand tiring from these silly notes on this round-and-round conversation that was going nowhere, "we can't keep you on after everything you did with Thomas Cook—"

"Which was nothing—"

"And certainly you should feel ashamed to even be in public right now after all that scandal—"

"But I didn't do anything!"

"Some time off might be exactly what you need. So I suggest you quit fighting it, sign your termination agreement, and clean out your desk."

But Sam didn't flinch. "Because of something I didn't do? What about Thomas Cook?"

"What about him? He owns you, Samantha. He's untouchable. As most men are. Haven't you learned that yet?" Mel asked.

Sam looked at the termination agreement and picked up the pen, hovering the tip over the signature line. She found it ironic that when it came to her pay raise, it required her nonexistent husband's signature, but when it came to getting fired, hers would suffice.

Ding dong, Mel cheered silently as Sam pressed the pen tip to the paper. *The queen is dead!*

Then Sam grabbed the paper, tore it in half, and stormed out of the office.

Women's House Magazine March 1972 Issue

SAMANTHA SAYS…

Q: Dear Samantha,

Your column has inspired me in so many ways, from my mental health, to my physical health, and even in my family life. Last year I reconnected with a long-lost family member after reading your column about the toxicity of unforgiveness and bitterness. After thinking over your advice, I chose to forgive him and it was like a weight was lifted off my shoulders.

So now I'm trusting you with my heart. I'm in love with someone, and I'm pretty sure he loves me back. He is brilliant, encouraging, funny, and irresistible to be around. I ache to marry him, but I'm not sure he feels the same way about marriage that I do. I'm over forty years old, and according to my mother I'm past my prime and destined for spinsterhood. Thus I feel the urgency to act fast.

How do I handle this situation? Is it okay for a woman to profess her feelings? And if so, do I tell him how I feel... even if it means he might break my heart?

Sincerely,
Aching Agnes

A: Dear Aching Agnes,

Heartbreak is a sad reality of life. It cannot be avoided, no matter how much we strive against it. My own heart breaks to tell you that I have been formally fired, and this will be my last column, so I'll try to make it as brutally honest as I can.

I dared to dream big and ended up crushed. The old Sam would have told you to screw fear and chase that dream with reckless abandon, because not knowing is the worst heartbreak of all. But the new Sam knows better than this. The new Sam knows that if you have to fight so hard for it, maybe it's not meant to happen.

I wish you better luck than I have. And there is nothing wrong with being a spinster. It's become my life goal.

Sincerely,
Samantha

Chapter 36

Thomas Cook's home office overflowed with case studies and science journals and research notes written in illegible shorthand. Carpenters' "Superstar" playing from the turntable was punctuated by a mix of woeful sobs and self-congratulatory noises one might utter when making a million-dollar discovery.

"Guadalupe, I've made the discovery of a lifetime!" he yelled. "This will change everything!"

His voice echoed down the empty halls of his mansion, eventually reaching Guadalupe in the kitchen, where she rolled her eyes.

After forcing his housemaid Guadalupe to also serve as his private therapist to help him get over Sam, she had advised him to focus on improving himself. While Guadalupe meant for him to find a new hobby, he took it as a challenge to create "the ultimate man drug."

Years ago he had undergone every innovation of "sex therapy," including the only sheep testosterone treatment available, but when that proved ineffective, he had even begun looking into goat gland implants to solve his little problem that not even Guadalupe knew about. But when the medical board shut down livestock therapies, Cook took it upon himself to find his own cure.

One that would make him irresistible to women, Samantha

Stanton in particular.

Rumors of a penis pump implant on the horizon had been circulating among the medical community, but they were years away from putting it on the treatment menu. So Cook, using his vast knowledge of chemical reactions and his personal drive for a working appendage, set out to create the first erectile dysfunction drug… and he was darn near close. If only the side effects didn't include explosive diarrhea and excessive defecation. Nothing soiled an evening of passion like soiling the sheets. A few more tweaks, however, and he would have created the drug of the century. Who cared about curing cancer when you could have a great sex life with the girl of your dreams?

A man needed his masculinity in order to control the weaker sex, after all. And what did women want more than riches? A masculine man.

Finally Samantha Stanton would be his.

His plan had been flawless, so he thought. When kindly requesting a date from her didn't work out, scare tactics that condemned her integrity seemed the logical next choice to force her to succumb. But when he heard about her stint behind bars, her felonious cellmate eyeing her like a human-sized voodoo doll, he quickly retreated.

He had never intended for Samantha to actually go to jail; she was of no use to him in prison. Charges dropped, he expected her to come running, grateful for the reprieve. But no, still she resisted him, even when he returned her potted plant as an *I'm sorry, please take me back* gesture.

When an Italian investor from the Gaslight Club, who Thomas conveniently overlooked as an associate of the Gambino crime family, suggested a little greenhouse sabotage to motivate Samantha, it seemed like the perfect solution to force a confrontation.

That had been a year ago.

He had even put off shuttering the doors of *Women's House Magazine* for her. The rag had been a loss leader for years and was overdue for cutting it from the budget. The night he met Samantha and found out she worked for the doomed magazine, he had even felt guilty about the possibility of taking her job from her—it was the first time he really felt guilty about anything. So he postponed the closure.

And then Samantha's magic touch happened. She singlehandedly turned the periodical around and made it profitable. More than that, she made it innovative. And there was nothing Thomas appreciated more than innovation.

Oh, and a working penis.

But now he was tired of giving Samantha excuses to avoid him. An impatient man, Thomas Cook grew tired of waiting. If wooing didn't work, and incarceration didn't nudge her, and personal property destruction wasn't effective, maybe job loss and desperation would do the trick.

Yet a lingering doubt arose that perhaps she would never be his, for she was something of a female anomaly. Feminists— they simply *had* to be independent, didn't they? And that was the whole problem. Most women he met weren't independent, or at least didn't want to be. They wanted to be wooed, dinners paid for, doors opened, doted on, marriage, a picket-fence house, kids, a perfectly appropriate life. Not demanding, but not demeaning either. They were the women who made up the majority of his social circle—*aspiring* but not *inspiring*. Women who weren't going to blow his mind, but neither were they going to start a revolution.

With Samantha off the table, it left a small pool of desirable women left. More like a shallow puddle. In fact, not a single woman compared to Samantha—*Sam*, she had insisted, which made him smile.

The only other issue holding him back, besides his receding hairline, was his failure to fix his *manhood* problem. And once he did, world domination was his.

The drug trial results sat on his desk, along with a stack of other confidential paperwork he needed Guadalupe to file for him as his housekeeper plus therapist plus secretary. Although the trial had only included seventeen men, every single one of them saw tangible results… along with the blushing nurse staff. Seventeen subjects seemed like a quantifiable number to support his theory that the drug was effective, and safe, so he could push the drug through. With enough financial encouragement, he was certain the FDA would agree.

"Guadalupe, where are you?" Thomas called out again.

A couple minutes later the housekeeper bustled in, out of breath. It took a solid three minutes to sprint from one side of the house to the other, then compose herself in order to appear unruffled. A true lady didn't sweat, after all. She *glistened.*

"Congratulations, Dr. Cook. I heard your news," she huffed.

"I need you to file all of these documents for me. Post-haste. And once you're done with that, I need you to draft up an employment offer for Miss Samantha Stanton."

Guadalupe's eyebrow rose. She had been following *Samantha Says* since its inception, and read her latest column that didn't sound quite like herself as she announced her termination before shrugging off the advice-seeker's question with a reply more befitting a man. Clearly Sam wasn't taking her termination well.

"What's the job position?" Guadalupe asked, taking notes on the notepad she always kept in her uniform pocket for exact moments like these.

"Editor-in-chief."

"For what magazine?"

"*Ladies Home Journal*."

"In New York City?" Guadalupe clarified.

"It's the only way to get her away from that guy she's seeing—Raul Smothers. Once she finds out that he betrayed her, she'll certainly break up with him. And who will be there to dry her tears? Me. Then I can whisk her away to her New York City where she'll forget all about Raul and we can finally have our happily ever after without any other distractions tearing us apart."

Guadalupe looked up at him with judgement in her eyes. "That's quite deviant, even for you, sir."

"A man's gotta do what a man's gotta do," he replied.

"Have you told your current editor-in-chief he will need to step down?"

"Oh, I don't plan on actually giving Samantha the job. Just offering it to her. But once we're settled in the city, I'm sure she'll come to realize she doesn't need a job when I can give her anything and everything she wants. She won't ever have to lift a finger again!"

"What if she wants to keep writing and helping people, Dr. Cook?"

Thomas laughed. "No woman in her right mind would rather have a career over a cushy life, Guadalupe. Are you telling me you'd rather clean up after my mess than sit at home being taken care of?"

"Well, if given the choice, I actually always wanted to be a lawyer."

"Ha! A lawyer? Why—so you can enact laws that help your people overrun America?"

"My people, sir?" Guadalupe didn't know any fellow Spaniards eager to immigrate to America, let alone take it over.

"Illegals. You know, Mexicans." He paused, giving his wording a second thought, then said, "No offense."

Not that there should have been any offense to the word *Mexican,* if indeed Guadalupe was Mexican. But she was Spanish-American, which she had told him at least a dozen times. So she rolled her eyes as she did every other time she had corrected him about her ethnicity, but this time she didn't bother to respond.

"Why are you so obsessed with winning this woman over, Dr. Cook?"

"Because I *don't* lose. I never have, and I never will."

Chapter 37

It had been everyone's expectation—everyone being Raul, Bernadette, and even her mother Minnie, who desperately hoped Sam would forego the whole career aspirations fad and marry Raul instead—that Sam would be swimming in a sea of job offers after her termination. But the only employment opportunity that arrived came on a piece of Dr. Thomas Cook letterhead, and accepting the prestigious dream role of editor-in-chief meant moving back to New York City. The city that had spit her out in the first place. And the city where Raul was not.

It didn't help her job search that Sam's name had been permanently smeared across every Pittsburgh tabloid due to her "scandalizing revenge campaign" against Cook Pharmaceuticals. Or that she had been incarcerated for theft and forgery, which they never bothered to publicly retract after the charges were dropped.

Her phone calls went ignored. Her résumés were returned to sender. She was a failed journalist by day, and a homeopathic quack by night. And so Sam slipped into the tired cliché attached to every woman: that she was being "too emotional" and couldn't be taken seriously. The only Samantha Stanton anyone was interested in was the one who'd made a public spectacle of herself. Finally the world had won as Sam learned to take her medicine and give up.

Sam and Raul were wandering around Kaufman's Department store browsing the men's section. Raul had invited Sam along to help him update Mr. Rogers' wardrobe, but Sam was quite fond of the one he already had. Clothed like a sweet grandfather a child would snuggle up with while he read a story, or a kindly uncle who played with puppets.

They had been discussing Sam's jobless fate between aisles of pleated pants and button-up shirts.

"What do you want to do?" Raul asked while nixing everything he saw as outdated or old-fashioned.

"Little kids don't need trendy fashion. They want comfort. Safety. Something that says *trustworthy*." Sam held up a red zippered cardigan. "What about this one?"

"Red? Isn't that too bold for a grown man?"

"I don't know. I think it makes a statement," Sam said, carrying it to the register despite Raul's protests.

Raul hadn't been keen to go shopping, but when the studio stagehand Michael Keaton asked Raul to pick up a couple extra shirts to have on hand, Raul asked Sam to join him. No one said no to the Flying Zookeeni Brother that always kept the production team laughing. A star in the making.

"You didn't answer me," Raul reminded Sam.

"About what?"

"What you plan to do."

"I don't have an answer."

"Does that mean you will consider staying in Pittsburgh?"

"I don't have a job here."

"But you have me."

But Sam had never tied herself to a single person, with the

exception of her sick father, and she wasn't confident she should start now. New York had a job, Pittsburgh had Raul.

What if Raul wasn't enough reason to stay?

Chapter 38

After Sam had forced Raul to purchase the cardinal red cardigan that Raul doubted Mr. Rogers would wear, Raul drove them back to Sam's house, finding Miss Posey standing on Sam's doormat in a tizzy.

"What did Fido do now?" Sam groaned as she mounted the porch steps expecting the worst.

"No, it's not Fido's antics this time," she said, her voice warbling. "I… I… I almost died!" she exclaimed, at which point she broke down into tears, pulling tissue after tissue from her sleeve like a magician with a silk scarf. "But I don't want to talk about it."

Sam was about to ask her what happened—clearly Miss Posey wanted to tell all about it; why else would she be standing on Sam's doorstep announcing it to all the neighborhood?—but Miss Posey trembled and sputtered.

"It's too horrible to put words to," she said between sobs.

"Would you like for me to make you some tea?" Sam offered.

"Tea? I can't possibly stomach tea when I'm in such a state. Didn't you hear me? What would poor Archibald Maverick Emerson Posey the Sixth do without me?"

"Are you sure you don't want to talk about it?"

"No, it's too traumatic to speak of what happened."

"Okay, I won't press," Sam surrendered, nudging past Miss Posey toward her metal screen door.

Miss Posey's hand flew out and yanked Sam's arm to stop her, then she spun Sam around to face her.

"If you're going to insist on being so nebby, Samantha, fine, I'll tell you." From there she launched into storytelling mode, which for Miss Posey was every mode. "It was earlier this afternoon, and I was on my way home from the dry cleaner, getting the stain out of my fur coat from when Betty—do you know Betty, who lives four houses down?"

Sam had lost count of all the Bettys in her life, but she nodded nonetheless in order to move the story along.

"Anyway, a couple weeks ago Betty spilled wine on my beautiful fur coat that my late husband—God rest his soul—had bought me for our first anniversary. Would you believe the dry cleaner said it was one of the toughest stains he had ever encountered?"

"Yes, I would." Sam prodded her, saying, "Now about your near-death experience?"

"I'm trying to tell a story, dear. The details are important."

Sam wasn't sure how a tough wine stain was pertinent to her brush with death, but she couldn't wait to find out.

"So I was driving home when a deer darted out in front of my car. I careened off the road into a ditch, blowing my tire. While the car was rattling off the road, I knocked my head pretty badly against the window. Then when I glanced down at my coat it was covered in what looked like blood! The sight almost caused me to pass out, when a policeman came to my rescue."

"Oh, that's wonderful," Sam said, assuming the story was over. But Miss Posey was only just getting started.

"He was my guardian angel sent by the Lord Himself, I believe. Even the name he wore said *love*. That man fixed my tire and escorted me home. A personal escort, would you believe it? So here I am, still clinging to life, with a whole new appreciation for each moment, I might add."

While a blown tire didn't seem quite like a brush with death, to each their own, Sam supposed. At least Miss Posey walked away from the trauma with a new attitude toward life. Perhaps this newfound zeal would help her cut the Breedlove family some slack.

"What about the stain?" Sam belatedly remembered.

"Oh, that. Yes, well, when my car shook from the tire popping, my grocery bag with a bottle of wine in it broke and spilled all over my freshly dry-cleaned coat! Turns out it wasn't blood on the coat but red wine. Can you believe that? Now I have to take it back to get cleaned again. How embarrassing!"

"Not any more embarrassing than fainting from seeing a stain," Sam offered with a smile.

All this time Raul hadn't spoken a word, because he knew better than to start a conversation with Miss Posey, whose favorite topic was his singledom and why he hadn't taken Sam to the courthouse to marry her yet.

"Well, I'm glad you're alive, Miss Posey. But we're running late and have to go." Sam inched toward the door, attempting a sly getaway.

"Oh, do you need a chaperone?" Miss Posey's voice rose with playful octave as she eyeballed Raul. "I don't mind joining you."

"We wouldn't dare impose on you like that," Raul nearly shouted feverishly. His tolerance for Miss Posey was very low, and already he had met his quota of her for the day. "I meant, no thank you, ma'am. We're simply dining with the neighbors."

As if the universe wanted to aid and abet Raul and Sam's getaway, Bernadette called from her window, "Supper's ready when you are, lovebirds!"

Miss Posey cast a disapproving scowl at Bernadette's house. "You're not befriending the terrorist family, I hope?"

"They're not terrorists, Miss Posey."

Sam nudged Miss Posey off the porch, shooing her back home, when she noticed a large, unmarked manilla envelope sitting on the doormat Miss Posey had just vacated. She picked it up, examining both sides, which were void of any kind of address or markings. Apparently it had been hand delivered.

"What's that you have there?" Raul asked, looking over her shoulder.

"I don't know. Knowing my luck, it's bound to be something bad. I'm probably being tried for treason. Goodbye, cruel world!"

Raul reached for the envelope, but Sam pulled it away and shoved it in her purse.

"I can deal with it later," she said, though in truth she wasn't sure she could. Good news, bad news... Sam was news-ed out.

"Maybe it's best you not deal with it at all. I can handle it for you, if you want." The cryptic way Raul spoke sparked Sam's curiosity.

"Why? Do you know what's in this package?"

"No, of course not."

"Then why are you acting so strange?"

"I'm not acting strange."

"Elusive."

"Cautionary, maybe."

"No... guilty." Sam watched his features shift, cheeks blush, eyes dart. "What did you do, Raul?"

"Nothing."

"Something is up. I can tell. You're easier to read than *Flower & Garden Magazine*."

The comparison was lost on Raul, who didn't find anything easy about reading *Flower & Garden Magazine* as he confused hydrangea with hibiscus, and peonies with pansies. And don't get him started on plant propagation versus stem grafting.

"I promise you, Sam, nothing is up other than my heartrate after seeing you looking so fine tonight."

Sam rolled her eyes at his over-the-top compliment, but she was right. Raul was hiding something and couldn't tell her the truth. It would certainly end things between them—whatever the fragile thing was that they had.

Chapter 39

"Supper's ready when you are, lovebirds!" Bernadette poked her head out of her kitchen window, waving Sam and Raul over.

She had been looking forward to meeting *the* Raul Smothers ever since she detected the adoring lilt in Sam's voice every time she mentioned him. Which was growing more frequent by the day.

"Raul told me the funniest joke today..."

"Raul wrote the most insightful article for the Times *about that..."*

"Raul surprised me with a moss ball..."

To which Sam had to further explain was a little-known aquatic plant symbolic of love.

When Bernadette discovered Raul was a journalist—*former reporter*—for the *New York Times*, an idea formed, and soon a dinner invite was extended. Reporter meant connections, and connections meant money, and money meant change.

She had hoped to pick Raul's brain about the hostile takeover of the neighborhood and if there was any way to peaceably reach some kind of agreement to stop the vandalism and threats. Sam teased that there wasn't much in Raul's brain to pick at, but one never knew what they'd find while digging around in his dark matter.

"We made soul food." Bernadette ushered Sam and Raul

inside, giving Raul a quick once-over as he paused to greet her. She nodded her approval to Sam.

"Soul food?" Sam asked.

"You know, food that's good for the soul. Fried chicken, okra, cornbread, collard greens… deep south African-American cuisine. Anyway, I'm going to help you expand your culinary horizons tonight."

"What's good for the stomach is good for the soul." Raul patted his belly that had gone up one size ever since Minnie started cooking for him and Sam every week. "Especially when it includes fried chicken."

When they entered the Breedloves' home, Alonzo Sr. was already in the kitchen breading the fresh okra—barefoot—perching their newest addition—already six months old, how time flies!—on one hip. Raul glanced at Sam, remembering her promise from so long ago.

"Hm, look at that, Sam. A husband barefoot in the kitchen with a baby on his hip. Does this mean you'll finally marry me?"

Bernadette's eyes widened with surprise as Sam flushed with embarrassment.

"If that was a proposal, Raul Smothers, I suggest you try a little harder and get a little more creative, honey," Bernadette chided.

It was the tastiest chicken Raul had ever eaten, and the most entertaining dinner Sam had ever enjoyed. They spent the evening eating and drinking and laughing and sharing. Stories of how Alonzo Sr. and Bernadette met when she was trapped on a carnival Ferris Wheel that broke down just as her pod reached the top and Alonzo climbed to her rescue.

Followed by tales of how Sam and Raul got stuck on a ferry

during a storm on the way to visit the Statue of Liberty, which was the last time Raul stepped foot on a boat.

Alonzo Sr. regaled them with memories from his beat cop days, and Raul entertained them with celebrities he interviewed from his reporter days. They ended the evening with a game of *Clue* after Alonzo Jr. tuckered out on a competitive round of *Chutes and Ladders*, and Sam realized she had laughed so hard that her cheeks ached.

"So, Raul," Alonzo Sr. began as they sat around the living room sipping the cheap red wine Sam had picked up at the liquor store that had a low enough alcohol content that even Bernadette, who was still breastfeeding, poured herself half a glass. "I read something interesting in the papers the other day. About you."

Raul's mouth dropped, eyes widened, and he stumbled through a hasty reply. "As much as I'd love to hear about it, I just remembered that I have to get back to the studio."

"Tonight?" Sam asked.

"Yeah, I need to drop that cardigan off for tomorrow's taping. As they say, time waits for no man."

"Oh, okay." But Sam didn't believe him.

Had Raul not rushed off in a peculiar hurry, he would have heard Alonzo Sr. go on to explain that the *interesting something* he was referring to was a television critic's praise piece on the children's show that Raul worked for.

As Sam speculated what on earth Raul could be hiding, she remembered the folder that had been left on her doormat and now bulged out of her purse. Peeling it open, she reached inside and pulled out a thick stack of papers with Cook Pharmaceuticals' name all over it, and a red CONFIDENTIAL stamped across the upper corner. Sam didn't need to read much more than the first page to learn it was a photocopy of a drug trial.

"What is all that jargon?" Bernadette asked, tossing a quick glance at it while she bustled around the kitchen reaching for dessert plates and silverware.

"You'll never guess."

"You're right. I won't. So just tell me."

"It's all the proof I need to clear my name and bury Thomas Cook."

"Girl, you're trippin'!"

"Here, look."

Sam pointed to the long document packed with details about the Nosartin heart pill clinical trials, which stated as clear as day that the case study only included 80 *severe* heart issue patients. Of those test subjects, the medicine was only 69% effective for patients with severe heart damage, but most died from other "unrelated" health issues within five years of the study. The conclusion stated that the heart medicine was indeed effective, but it couldn't be proven to offer long-term impact.

No study had been carried out on those with only *mild* heart damage. According to doctors who reported side effects from heart disease patients, Nosartin proved ineffective for 25% of mild cases, and the number of deaths due to heart-related issues was substantial.

"I don't understand what any of this means," Bernadette concluded after skimming it.

"It means that the trials used a negligible number of test subjects, and they didn't even fit the profile of the patients doctors were prescribing this heart medicine to."

"Laymen's terms, honey."

"They didn't study Nosartin's effectiveness for people with mild heart issues at all—like what my dad had. In fact, it may have even made their condition worse. Almost a quarter of the patients who used it ended up dead. So it never should have been approved by the FDA to be used for people like my dad."

"Whoa."

"Yeah, whoa."

"You know what that means, don't you?"

"That I should never take your advice to stay out of trouble?" Sam said with a smirk.

"Okay, sure, honey, but it also means you didn't kill your dad with grapefruit like you thought you did."

While Sam would never know for sure if the grapefruit had contributed to it, at least when she exposed this information she could give peace to all the families who might also be blaming themselves for the deaths of their loved ones.

Bernadette flipped the page to another study stapled to the back. "What's this one about?"

"I don't know…" Sam mumbled, reading to catch up.

"Wait. Check this out." Bernadette pointed to the all-too-familiar acronym DES. It was the same drug she had taken while pregnant with Alonzo Jr. that she had fought her doctor about taking.

"Oh, geez Louise." Sam read the incriminating medical review summary with a horrifying understanding that this could be referring to Bernadette. "At least I can finally put a stop to the drug with this."

The original study for DES was dated thirty years ago, in 1940, branded under a different pharmaceutical company. But it appeared that Cook Pharmaceuticals had launched a generic version of the drug diethylstilbestrol, also known as DES, and resumed distributing it to pregnant women, despite questionable evidence of its effectiveness. Then last year, in 1971, a significant number of cervical cancer cases were found linked to the drug. And yet it was still on the market, still being pushed by doctors, and even listed in Thomas Cook's ledger.

"You're not just going to clear your name with all this, Sam. You're going to take Cook Pharmaceuticals to court. Probably even get a settlement."

"I am?"

"You sure are, honey. And I'll help you do it."

Sam wondered if any lawyer would dare take the case, considering most of the city was in Thomas Cook's pockets, and deep pockets they were.

"Do you think the women who were impacted can win against Cook Pharmaceuticals?"

"If we can find someone who will go up against him, a multi-million-dollar class action lawsuit is sure worth a try."

"But I have no way to get this story printed. I lost my job at the magazine, remember?"

Sam's gaze settled on the flower pot of unkillable dead aloe that Bernadette had defied all odds to kill. The flower pot reminded her of the priceless vase she had given to Betty Number Five. And the thought of Betty Number Five reminded her that the secretary still owed Sam a favor! It was time to call it in.

"Mind if I borrow your phone?" Sam asked.

"As long as it's not long distance."

Sam dialed the receptionist desk for *Women's House*

Magazine, asked to be transferred to Betty Number Five, and half of a Cher song later Betty picked up the line. Sam reminded her of their vase-favor transaction, to which Betty had a hazy memory about the deal.

"What do you want me to do?" Betty finally agreed.

"I have one last column I need you to run for me. Don't tell Mel. Just take it to the production manager and he'll run it for you no questions asked if you flirt with him."

"Has that ever worked for you before?"

"No, but I'm not you."

"What makes you think that will work for me?"

"There's a reason they called you *Babelicious Betty*. So will you do it or not?" Sam asked.

The dead silence on the line lasted so long Sam thought the line had disconnected.

Finally Betty whispered, "You're lucky Mel made a pass at me and threatened to fire me if I turned him in, or else I wouldn't be risking my job for you."

Women's House Magazine April 1972 Issue

SAMANTHA SAYS...

Q: Dear Samantha,

I'm a huge fan of yours, and I was devastated to find out your magazine will be shutting down. I truly hope you have plans to continue sharing your knowledge and passion at another larger national magazine, because I will surely follow you wherever you go!

Speaking of following, I've had a bit of a stalker situation. I'm a woman living alone downtown, and over the past several months I've been pursued by a man to no end. Even after confronting him, explaining in no uncertain terms that I'm not interested, he persists. Love letters, flowers, phone calls, randomly showing up at my door... he even tried to force himself on me when I was walking home from the bus stop one night. I find myself always looking over my shoulder, searching the shadows for him. It's become a terrifying existence to be the object of his relentless affection.

No one seems to believe me, and those that do blame me for "leading him on" because of the clothes I wear. I sought protection from the police, but all they see is a single woman in a short skirt and her doting love interest. Instead of arresting him they urged me to give him a chance since "it's not safe for a woman to live alone." It is men like this stalker who make it not safe to be alone!

Any final advice before your column bids us adieu to help me get rid of my problem?

Sincerely,
Freida the Fan

A: Dear Freida the Fan,

I've recently had my fair share of stalkers, and it turns out they're a resilient breed of human that is difficult to eradicate. For my own stalker I once fantasized about inviting him out for coffee, then spiking his drink with wolfsbane—its purple flowers are easy to identify in the mountainous Pennsylvania woodlands. The side effects of ingestion are swift and can be severe, including heart arrythmia, vomiting, and respiratory system paralysis. In fact, 20 ml of tincture could prove fatal. So unless you fear for your life, or he's really getting on your last nerve, I wouldn't advise that route.

Thank you for your encouragement to persist, a determination I had lost recently as I began to doubt my own calling. Although I feel as if I have failed you, my readers, I want to leave you with one last piece of ammunition that might help women force a necessary societal change. This will likely also pound the final nail in my columnist career coffin, but it's a sacrifice I must make.

I recently discovered that Cook Pharmaceuticals has been manufacturing a drug that is known to cause cancer in women and their babies. If you are pregnant and your doctor has prescribed you DES, it is urgent that you stop taking it. If this has impacted you, please join me in my last battle against this mammoth company that has faked their drug trial results and led to the death of hundreds of thousands of women.

I will be loud. I will be proud. And I will expose the wrongs thrown at us. Men merely fight to win, but women fight to survive.

Sincerely,
Samantha

Chapter 40

The radio could be heard through the screen door and open windows as Sam toiled under the summer evening sun rebuilding her greenhouse. "Everybody Plays the Fool" by The Main Ingredient had segued into the "dad-ee-o of the rad-ee-o" Porky Chedwick's news segment. He was saying something about a man dying unexpectedly in front of a café in downtown Pittsburgh. Investigators suspected it was poisoning. Unfortunately, the only witness, a woman by the name of Freida, wasn't able to revive him before calling for an ambulance.

Freida. The name held a strange familiarity, and Sam instantly thought of her last advice column that Betty had managed to publish, as promised. Certainly it couldn't be Freida the Fan with the stalker? And if so, how did she get her hands on wolfsbane so quickly? Sam couldn't help but be impressed with the woman's efficiency in problem-solving.

"Such a shame," Miss Posey lamented from her back porch while she oversaw Archibald Maverick Emerson Posey the Sixth running along the fence line after Fido in a game of catch me if you can, which Archibald continued to lose and Fido continued to win.

"The world is going to hell in a handbasket," Miss Posey added with a dramatic sigh.

The statement was clearly intended to bait Sam into conversation, and since Sam was a goodhearted gal who knew a cry of loneliness when she heard one, she left her greenhouse construction in progress and approached the fence dividing their yards.

Sam dusted the wood shavings off of her pedal pushers, sniffed the armpits of her psychedelic t-shirt, and pushed her sweaty bangs off of her face. She would need to finish the greenhouse within the next couple of weeks if she was going to have any kind of herb harvest to carry her through the winter. With her budget sapped and no job to fund it, the deadline didn't look promising.

"What's got you in a funk today, Miss Posey?"

"The news, that's what. Tragedy after tragedy. Men dying in droves from poisoning."

"Oh, there's another one?" Sam asked, hoping she hadn't spurred a wolfsbane murder spree across the city with her latest column.

"Sadly, yes. A couple days ago a husband dropped dead in the middle of eating his Watergate cake. The cops have no idea what killed him, but his poor widowed spouse, Sally something-or-other, sounded devastated when they interviewed her. She must be heartbroken."

No, it couldn't possibly be Supper Sipper Sally that had written her a year and a half ago. Suddenly Sam felt the weight of responsibility for advising all of these women to essentially kill their husbands. That hadn't been her intention at all—well, not explicitly—but it wasn't as if the world wasn't better off without cruel people.

"What if those people deserved it?" Sam wondered aloud.

"What could possibly make someone deserve to die?"

"Oh, I don't know… abusing or terrorizing women?"

Miss Posey sighed and shook her head. "You have no idea how good you modern girls have it, Samantha. You women these days are so fragile. The slightest breeze and you break. You know, when I got married I nearly lost my citizenship over it and could have been deported. But you didn't hear me moan and groan about it."

"How on earth did you almost lose your citizenship? Did you marry a treasonous enemy?"

"Close. I married a Thai man. Back then, a woman lost her United States citizenship if she married a foreigner, since they saw it as a woman assuming the citizenship of her husband. But lo and behold, that law did not apply to citizen men who married foreign women. Yet another double standard against women."

Obviously Miss Posey didn't lose her US status, unless she was an illegal alien in hiding. "So what happened?"

"Luckily, shortly after we married a new law changed that—but it was touch-and-go for a while trying to duck the US Government during our honeymoon to Niagara Falls."

"Considering what you went through, don't you think women should be treated as equals? You sound like you think we should just suck it up and accept it."

Miss Posey shrugged and leaned against Sam's fence, her hair curlers slowly slipping. "I don't know, dear. That's a big change. Once we embrace equality in the workforce and politics and everywhere else, we lose chivalry. I liked being a homemaker and having a husband who took care of me. I don't want that to change."

"That's the whole point, though. Women should get to

choose that life, not be forced into it. Because of male chauvinism, I lost my job. How is that fair?"

"You weren't fired for wearing pants, were you? Because I heard that's illegal now."

"What are you talking about?"

"I'm talking about how I got fired from my first job for wearing pants."

"Are you jive-talking me?"

"I kid you not." Miss Posey adjusted a pink roller that bumped against her forehead. "There was an actual law that allowed employers to fire women for wearing pants. It was only maybe a decade ago when they passed a new law that forbade employers from terminations related to wearing pants… but most employers still enforce that rule."

By now a whole row of curlers were blocking Miss Posey's vision as she fidgeted to push them back in place.

"Anyway, welcome to womanhood, Samantha. You're lucky to be young in this era of free love and free pants, or whatever you want to call it. Discrimination is nothing like it used to be."

But the universe was at it again. As if to make its point, it was that exact moment when Bernadette waved from the other side of Sam's yard carrying her daughter, another month older and a onesie size bigger, while Alonzo Jr. carried a carrot for Fido.

"I hope you don't mind if Alonzo Jr. gives Fido a snack."

While Bernadette fiddled with the gate lock, Miss Posey leaned over the fence with a conspiratorial whisper. "I see you've met the," Miss Posey cleared her throat, "neighbors." She shook her head woefully. "You might as well invite them to rob you, giving them full access to your property."

By now Miss Posey's whisper was loud enough to draw a glare from Bernadette, who hung back while Alonzo Jr. climbed on Fido's bare back. Fido, happy to have a rider, lifted his head high and his tail even higher as he pranced around the yard while Alonzo Jr. gripped his mane like a rodeo master.

"You really should be careful hanging around them. The neighborhood is liable to find out."

Sam propped her hands on her hips. "I thought you just said discrimination isn't what it used to be, Miss Posey."

"Well... sometimes it's warranted, Samantha."

"On what basis?"

Miss Posey gasped. "On the basis of them..."

"Having more melanin than you?" Sam stepped back angrily, tired of the nonsense that made people do nonsensical things. "Or do they deserve it because they enjoy soul food? Or have an afro? Or enjoy the music of Roberta Flack?"

"Hey there, I enjoy 'First Time Ever I Saw Your Face' as much as anyone else."

"Then why did half the neighborhood disappear when a Black family moved in?"

By now Sam's face was pink with indignation and Miss Posey's face was pink with humiliation.

"Honestly..." Miss Posey hesitated, then stuttered, "I really don't know."

"Shame on you all for making Bernadette Breedlove and her family feel unwelcome! You're no better than men like Thomas Cook who use their power to hold back women."

The name rang a bell as Miss Posey grabbed Sam's wrist. "Did you say *Breedlove*?"

"Yes. Why?"

"Remember the story I told you about the policeman who saved me when I almost died in that horrific accident that almost cost me my fur coat?"

"Yes, I recall the story of when your tire blew."

"Strange. That was the name printed on his uniform name tag: *Breedlove*."

By now Bernadette was determined to confront the leader of the gang that was making her family's life a living hell. If she couldn't set this woman straight, maybe she could at least ask for a cease-fire.

"Hi, I'm Bernadette Breedlove." Bernadette extended her hand coolly as a peace offering, which Miss Posey hesitantly shook. "And they boy riding the pony is my son Alonzo Jr."

Already Miss Posey noticed the exhausted mother with two young children and no husband to speak of. *Typical*, she thought to herself.

"Where's Alonzo Sr.?" Sam asked.

"Working a double shift. They're shorthanded and needed extra officers to direct traffic for the Steelers game."

"Your husband is a police officer?" Miss Posey asked with surprise at not only the fact that Bernadette was married, but that her husband was a man of the law. The neighborhood gossip gang couldn't have been more wrong.

"Yes, ma'am. He's been serving and protecting this city for almost a decade now."

"Oh my dear." Miss Posey cheeks flushed an even deeper shade of pink. "Did you say his name was Alonzo Breedlove?"

"That's him. Why? Have you met him?"

"Well, yes, he saved my life." Miss Posey recalled the

incident play by play, from Betty's wine stain on her fur coat to the deer dashing out in traffic, and the rumble of the car onto the berm, and the moment her skull smacked the window. She praised Bernadette's husband for his God-ordained appearance at just the right time and just the right place to come to her rescue. "I'd like to bake your family an apple pie to thank him for his life-saving efforts. It's a family recipe."

"Oh, that's not necessary—"

"I insist, Mrs. Breedlove."

"You can call me Bernadette. And you are—"

"Everyone knows me as Miss Posey, but you can call me Hannah."

Sam grinned, as to date she had never gotten Miss Posey's first name.

"And who is the little bundle of joy?" Miss Posey leaned toward the baby, offering an index finger for her to wrap her tiny hands around.

"Kristin Eleanor, a bundle of joy? No one has accused her of that since she was twelve weeks old. You must not hear her screaming her lungs out at two in the morning, then four, then six…"

"Oh, colic, is it?" Miss Posey asked, as if she, too, had an infant with a similar predicament. "My son went through the same thing until he was almost two years old."

"God help me, it better not end up lasting that long!"

"I had a trick that seemed to help. I'll show you," Miss Posey paused, glancing at Bernadette hopefully, wanting any sign of forgiveness for her ignorance, "if you don't mind?"

"I'd love to try anything. Thank you."

"If you want to come over right now, I just baked some

cookies. Do you like cookies, Alonzo Jr.?"

At the word *cookies,* Alonzo Jr. hopped off Fido's back and came sprinting. While Miss Posey showed Alonzo Jr. to the gate, then led him by the hand to her back porch, Sam stopped Bernadette.

"How can you do that so easily?" Sam asked.

"Do what?"

"Forgive her for all the hurt she's caused you, trying to push your family out of the neighborhood?"

Bernadette thought for a moment then said, "If Congresswoman Shirley Chisholm could visit her segregationist and Jim Crow-supporting rival George Wallace in the hospital after his shooting last year, I can visit an old lady in her home who genuinely is trying to do better. Both love and hate can't abide in the same small space, honey. So I guess I'm gonna choose love."

And just like that Bernadette and Miss Posey had mended a fence that Sam thought was beyond repair.

Chapter 41

"Last mail call!" Mel shouted as he dropped the final bag of *Women's House Magazine* reader mail for *Samantha Says* on her desk empty of all personal possessions, and where only her green typewriter and matching telephone remained.

Mel had called Sam back to the office to collect the last batch of mail, only because he didn't feel like dealing with it himself. The bonus was that it completely inconvenienced her.

Most of the typists had already cleared out their things, and personnel had processed half of the company's termination paperwork. One half of the bullpen was full of bare desks where a few lingering employees mulled around trying to look busy for the last issue they would be publishing. Across the other half was a scuffed linoleum floor full of endless brown cardboard boxes ready to transfer to the New York City headquarters.

"May you drown in your letters," Mel added with a growl.

Even after the stunt she pulled, sneaking in April 1972's column after her formal termination, he had allowed Sam to return one last time. It wasn't on his own kindly merit, however. One call from Mr. Getty reminded him that the magazine had to go out with a bang, with Sam at the helm—or else. Mel losing any chance of relocating to New York City was the *or else*.

"Would I be permitted to keep my typewriter?" Sam asked hopefully.

She had grown quite attached to her portable Smith-Corona, which boasted unprecedented typing speeds. Sam recalled that very first sentence she had ever typed: *The quick brown fox jumps over the lazy dog.* Every letter of the alphabet captured in a single sentence, and the day her fingers first gained familiarity—and love—for the expression of language. That sentence met its master as the advertising slogan said, *"No other portable has the power to make fox fur fly like the Smith-Corona electric."* How true it was, as Sam had sent a lot of fur flying recently.

"Fine," was Mel's one-word answer.

"Why do you hate me so much?" Sam asked, looking up at Mel.

She already knew why. She was better at his job than he was, and he couldn't stand to accept it. But she wanted to hear it from his lips. Or at least whatever version society had been spoon-feeding him to believe.

"Miss Stanton, you are not even on my radar enough to hate. You're nothing but a simple-minded, status-climbing, underhanded feminist who thinks she is better than everyone else at this rag all because you make up facts about medicine and managed to get the owner to fall in love with you."

"They wouldn't be called *facts* if they weren't true. That would be called *fiction*."

"I'm so tired of ugly spinsters like you thinking you know what women want better than their husbands do!"

"As a woman, I would think I would have a natural advantage."

"I almost forgot to add that you are a smart-aleck too, Samantha."

"That part may be true, but it's not intentional. It's not like I go out of my way to be *smart*. I just naturally am."

"You make my point for me." Mel began to walk away, then he stopped and turned. "Never seeing your smug face again will be the second-best day of my life."

"And the first best day?" Sam asked as she leafed through the letters, reading one plea for advice after another.

One letter in particular stood out. It was the perfect way to end things.

"The day I watch you lose everything."

With those words ringing in her ears, and the letter's content guilting her soul, Sam knew exactly what her final advice column would be.

Women's House Magazine
May 1972 Issue

SAMANTHA SAYS...

Q: Dear Samantha,

You may remember me as the reader who sought your advice about my temperamental husband. To refresh your memory, if supper didn't appeal to him, he would blend it and force me to drink it so I might aspire to be a better cook.

Back then you advised me to offer him nux vomica seeds—also known as the "poison nut," treated by soaking and boiling them in milk to remove the toxic poison. Your sage advice did indeed cure his irritability and quell his anger. Unfortunately it didn't cure mine until the tragic day I had forgotten to pre-treat the seeds before sprinkling them on his slice of Watergate cake. Needless to say, the funeral was beautiful.

Today I come to you again seeking advice after hearing the terrible news about your fate. More than that, you had filled me, and countless others, with a hope for something apparently unreachable.

Freedom. Self-worth. Equality.

Perhaps that is the hardest pill to swallow—nothing will change, and the more we fight for it, the more we bleed. This reality has resulted in my depression and an accompanying prescription for Tofranil, which only adds to the weight I carry—literally. Gaining four sizes and plagued with vertigo have done little to boost my spirits.

So my final enquiry before your column closes for good: What is the cure to all that ails me?

Sincerely,
Supper Sipper Sally

A: Dear Supper Sipper Sally,

Thank you for your condolences on the doom of my advice column. Despite everything that's happened, this is not the last you'll see of me. I do not give up that easily, and neither should you.

Do not feel alone—we all struggle with feelings of anxiety or depression at some point, and it should be perfectly acceptable to discuss the messiness of life, no matter what social norms dictate. One of my preferred treatments is ashwagandha, a natural plant-based supplement that contains antidepressant properties as it increases dopamine and serotonin, thus boosting mood. Within a few days of taking it you should notice those dark thoughts shrinking, along with your waistline.

You mentioned equality, a sticky word that

clings to my fingertips but remains out of my grasp. I thought I had found it once on a brisk March day two years ago, but it ended up costing me more than this column: my confidence, my reputation, and the love of my life. But as someone, perhaps naïvely, once said, "Choosing silence is choosing death. As long as we padlock our tongues, we will all continue to wear chains, even if some rattle louder than others."

Unlock your tongue. Bleed if you must. In the end, it's life or death, freedom or fetters. What else do you have to lose? I may have lost my voice today, but you'll see—The Man hasn't silenced me yet.

Farewell... for now.

Sincerely,
Samantha

Chapter 42

When an earthquake happens, you might feel the earth shudder as the tectonic plates shift and move. But the resulting tsunami can take hours, even days, to make its way across the ocean before crashing onto an unsuspecting shore. The earthquake was Samantha Stanton's exposé on Cook Pharmaceuticals, the tidal wave was the public interest, and Sam's life as she knew it was that unsuspecting shore.

Within one month of her final advice column hitting May 1972 newsstands, Sam found herself back on top—if *on top* was a wobbly and uncertain spinning top. Her name had been cleared after she blew the whistle on Thomas Cook's schemes, and open job positions poured in from every national magazine and big-city newspaper from sea to shining sea. Everyone wanted a piece of Sam.

Including the vengeful Thomas Cook.

Within two months she had already turned down half a dozen interviews about how she had uncovered the truth about the Nosartin case studies. News outlets wanted Sam as their next investigative reporter, but still Sam wasn't interested. Sam only wanted one thing, and that was getting *Samantha Says* back. But it seemed like the one thing she wanted was the one thing she couldn't have.

Despite the minor setback of *Women's House Magazine*

shutting down for good, life wasn't all bad. She was settling into a welcoming new level of relationship with Raul that was genuine, comforting, and most importantly, honest.

Sam had gotten home late last night from an evening at the comedy club with Raul watching his new friend Michael Keaton perform. She had walked right past yesterday's newspaper laying in the driveway, and ambled to the bedroom without checking her phone messages. She had barely given Fido his nighttime muzzle nuzzle before crashing into bed. So when Sam awoke to her mother arriving with freshly baked scones and cream, she barely noticed the coffee brewing or her mother humming or the PhoneMate blinking.

"My goodness, Samantha. Do you ever check this?" Minnie commented, gesturing to the glowing answering machine button. "You do know how to use it, don't you?"

"I got home late last night and was too tired to check."

"Oh? You're weren't up to something scandalous, I hope."

"I went to a comedy show with Raul, Mom. That Michael Keaton—he's destined to be a star someday."

"Hm, I'll take your word for it. You know who's going to be a star? The guy who played Ward Cleaver. What a handsome fellow."

"From *Leave It To Beaver*? Mom, he had a stroke and retired from acting earlier this year."

"Oh, well, anyway, I'll check your messages for you while you have some breakfast. Sit and eat."

Sam had already been sitting, and her mouth was already half full of scone and cream.

Minnie secured the earphone to her ear and pressed the play button, with message after message from reporter after reporter.

"Uh, Samantha, you need to listen to these," Minnie warned.

Sam scooted over to the device and replayed the messages from the beginning, surprised to discover that this time they weren't the job offers or interview requests that she had gotten used to turning down. This time caller after caller asked her to comment on an article that had come out. The only problem was Sam had no clue what article they were referring to, and after noting their dire tone, she wasn't so sure she wanted to find out.

The newspaper was still in the yard where she had forgotten it last night. After a mad dash in her nightgown down the driveway and back on this misty morning, her cup of coffee sloshing brown stains all over the pink ruffles, she slammed the door behind her, hoping she hadn't just given a free peep show. Then she sat down and opened the dew-damp paper, leafing through it until she stopped dead on page 3. Now she knew what all the commotion was all about.

Printed in black and white was Raul Smothers' name next to Raul's smiling picture next to *her* big headline. The article was giving him full credit for breaking the story about the pharmaceutical faux pas.

"Oh, Samantha. That can't be true. Raul would never take credit for your story. There has to be an explanation for this," Minnie said. "Why on earth would he do this?"

Sam knew Raul, and Raul was first a reporter, second a human with a heart. Anything for a story, right? Even if it required stealing it from the girl he claimed to love.

"He's an investigative journalist who is no longer an investigative journalist. He probably did it to get his foot in the door for a job."

"I thought he was done with all that."

"So did I, but apparently not. He told me that he had tried taking Thomas Cook down shortly after Dad died, but he gave up the story. Just like every other male, he probably couldn't stomach letting a woman do the job that he couldn't get done. God forbid I succeed at something! There he was, Mr. Big-Shot Journalist who couldn't get the dirt on Cook Pharmaceuticals. Then here I come, a nobody, and break the biggest story of the year. But no, his ego can't handle that, so he steals the credit for himself."

Minnie puckered skeptically. "That's an awful lot of speculation about a man who left his high-paying job in New York to follow you here and work for a children's show all because he loves you."

"His pride is bigger than his love, Mom," Sam added sadly. "Besides, how would the papers know about Raul's connection to me, to this story, unless he's the one who told them?"

"You've been in the papers a lot lately, dear. As easy as someone can talk, they can make up a story. You of all people should know that after all the lies Thomas Cook spread about you."

As Sam tossed the paper in the garbage, too angry to even repurpose it as newspaper pots for her seed starters. Tears stung her eyes as she headed to her bedroom to be alone.

The phone rang. She could feel it was Raul. Of course he would be reading the same exact paper at the same exact time.

"Do you want me to get that?" Minnie called to Sam down the hallway.

"No. It's Raul. I can't speak to him right now."

"Maybe you should talk to him?" Minnie had already

328

picked up the phone and answered.

"No, please don't—"

"Miss Stanton's residence. How can I help you?" Minnie announced into the receiver. Then a moment later, "One second, Raul." Minnie turned to Sam's open bedroom door, where Sam fervently shook her head. "I'm sorry, Raul, but she doesn't want to speak with you. I assume this is about the article?"

But before Minnie could push another syllable out, Sam stomped into the living room, yanked the phone out of her mother's hand, and slammed it down on the base. She grabbed her car keys.

"Where are you going, dear?" Minnie begged.

"There's something I need to take care of."

"Are you sure you should be *taking care* of anything in your current state?"

"Don't worry, Mom. I'm not going to confront Raul."

"Then what are you doing?"

"Honestly, my life is already on fire. I'm going to finish it off and let it burn."

Then Sam stormed out of the house—out of her mind and out of control.

Chapter 43

Sam's hand trembled as she gripped the lion's head knocker. It mocked her with its bronze teeth bared, as if snarling at her for being beneath it. One, two, three bangs of the metal handle before the door creaked open.

"Miss Stanton! You're like a celebrity in these parts," Guadalupe exclaimed upon seeing her. She stood in the gap, surprised to find the most unexpected company to dawn Thomas Cook's doorstep, today of all days. "Come inside."

"Oh, that's not necessary. I just need to speak with Thomas—Dr. Cook—for a moment. I'll be quick."

Guadalupe glanced up and down the street. "No, really, Miss Stanton, this might be a conversation best had behind closed doors."

Sam played enough Clue to know that house staff wasn't always so innocent. Would Sam die from a bludgeoning at the hand of the housekeeper, in the library, with a candlestick?

She wasn't fond of the idea of locking herself inside with a man who might want her dead in a house so big that even the next-door neighbor wouldn't be able to hear her scream. But something about Guadalupe felt trustworthy, so she stepped inside. Guadalupe disappeared, and returning in her wake was Thomas Cook looking as haggard and helpless as a stray dog.

"I never thought I'd see you again. Come," he insisted,

gesturing her to follow him to the formal living room.

Further into the mammoth house she went, wondering what kind of hiding places this house had to stash a body, and what the sound range was if an echo could reach Guadalupe's ears.

"Are you here to finish me off? Destroy what's left of me?" Thomas cut to the chase. It was what made him so menacing, his ability to put tact aside for the sake of brevity.

"I should ask you the same question. I know you own *Women's House Magazine*," Sam started with.

"*Owned*. Past tense," he corrected. "It's been dissolved."

"Right. Thanks for that, by the way."

"It was just business. A financial loss."

"It was more profitable than ever before, and you know it. And shutting it down wasn't business, it was personal. Against me."

"Wow, you really think that highly of yourself?"

"Should I not?" Sam dared. "Every man is permitted to think highly of himself without judgement. Why can't I?"

"Touché. And yes, you're correct. I did close it down in the end because of you."

"Do you care to tell me why? What did I ever do to you that deserved slandering my name across the papers, accusing me of forging the ledger, and sending me to jail for theft?"

"First of all, I never accused you of forgery. That wasn't me. The rest, however was true."

"So because I stole evidence that proved you had committed a crime, you figure it's okay to shut down a successful magazine, putting hundreds of people out of work?"

"I offered them all other jobs."

Sam clapped slowly. "Good for you. You have a heart after

all."

"Yes, the same one that you broke."

"So this was all about revenge?"

"No, it was about desperation."

Desperation? Was Thomas becoming vulnerable before her very eyes as he confessed what Sam assumed to be a weakness he had never exposed before? For the briefest of moments, he endeared himself to Sam over this professed desperation... until he continued speaking.

"I wanted to bring you to a point of desperation so that you had no other option than to be with me."

Nix that whole endearing trait.

"Did it work?" he asked.

"Did what work?"

"Did you break up with that Raul Smothers character?"

Raul Smothers character. Now the pieces were beginning to click into place. Somehow Thomas had found out about Sam dating Raul—which was easy enough to do when you could afford to hire a private investigator... or the entire Pittsburgh Police Department. He must have plotted to break them up. What better way for a media mogul to break up a couple than to go the extra mile with his smear campaign? All it took was a little redirection of Sam's ammunition against Thomas, instead putting the smoking gun in Raul's hand.

Raul got the credit, Sam got the curb, and Thomas got the girl. Pure evil genius.

"Even if it did work and I broke up with Raul, it wouldn't have made me ever date a man like you."

"A man like me? You mean wealthy, powerful, and in control."

"No, I mean insecure, egotistical, and terrified of losing control."

Thomas gawked. "If you didn't come here to get in my pants, then why are you here?"

"Because I wanted you to know that I forgive you."

Thomas scoffed. "For what? I never asked for your forgiveness, and I didn't do anything to need it."

Of course Thomas would think that. Luckily for Sam it wasn't about him.

"It's about me… needing to release you. You've had a hold on me for too long."

"So you *do* love me too! You are professing your love for me, right, Samantha?" For someone as intelligent as Thomas Cook was, he sure could be dumb.

"No, if you would just listen! I've been angry at you for a long time for your part in my dad's death with your mis-prescribed Nosartin, and forged drug trials, and paid-off doctors, and attempts to ruin me. I fought as hard as I could to bring justice, but I could never win against you. I thought I could make you taste just a bite of the pain you put me through, but you're right—you are untouchable."

"You're starting to get it…" he interrupted, before Sam placed a finger on his lips to shut him up.

"But not because you are rich or powerful. You can't be touched because you have put up walls so high around you that no one wants to even try to break through them. Since I refuse to fight dirty like you, I forfeit. I forgive you so that I can be free of you and finally let my father rest in peace, because he never wanted my life to be this hard. So I'm doing this partly for me, but also for my dad."

Thomas couldn't think of a befitting retort. In fact, he couldn't think anything for a long moment, possibly the longest he had ever been quiet. When he spoke, it was sincere, possibly the only time he had ever been genuine.

"I'm sorry about your father, Sam. It sounds like he was a good man. I know what it's like to lose someone good…"

"My father wasn't just good; he was the *best*. Full of compassion, and humor, and he treated me and my mother with every bit of love in his arrhythmic heart. He's an example all men should strive to be more like."

Thomas returned to his silence, then nodded. "I never had a father like yours. Mine was unloving and greedy and distant, and now I'm starting to see maybe I'm more like him than I thought."

"You don't have to be." Then Sam suggested something that would blow Thomas's mind, more than any medical discovery ever could. "You could be one of the good ones. Heck, maybe even one of the best ones."

Another beat of silence later, Thomas finally whispered, "I need to make amends. It was the one thing I wish my father would have done with me before he died. I always wanted to be different from my own scheming, money-grubbing family, but like father, like son. I turned out just like him. I need to stop this cycle… starting with you."

No one intimately knew the dreadful way Thomas Cook's own father had abandoned his family after relocating to Pittsburgh to escape the bad press—and multiple lawsuits—that he had left behind in Boston. Or the way he drove his wife to take her own life. As a child, all Thomas wanted was an apology, but instead he got a goodbye. Which turned into the obituary of a man he hardly knew or cared for.

"I want to settle," Thomas declared. "Out of court. I'll take Nosartin and DES off the market immediately and pay everyone who was hurt by the side effects. You'll need to hire a trustworthy lawyer to draw up the settlement, though. Someone not on my payroll."

But where would Sam find such a rare, trustworthy attorney?

"I can do it," a voice echoed from the hallway.

Both Sam and Thomas pivoted to find Guadalupe standing under one of a dozen chandeliers, holding a duster, hand propped on her uniformed hip.

"You?"

"Yes, sir. I passed the bar exam this past spring."

Thomas bellowed laughter, but Guadalupe held a fixed glare. "I'm sorry, what's so funny about that?"

"My maid—a lawyer? That's a good one, Guadalupe. I never knew you to be a jokester."

"I'm not joking. Where do you think I've been going every night? Did you ever once hear me when I told you why I couldn't work evenings for your parties?" He probably listened as well as when she told him she wasn't Mexican but Spanish-American.

"I just assumed you had a family somewhere."

"Sir, I *live* in your maid's quarters! How on earth could I have a family somewhere else?"

"So… you're telling me that you have a law degree?"

"From Duquesne University, sir. You would know that if you ever listened to a thing I say."

"I'm sorry—"

But Guadalupe was a vented pressure cooker now and wasn't stopping. "You know what really irks me about you? You never bother to pay attention to anyone else but yourself, and I'm not Mexican, I'm SPANISH!"

While Thomas did pay attention and notice her disappearances, it was only when her absence caused an inconvenience to him. He had never cared to ask where she went or what she did in her free time.

"But we can't hire you."

"Why not?"

"Because you're on my payroll."

"Not anymore I'm not," she stated, dropping the duster to the floor.

Only now that he discovered she was officially a lawyer did he come to another realization: she would be leaving him. His natural instinct was to get frustrated at this untimely nuisance, but the new Thomas took over and smiled.

"You're Spanish. Got it. And congratulations on the bar exam. I want to host a celebratory party for you, Guadalupe. You have waited on me hand and foot for a long time. It's the least I can do before this lawsuit makes you rich."

It really was the least he could do, considering he had never given her a raise during her fifteen years of service.

"As long as I won't be responsible for organizing the party or cleaning up," she agreed. "So am I hired?" Guadalupe turned to Sam.

"You've got the job!"

It would turn out to be one of the biggest pharmaceutical settlements led by a woman not just in 1972, but in history.

Sam's father would have been proud. He set the bar high

when it came to men, and there was only one other man in Sam's eyes who came close to being as wonderful as her father. She wouldn't let anything get in the way of that again.

She had said what she came to say and marched down the long Morewood Heights driveway, past a Rolls-Royce and impossibly green grass and excessive marble archways, glad that none of it was hers. For what she truly wanted wasn't found in the novelties behind that lion's head knocker, but in a much simpler, homier place.

At the end of the driveway she hopped in the muscle car her father had never gotten to fully enjoy, knowing the last check payment for the car had officially been cashed, leaving her with $4.16 to survive on until she found another job.

She wouldn't worry about money or a job or her near-empty bank account today. It was a beautiful summer afternoon, the convertible top was down, the sun speckling her fair skin, and she would enjoy her dad's car for him as she raced back to the only thing she knew beyond a doubt that she wanted—more than her column, and more than justice.

Chapter 44

Raul's apartment doorknob rattled but wouldn't budge when Sam twisted it, so she knocked, then yelled at the door until several residents popped their heads out into the apartment hallway wondering what all the ruckus was about. Only after agitating a dozen tenants did Sam remember the spare key Raul had made for her in case she ever needed to get inside when he wasn't home. Today was one of those days.

In the modest apartment of a downtown building overlooking the Allegheny River, Sam paused to take in the scene. It was nearly a beautiful view, despite her fear of heights. Overlooking the murky river bridges that shot out from the mountains hugging the city, she grinned down at a roll of smog that almost resembled a sunset-hued fog hanging over the skyline.

She backed away into the kitchen, searching for a pen and paper near the telephone that hung on the wall. She needed to end this cold silent war she had waged unjustly against Raul for the credit he hadn't stolen. She should have known he would never sabotage her success for his own personal gain. She should have asked before jumping to assumptions that he would betray her. Raul Smothers was a man of integrity, and if only she had considered his character before reacting, she would be telling him how much she loved him in person rather than on this silly apology note.

And that's exactly what she wrote on the note pad that she left on his kitchen counter.

Deciding to wait to tell him in person the good news about the Cook Pharmaceuticals settlement, she tucked the corner of the note under his half-full mug of that morning's coffee, then grabbed her purse from the counter. The macrame fabric caught a stack of mail, scattering it across the floor. Leaning down to pick each piece up, she noticed something interesting amid the advertisements and utility bill.

An open letter from *Newsbreak*, attached to an unsigned check to Raul Smothers "for services rendered," the memo declared. Wondering what services the no-longer-reporting Raul had rendered, she read the corresponding missive and gasped:

We appreciate your willingness to supply credible information regarding the Samantha Stanton and Thomas Cook controversy for our paper. Enclosed is a check per our agreement.

Sam glanced at the date on the check. It was issued in January of 1971, over a year and a half ago. The timeline matched when Floyd Jameson had published the article about Sam forging the ledger. Could Raul have been the one to put that reputation-ruining story in motion?

The rattle of a key in a lock startled Sam.

"There you are!" Raul exclaimed as he waltzed through the door blindly into a war zone. "I've tried calling you and I was just at your house looking for you."

Then he noticed the letter in Sam's hand, along with the uncashed check.

"What is this?" Sam demanded, wanting so badly for him to give an explanation she could approve.

"It's not what it looks like."

"It looks like you sold information about my ledger theft—correction, my *forgery*—to *Newsbreak*."

"Okay, it is what it looks like, but not for the reasons you might be thinking."

"I don't care about the reason, Raul. Was losing me worth—" she glanced at the check, "$500?"

"I never cashed it, Sam. I felt terrible about it afterward. I was just trying to protect you."

"Protect me by accusing me of forging a ledger?"

Raul held a hand up, but Sam would not be silenced.

"You destroyed my name! You crushed my career! You are no better than Thomas Cook or any other man set on squashing women who tried to rise up."

"It was never about holding you back, Sam."

"No, it was about publicly making me look like a liar, which is worse."

"I was trying to prevent you from being charged with theft!" Raul tried to reason with her.

"Which I never asked you to do," Sam reminded him.

"But it all turned out okay. You'll bounce back. You always do. This has happened to me too. People have short memories."

Yet Raul was missing one crucial ingredient to his logic: there was a difference between those who have already risen to the top and fall, and those who fall before they've even left the ground.

"Do you know how hard it was for me to establish any kind of respect, let alone after being publicly defamed? It was near impossible, Raul!" Sam felt angry sobs surging, and this time she wouldn't hold them back. "Here I was furious at Thomas Cook, even Mel, for vilifying me. Never in a million years would I imagine that my backstabber, the one who would in the end hold me back, was the love of my life."

Raul fell silent as he absorbed Sam's profession of love mixed with clashing hate. His defense was simple but stupid:

"I... I only did it so you wouldn't get charged with theft and end up in jail. You were playing with fire, and I was trying to extinguish it."

"By running my name through the mud. By taking my column from me. And I could have forgiven all of that, because you were more important than those things. But you did something unforgiveable, Raul. And if you truly know me, and love me like you say you do, you would know exactly what that unforgiveable thing is."

Sam didn't give Raul a chance to guess at what that *unforgiveable thing* was as she stormed out, determined never to again set eyes on the man who broke her heart, tore apart her soul, and left her love for dead.

Chapter 45

"Aaaand, action!"

Alonzo Breedlove Sr. shook off the nerves as he walked onto the set of *Mister Rogers' Neighborhood*. Even after over a decade of patrolling the mean city streets, both the object of fear for many young Blacks, and the subject of hate for many racist whites, he had never felt as anxious as he did right now. And yet his smile broadcast nothing but cool composure to thousands of living room televisions across America. His very own son being one of them.

A kiddie swimming pool sat in the middle of the set, with fake shrubbery and a picket fence encasing it. On a stool sat Mr. Rogers himself, his cardigan aside and a towel draped over his shoulder. In a matter of minutes the two men were washing their bare feet together in the tiny pool, a subliminal message of unity to the nation that Alonzo hoped would reach every child and their children's children one day.

The idea first came to Raul after Alonzo had shared his family's experience at their community pool last summer. Bernadette was bursting at the seams pregnant with their daughter at the time, cooling off under the shade of an umbrella, and Alonzo was playing with Alonzo Jr. in the shallow end. Even then he was always aware of the glares and stares, but he shrugged off the uncomfortable attention for the sake of his son and wanted more than anything to create a perfect July afternoon memory. Instead it turned into a nightmare that would haunt Alonzo Sr. for months.

A community center volunteer took it upon himself to pour toxic cleaning products all over Alonzo and his son while they swam, giving Alonzo Jr. a third-degree chemical burn that took weeks to heal. As Alonzo Sr. recounted this to Raul, and Raul mentioned it to Fred Rogers, the reaction was swift.

"Let's address it in our next show," the production team agreed.

And so they did, inviting Alonzo to join an episode. It took one week for Raul to persuade Bernadette, then another week for Bernadette to persuade Alonzo, but eventually he agreed. And now, as he sat beside a fellow activist, who used his gifts to spread kindness, Alonzo for the first time in a long time felt hope in a better future for his two children.

Sam stood with Bernadette on the studio floor, holding Alonzo Jr.'s hand while Bernadette bounced the baby to keep her occupied. A whispered name pulled Sam's attention from the set.

"Sam!"

She glanced over at the sound of her name and saw Raul waving her over. Still angry with him over his duplicity, she shook her head. But Raul wouldn't accept no for an answer. Not this time. Not when so much was at stake.

He tiptoed toward her and grabbed her hand, dragging her toward another stage across the studio that depicted the usual living room scene. He sat her on the red plaid sofa, knelt down in front of her on a brown oval carpet, and cupped her hands.

"I'm so sorry I jeopardized everything that was important

to you," he began, the words coming effortlessly from his heart. "I thought I was helping you by scaring you away from investigating Cook, but I should have known that you are too fearless to run. Too courageous to back down. Too determined to stop. And too bold to be silenced. Those things scare me about you, but they also are what I love most about you."

Sam sat, breathless. Once again, a wordsmith without words.

"You didn't think I knew what unforgiveable thing I had done, but I do know you, more than anyone else knows you, and I do know what that is."

Sam waited for his answer. It would tell her everything she needed to know.

"I lied, Sam. The one thing you told me you needed from me—honesty—I didn't give you. So I understand if you can't forgive me. But I just needed you to know that I know you, because I have always loved you since that first day I saw you in that New York deli, and always will love you, bad haircuts and terrible fashion and all. I followed you 350 miles, Sam, and I'll follow you however many more miles it takes just to linger in your shadow."

Raul hadn't felt the tears come, and Sam hadn't noticed them either until he wiped them on the back of her hand. Then he kissed her knuckles and stood up.

"Is that all?" she asked colder than she had intended.

The truth was, she still loved him, but sometimes she felt as if no one could ever truly love her because no one ever truly knew her. Except Raul. And he just so happened to be the one person who could break her heart.

"Yes. That's all."

"You're not going to ask me to take you back?"

"No, Sam. Because ultimately, you don't need me. You never did. I could beg and plead for you to be my girl, but isn't that just another form of me trying to manipulate you? I'm not going to do that to you. I don't want to be the thing that gets in your way. I'm happy to sit on the sidelines lifting you up… though the good Lord knows you're plenty capable of supporting yourself. But I do have a surprise for you. It was the only way I could think of to right at least a few of my wrongs."

As Raul stepped back, a hoard of people bustled onto the set, primping and instructing into a moving chatter filling the gap of his empty space.

"What's going on, Raul?" Sam blinked as a makeup artist brushed shadow across her lids. She winced as a stylist combed through her brown shag.

"Fred is going to interview you now, Sam. You're going to talk on public television about your passion for supporting women, and your desire to inspire alternative health options through homeopathy. And you're going to tell Fred—and all of the kids watching at home—a little bit about your column."

"Are you serious?"

"The world needs to know your name, Sam Stanton, and what you stand for, not the lies sold about you."

Raul gave her a little wave as the production crew began telling Sam what to expect while they powdered the nervous sweat from her brow and fiddled with hair that the makeup director eventually declared hopeless.

Then something occurred to Sam.

"Raul—wait!"

He stopped and turned.

"My fashion isn't that terrible. Especially coming from a man who wears crushed velvet elephant bell bottoms."

He winked, that brown-eyed gaze full of golden sparks she already missed more than she should. "Some might say we're a perfect match."

Sam tended to agree.

"Now go tell the world about your column!" Raul urged her as the makeup artist vigorously dabbed at Sam's forehead like she was slabbing spackle on a crude wall.

"But I don't have a column anymore."

He laughed, the warm comforting chuckle she had grown so fond of, so attached to over the years. The only sound that could calm her nerves and weather her storms.

"Oh, you didn't hear? Thomas Cook offered to sell you *Women's House Magazine* for $1, so it's yours if you want it. Unless of course you've decided to take the editor-in-chief job in New York instead..."

Reviving a dead magazine, or running the most coveted women's magazine in America? She could do so much with the circulation numbers and prestige attached to *Ladies Home Journal*, but that meant a long-distance relationship she wasn't sure her and Raul could survive...

Chapter 46

New York City was just as alive as when Sam had left it two and a half years ago, that brisk March day when she last stepped foot in the *Ladies Home Journal* offices. Her clogs tapped up the familiar stairwell—still no elevator for her—to the sixth floor, then through the glass doors that led into the lobby where she had endured her first formal arrest.

Sam idled up to the receptionist's desk. "Sam Stanton here for Calvin Dreyfuss."

The same Twiggy-haired receptionist ignored Sam as she leafed through a *Cosmopolitan* magazine, where every article seemed to be about keeping a man or staying thin. Some things never changed.

Disinterested in helping Sam, or any other visitor, Twiggy kept flipping pages until Sam slapped a hand on the article about how to look like the New Girl of the Golden West, whatever that was.

"Uh huh. I heard you the first time." Twiggy gestured to a row of plastic-coated fabric chairs while she rolled her eyes and picked up the phone. She glanced at her appointment book, then did a double-take of Sam. "Yes, sir, Sam Stanton is here for you."

A moment after she hung up the light bulb went off.

"Excuse me, but are you the *Samantha Says* columnist?"

The receptionist held up an old issue of *Women's House Magazine*, then flipped to the page where Sam's face smiled from a black-and-white photo at the bottom of the column. She held it up against Sam's real-life scowl, comparing the two with a scrutinous gaze. "It *is* you! It's a pleasure meeting you!"

"We've actually met before. Remember the sit-in?" Sam reminded her. "And I worked in this office for years before that."

"Oh, right. All I recall from that day is you getting hauled off to jail. And before that... well, you weren't famous or memorable back then."

That tended to be the nature of memories, clinging to all the dirt and grime and filth and things we wanted most to dust under the rug and forget. But sometimes those very things we wanted cleaned from our past were the very things that made us who we are. Relatable. Redeemable. Relevant.

"Mr. Dreyfuss is ready to see you now."

Sam walked through the doors that separated the waiting area from the bullpen and found Calvin Dreyfuss's office exactly how she remembered it. Still as red-faced and shiny and rotund as ever, Mr. Dreyfuss grumbled upon seeing her in standard *Callous Calvin* fashion.

"Are we all set?" Sam asked.

"Everything is ready for you, Sam."

Ah, and there it was. He had finally gotten her name right!

"I'm very excited about this opportunity," Sam admitted.

"And I know you'll make the most of it. Despite how much of a pain in my butt you were, I applaud you for being a woman of conviction. Darn respectable, too. You earned this, Sam. Make me proud."

Except Sam wasn't there to make Mr. Dreyfuss proud. Or to organize another sit-in. And she wasn't there for a job, either. She was there to claim the keys to her new kingdom.

Mr. Dreyfuss handed her the signed contracts in Thomas Cooks' stead, since he was doing a year in prison for fraud. Twelve months didn't seem like a sufficient sentence for the countless lives he destroyed, but at least he went willingly. And the payouts to all the families who suffered would at least help float them through the unstable economy... and a good fifty or so years longer.

Sam glanced down at the signed, sealed, and delivered contracts. Samantha Stanton was the proud new owner of *Women's House Magazine*, an all-woman staffed magazine that the media was calling a "literary trend-setter."

The first issue would prove to be a record-setter in magazine sales. Guadalupe's first article was a hit, offering exclusive coverage of all the legal ramifications of the FDA's investigation into Big Pharma, along with the settlement details she had negotiated for the countless women who had taken DES. And no one could forget about all the patients who suffered adverse side effects from Nosartin, which was effectively pulled off the market.

The other sweet surprise was Bernadette's interest in writing a column about the Black woman's experience, which garnered national interest as she shared anecdotes and maternal encouragements to her readers.

With a final handshake, Sam left Mr. Dreyfuss' office and headed back downstairs, out into the busy sidewalk on 54th street, where Raul Smothers argued with a meter maid, who had slid a pink parking ticket under the windshield wiper of Sam's father's newly paid-off 1965 Chevrolet Impala SS, once again parked in the middle of the street.

"You can't park here!" the meter maid yelled.

"The car was idling, not parked!" Raul argued back.

The irony wasn't lost on Sam that everything had come full circle—the parking ticket given in this very same spot two years prior was the moment everything was set in motion. Now it signified the end of that very long, very arduous journey.

She giddily walked toward them to interrupt the dispute over the nuances of road rules, when two men stopped her halfway across the sidewalk.

"Samantha Stanton?" one of them asked.

"Yes?"

First she noticed the Portapak with the no-name news station hanging from his shoulder. Then she recognized the thin mustache of the cameraman who had hassled her in this very same spot—and whom she had retaliated with a well-deserved slap to the face—all those years ago.

The reporter stepped forward, his hand outstretched holding a microphone. "I wanted to ask if you'd be willing to let me interview you."

Sam glanced at the cameraman. "I thought no one was interested in my '*silly little ra-ra-rally*,' as you called it."

"He may have misspoken…" the reporter apologized for his tightlipped colleague.

Sam shrugged him off. "I'm sorry, I have far more important matters to deal with, like this meter maid giving me a parking ticket…"

"I'll pay it for you," the reporter insisted.

"I'm dying to know what suddenly makes me newsworthy."

"You singlehandedly took down Thomas Cook's pharmaceutical company and relaunched *Women's House Magazine*—the first all-women-run magazine. That's news if I ever saw a story! So is that a yes?" the reporter asked.

"Only if your cameraman apologizes to me," Sam offered. "For harassing me on March 18, 1970."

"Uhhh, that's a very good memory you have," the reporter muttered, then tossed a pleading glance at the cameraman, whose mouth dropped open in disbelief.

"Getting a black eye and going to jail because of him are extra memorable," Sam explained. "So? Do we have a deal?"

The cameraman stepped forward, forced to wave the white flag of defeat if he wanted this much-needed interview. "I am genuinely sorry. I'll have you know I never heard the end of it from my girlfriend after I told her I was at your sit-in and got you arrested. She almost left me over that."

"And not because you were hitting on another woman while you had a girlfriend?"

"Well, I didn't tell her *that* part. Anyway, we're married now and she's a big fan of your column, I should add. So, I can say with absolute honesty that I regret what I did."

The interview only lasted ten minutes, eight of which were dedicated to asking questions about Thomas Cook and his crimes. But those precious remaining two minutes spotlighting her *real* work in renovating an all-female-run magazine would become the first of many.

"Everything good?" Raul asked as Sam handed the cameraman her parking ticket, then hopped in the driver's seat.

A passing breeze winded through the skyscrapers. It whipped her newly grown brown bob—which even Sam preferred, as it was almost long enough to pull back into a ponytail—and wafted over her the faint fragrance of her mother's borrowed Ô de Lancôme that Sam still wore and had no plans of returning.

"It's more than good. It's perfect," Sam said. "And by the way, as one journalist to another, I understand why you did it the way you did—protecting me by slandering me, which I suppose fit your *modus operandi*. So I forgive you, and I hope you can forgive me for keeping mum about your dad. You had your secret, and I had mine. But going forward, I hope we can skip all the subterfuge and just call it even?"

"Even Stephen," Raul answered, though he was more hung up on her phrasing *going forward*. They had yet to formally establish the nature of their reunion—Friends? Lovers? Pen pals?—as Raul was too nervous to ask directly and Sam had only hinted vaguely.

"Now, are you ready for the biggest adventure of all?"

"I think so." Raul nodded, but he felt sick to his stomach. He wasn't sure meeting his estranged father and brother was the best idea. After all the hurt and all this time. "Thank you for planning this and setting it up. I couldn't have done it without you. I'd have chickened out. You make me stronger, Sam."

Sam squeezed his shoulder, as she had done a lot recently, playing the role of Raul's pseudo-therapist while she talked Raul down from his fearful ledge the past few days every time he felt the urge to cancel on their trip. He would give a million reasons why it would only end badly, but Sam continued to give him one reason that always outmatched his: *No matter what happens, I will be right by your side.* Her being here was all Raul needed to feel okay again.

"I promise you'll like your dad. Gabriel Smothers has been waiting a long time to see you." When Sam had called long-distance to see if Gabriel would be interested in meeting Raul while they were already in New York signing the magazine paperwork, he eagerly jumped at the chance.

"Got any sage advice to make sure he likes me?"

"He's already obsessed with you! Did you know he watches *Mister Rogers' Neighborhood* every day just to see your name on the credits?"

It was a beautiful image, his father, now an old man, sitting by the tube every evening for thirty minutes, venturing into the Land of Make-Believe along with thousands of children, anticipating the closing song just so he could see his son's name roll up the black screen in the credits. For so long it was the closest Gabriel could get to his son. The thought made Raul smile as he unfolded the atlas for directions.

"Do you know where we're headed?" Raul asked as Sam cranked the ignition.

Although that wasn't the question he truly had on his mind. At least not in the directional sense. He wanted to know about them, where they were headed: If they were, or ever would be, *Sam and Raul* or *SamRaul*.

As if understanding the question buried under the question, Sam answered, "Does one ever really know where they're going?"

"I guess not, but I'm guessing the unknown doesn't scare you."

"The unknown is what makes life exciting."

"And treacherous."

"And full of surprises."

"But you hate surprises, Sam," Raul reminded her.

"Yes, but sometimes we don't realize we need them. And they do make everything more interesting, don't they?"

Sam shifted the gear into drive and touched the gas. They lurched forward to the next intersection, slowing at the red light.

"So…" Raul began tentatively, "I know we're not technically going steady anymore, but what word should I use to describe you in case my father asks? My quirky best friend? My road-trip navigator? My therapist?"

They sat for a moment as the stoplight turned green and a yellow taxi honked behind them. With Raul, Sam had never felt like she had to smile to look pretty, or hide her quirks to fit in. Sam knew without a shadow of a doubt that a dose of Raul Smothers was the only medicine she would ever want, or ever need, his love the pill that kept her heart beating. Only for Raul would she finally, yes, take her medicine like a *woman*.

There were a million words Sam could have offered Raul in answer to his question of who they were to each other, but only one came to mind:

"What do you think about the word *fiancée*?"

Women's House Magazine
October 1972 Issue

SAMANTHA SAYS…

Q: *Dear Samantha,*

I'm glad to see you're back! You may remember me as the reader who was stuck in an unrequited love. Well, I didn't take your advice and instead professed my love. As it turns out, he rejected me and I was mortified. So I turned to my best friend, a boy I had grown up with, and discovered a love I had never seen coming.

As it turns out, losing the object of my affection brought me something much deeper… my best friend, and the one I want to grow old with. So while I don't need your relationship advice anymore (it was pretty terrible, if I do say so), I am interested in any natural ways to deal with morning sickness! Yes, we are expecting, which doctors claimed was miraculous, given my "advanced age."

For any readers who may feel alone like I did, trust that love comes in unexpected forms and unexpected times.

Sincerely,
Aching Agnes

A: *Dear Aching Agnes,*

You thought I had been beat, didn't you? Well, I did too. But it turns out women can't be stifled or silenced or put down as easy as they thought. It will take a lot more than a media scandal, a threat to my life, and a discontinued magazine to stop me. This is now your magazine, ladies, and you get to help run it!

Congratulations on the nuptials and upcoming baby! As for your morning sickness, I've been sipping ginger root tea every morning, which helps. Oh, and did I mention that I'm expecting too?

Stay tuned for new upcoming healthy options for mothers-to-be, including all-new therapies for anxiety, sleeplessness, irritability, achy back, swollen feet, weak bladder control, and even some health tips for the little ones!

Sincerely,
Samantha

Did you know that reading provides health benefits including better brain connectivity, lowering blood pressure, reducing stress, fighting depression, and increasing longevity? While the victims in my stories clearly did not read enough Pamela Crane books, you don't have to be one of the statistics. Enjoy a long, healthy life by grabbing your next read at www.pamelacrane.com.

Acknowledgements

This book. I don't even know what to say. So I'll just be bluntly honest with you.

As a mystery and thriller author, I never in a million years imagined I would write humorous women's fiction (though I did try to throw in a little mystery to stay sort of on brand... though I know it was a stretch!). But sometimes we need to step out of our comfort zone in order to challenge ourselves, and that's exactly what this book did for me.

When Sam's story first came to me, I decided to write it as a palate cleanser, and I enjoyed every minute of it. I based Fido on my own mini-pony (he was thrilled to get his fifteen minutes of fame), and I relished the research, characters, homeopathy (can you tell I love plants and horses?), and simply letting myself have fun writing without overthinking it (which is quite different from writing thrillers where everything is a clue or a red herring).

Still worried I was making a grave mistake venturing outside of my "thriller lane," I turned it over to my amazing beta reader team, who convinced me that I had made the right choice. Without further ado, I'd like to personally thank the readers who gave insights, feedback, and encouragement when I needed it most: Tammi Pieczynski, Earl Messer, Sherry Brown, Louise McCardie, Tracy Shultis, Judy Johnson, Teresa Collins, Susanne Galley, Lisa Wetzel, Kathleen Harris, and Shana Moore. And to you, my readers, thank you for letting me cut loose!

About the Author

To know PAMELA CRANE, you first need to know her husband. He sleeps with one eye open. He checks the knife block to make sure none are missing. Why? It could be because they have four kids and a farm full of mischievous animals. Or it could be because she writes murder mysteries, and about the occasional woman who has lost her marbles (not based on her real-life psyche, she swears!). Don't worry—her husband is safe... for now. Her books range from witty whodunnits to psychological suspense and even humorous women's fiction thrown in for good measure. She's a USA TODAY bestselling author of over a dozen novels (who's counting?), but her biggest accomplishment is keeping her zoo of animals alive... and her husband in check.

Grab a free book at
www.pamelacrane.com

www.ingramcontent.com/pod-product-compliance
Lightning Source LLC
Chambersburg PA
CBHW030552170726
48283CB00002B/285